WE MAKE YOU FEEL SANE

PHILIP SKIBA

PhysFarm Ink

Published by PhysFarm Ink, an imprint of PhysFarm Training Systems LLC, 57 South Main Street, Suite 105, Neptune, NJ 07753, USA.

Cover art by Jeffrey Everett

First Printing April 2026

ISBN: 978-0-9794636-4-8 (Print)

ISBN: 978-0-9794636-5-5 (Digital online)

1

———

Uncle Aldo mishandled the clutch, forcing the El Camino's engine from an unhealthy but steady knocking into a heart-attack stall, punctuated by the slam of his door. My cousin Fusilli got out on the opposite side, leaving me sweltering under the camper cover until they popped the tailgate and glass. I scooted out, reflexively squinting against the sun. Fusilli used the bottom of his white T-shirt to mop the sweat from his face. The temperature on the pixelating bank sign across the street read ninety degrees but failed to report the oppressive humidity or maggot stench of trash bags at the curb. I hated Brooklyn. I hated it even more in the summer.

"It'll be easier going home," Fusilli said. "We can split ourselves between the cars."

It took me a minute to place myself. I hadn't been to Mrs. Costa's apartment since the '80s. She'd been a nurse in Grandpa's unit during the war and later settled in the neighborhood with her husband. Widowed young, Mrs. Costa lived a hard life raising four children alone. My grandparents welcomed them into the fold, and I had vague memories of the youngest Costa kids as college students around the family bakery during my childhood. In middle school, Fusilli and I sometimes tagged along with Grandpa Francesco when he delivered bread. We would stop to visit Mrs. Costa and eat Cadbury chocolates from the crystal bowl on her coffee table, the carved glass like dinosaur scales under our fingers. She was British by birth and said American candy was "rubbish." The word always made me laugh, both old-fashioned and perfect when squeezed through her frowning lips and smiling eyes.

Aldo circled around from the far side of the car, smoothing his goatee and adjusting his small round sunglasses. He was my mother's brother and only in his late 40s at that time, but thirty years of chain-smoking Camels had taken its toll. His emphysema crackled like the static on Grandpa's old AM radio. Aldo pointed up at the red brick facade of the apartment building in front of us. Backlit by the sun, the stone took on the deep maroon hue of dried blood.

"She lives up top," Aldo said.

"I remember," I said, then gestured to the no-parking sign. "We need to move the car."

"Pull it into the alley," Fusilli said. "If it'll fit."

"The bread truck always did," Aldo said.

They exchanged a glance, then Aldo waved dismissively. He climbed back into the cab and cranked the engine, the oil-starved gears squalling in protest as he muscled the transmission back into first. I took the measure of my cousin as Aldo steered into the shadows. They'd told me Grandpa was having car trouble, but something was off. I could feel it.

Fusilli headed for the door before I could interrogate him further. I chased him through the entryway and past the brass mailboxes to a narrow staircase. The metal edging on the steps creaked and snapped with each of our footfalls, echoing in the mausoleum silence above. The walls were sorely in need of paint, the surfaces cracked and peeling and leaving a patina of leaded flakes on the tread. How much of that dust hung in the air? Was its weight what thickened the atmosphere as I trailed my cousin under the frosted glow of the fluorescent tubes overhead?

"Fusilli," I finally asked. "What's going on?"

"You were read into the mission brief," he said, trying and failing to keep the tone light. He quickened his pace and beckoned me to hurry.

It was always something with my cousin; always some "mission" involving girls he shouldn't be involved with or a shit-box car he shouldn't be buying. He reveled in it, forever in search of adventure and skating a pencil-thin (or entirely imagined) line between disaster and triumph. His nonsense had never involved our grandfather, however. Grandpa didn't have patience for it.

"You said Grandpa had car trouble," I said, my fuse shortening with the heat and the climb. "He's supposed to be getting chemo in Manhattan. What the fuck is going on?"

"Look," Fusilli said. "The car is fine. Grandpa got lost on the way to Sloan, and he's embarrassed. He stopped at Mrs. Costa's to be safe."

I'd only just finished medical school, but I knew enough to understand that Grandpa Francesco's bowel cancer was terminal. The treatment wasn't about cure but rather palliation: keep his guts running long enough for him to die of something else. A GI obstruction is a terrible way to go. Grandpa had worked in a field hospital in the Second World War and understood the importance of medical care better than most. He'd hoped to go to medical school himself on the GI Bill but had opted to work in the family bakery instead, out of loyalty. Now, at the end of his life, he wanted to do things his way. I respected that. However, he'd never become frankly disoriented before. We might need to take away the car keys. It would crush his spirit.

"So, what's the mission?" I asked.

"Aldo takes him to chemo. You and I pretend to get his car fixed. We bring him home, and we don't say shit to Grandma."

Reaching the top of the final flight, we found ourselves before the bright blue door for apartment 3B. Small cellophane stickers had been applied to the finish but were fading with age. To the left of the peephole was an American flag; to the right, a yellow ribbon that read "Support Our Troops." Fusilli knocked loudly, and the peephole darkened as someone on the other side decided if we should be granted entry.

"Jack? Donatello?" a woman said, her British accent muffled by the door. "Is that you, boys?"

"In the flesh!" I called, momentarily surprised by the sound of Fusilli's given name. The only person who called him Donatello was his mother, and only when he was in deep shit.

Mrs. Costa flung the door wide. Slighter and shorter than I remembered, her salt-and-pepper hair had gone white since our last meeting. It was still pulled into a tight bun that starched the lines from her gaunt face, the same bun that appeared brunette in my grandfather's pictures from the war.

I leaned down so she could kiss me. Her eyes were bloodshot, swollen, and slightly clouded by cataracts. "My God," she sighed. "You got so big."

"It's been a long time," I said, giving Fusilli the side-eye. "Grandpa's playing hooky with you, or what?"

"I'm so very sorry about all this," she said, her voice cracking as she gave Fusilli a squeeze.

"All what?" I asked.

"Your grandfather isn't well."

She stepped aside and pointed towards the back of the apartment, to a door half-open and spilling daylight into the long dark hallway. I stepped past her, the photos on the walls forming a blurred stream of foreign memories as I strode towards the glow ahead. The kitchen entrance flashed in my peripheral vision, accompanied by the briefest hint of garlic and tomato that cut through the stale, ammoniac air common to the homes of the elderly.

"Grandpa?" I called, my heels falling dead against the old shag carpet. "Is everything ok?"

No response. I paused as I reached the door, like a child frightened of monsters lurking in the closet. As the hinges creaked, my grandfather's clothes came into view, neatly folded on a chair in the corner. His houndstooth baker's pants, a linen short-sleeve shirt, a white T-shirt, boxer shorts, and socks. His form lay beneath a thin white sheet, the bedspread turned down to his feet. His bruised, chemotherapy-withered arms lay at his sides, resting atop the ghostly fabric that rippled in the breeze of the window fan. His mouth lay slightly open, his jowls hanging, his eyes closed. His shock of white hair had been carefully smoothed back from his brow. His chest was still.

It took me a moment to process the scene. My grandfather, married for sixty years, had died naked in another woman's bed. I could not wrap my mind around the idea that he had a *cumare*. He'd had no respect for the philandering of his brothers-in-law and always said he wouldn't want to confess that sort of thing to the priest. Yet here he was, his mortal remains frozen in the summer heat, his last moments having been spent with someone I barely knew.

There would be time for reckoning later. I did the only thing I could and allowed my medical training to take over. I stepped around to the far side of the bed and pressed my fingers to his throat, searching for a pulse I knew I would not find. He was still warm, his skin elastic under my fingers. His head lolled to the side with the pressure of my touch. Rigor had not yet set in. I knelt at the bedside as if in prayer, then placed my cheek above his mouth, waiting for a breath that would not come. His aftershave still smelled crisp, as though he'd just stepped out of the shower, but there was an undercurrent of women's perfume. I pressed my ear to his chest, the way I'd sometimes fallen asleep while watching the Yankees game with him as a child. His heart was quiet behind his ribs. Finally, I lifted one of his eyelids. His iris was as blue and clear as I had always imagined his conscience but did not react to the light. What more didn't I know about my grandfather?

Fusilli entered the room with Mrs. Costa, his arm around her as tears squeezed from her crow's feet. The droplets rolled slowly over her ruddy cheeks, then fell to her gray house dress and traced dark lines. Beside them, two photographs hung from the wall. In the first, Mrs. Costa and her long-departed husband, surrounded by their gaggle of children. In the second, my grandfather and Mrs. Costa in their Army uniforms, sitting on the back bumper of a jeep in the jungle. Had this been a sixty-year affair?

"Oh," Fusilli said. "Oh, shit."

Rising to my feet, I laid a hand on Grandpa's forehead, then glanced at my watch. "Time of death, 13:32. I have to call the coroner."

"No," Mrs. Costa said.

"What do you mean 'no'? He's *dead*. There are rules about this."

She looked at Fusilli. "This is why he asked me to call you, Donatello."

"It's going to be all right," he said. "We'll take care of it."

"What?" I said.

The gears turned behind Fusilli's eyes as he dreamt up his latest half-baked scheme. "We're going to put him in the back of the El Camino and bring him home. You and I will take his Plymouth. The girls will take Grandma to the store. We'll put him in bed for her to find later."

I'd only just gotten my medical license a couple of weeks before. I wasn't ready to surrender it in commission of the felony transport of our grandfather's corpse.

"Jesus. Fucking. Christ," I said. "Move a body across state lines? Are you out of your mind?"

"One last mission," Fusilli said.

"Maybe this family could try the truth," I said, trying to use my incredulity to tamp down my sadness. "Just once. Maybe see how that feels for a change?"

"No," Mrs. Costa said. "Your grandmother deserves better."

2

____

Ten days earlier, I'd accepted an ill-fated invitation to join Fusilli at the family summer house at the Jersey Shore. I was forced to take public transit after the demise of the Tijuana Torpedo, my mid-'70s wreck with a radio that had been stuck on a Spanish-language station for a decade. Though I'd only rarely taken the train in my youth, the metronomic click of the wheels felt familiar as I rumbled across the drawbridge to the barrier island. Emerging from a riot of cattails, the docks on the far side of the inlet came into sharp relief under the glow of the sodium lights. The berths lay vacant, the names of the rust-bucket fishing boats rendered in peeling white paint on wooden placards nailed to the piers: the Yellow Jacket, the Miss Sarah Beth, the Chicken Man. Grandpa and I had sailed on most of them over the years in search of striped bass or fluke. I always seemed to miss the really big fish, in their place Mr. Bateman's refrain from behind the bait shop counter: "Shoulda been here last month, kid."

At the far end of the train car, a pot-bellied conductor tucked his newspaper under his arm and reached for the microphone, his yellowed undershirt peeking between the straining buttons of his uniform. Our eyes met for a moment, then he waved dismissively without making the announcement. I was the last passenger. I gathered my things and made for the vestibule as we ground to a halt. He ushered me out into the darkness, admonishing me to "be careful, now" and "watch my step" as the air brakes hissed. With Grandpa sick and Memorial Day approaching, Fusilli and I were tasked with opening the family summer house for the season. However, neither Fusilli nor I knew the first thing about home improvement. I had just graduated from medical school and would be starting my internship in July. Fusilli had just finished his master's degree in archeology and would soon be off to Rome to start his PhD. He hadn't been stateside in more than a year. This would likely be the last we saw of each other for a long time.

Outside, night hung like the condemned. There might have been stars above, but their cold fire was drowned by the neon of the boardwalk rides, the bright colors turned a sickly gray green by the salt mist. Somewhere under those false northern lights lay the rigged games and fortune tellers that held romance and adventure for Springsteen, but mostly drunk tourists and rent-a-cops for children of the '80s. Despite this disconnect, the warped carnival music of the carousel still brought a smile to my face. Some things would never change.

I centered my backpack and struck out to the east, giving the amusement pier a wide berth and following the darkened side streets on a diagonal. Beyond the reach of the circus racket, the salt breeze drew me through a break in the dunes and across a thin ribbon of sand. Kicking off my sandals, the ocean stroked my feet in welcome. I wet my fingers, then brought them to my lips. It tasted like home.

It was an hour walk to my street, then two blocks west through a flotilla of cottages to our bay-front house. My great-grandfather Mario called it *Villabaia* because of its proximity to the water. He bought it from an elderly sea captain. Family lore held that the captain turned down better offers because Mario came from Naples, a city of great fishermen. For his part, Mario was proud to have purchased something truly American. The house had classic two-story Cape Cod architecture, with white-washed cedar shake siding and tall, broad windows dressed in linen curtains. A widow's peak or tower comprised the right side of the house, rising from the brick foundation and reaching an additional half-story above the roofline. Tourists occasionally mistook it for an old lighthouse. Before the onslaught of McMansions, it was one of the tallest structures in town.

My feet crunched across the pebble lawn, then quieted as I climbed the staircase to the open-air porch. Mia and I had spent dozens of nights dozing on the bench swing under the eave. Other times, we went up into the widow's peak and named the stars until we got tired. Or at least, I did. Mia loved the view but wasn't always one for the science. I closed my eyes for a moment and allowed my fingers to drift across sand-blown shingle braille that recorded the best years of my life. It was good to be back in my sacred place, to feel the ghost of my younger self within me.

My reverie was broken by a *thump* behind the jalousie glass of the screen door, like luggage being dropped to the carpet. Unable to see past the glare, I tugged the handle. The apron scraped the stoop like a masonry trowel over drying cement. Inside, the armchairs drifted in the gloom, the dust covers lying in a ghostly pile in the corner. The ochre sleeper couch on the far wall was open, the mattress made up with sheets and a pair of pillows with mismatched cases. The vague scent of the fire-place was puzzling; it had not been used in living memory due to some alleged problem with the flue.

"Hello?" I called, reaching for the light switch.

A whisper from the floor startled me. "Jack! Get down!"

Dropping to my hands and knees, I found Fusilli peering at me from the shadows under the pull-out, so tanned that he almost blended into the night. The bright whites of his eyes showed his pupils in negative space, darting about the room.

"Fusilli, you scared the shit outta…"

"Quiet!" he said, the alcohol on his breath curdling with the funk of the braided area rug. "She followed me…"

The wave of anxiety in my chest crested with a tapping sound from the back door. A hushed voice followed, husky but probably female. "Don? Don, are you in there?"

If she knew his Christian name, it meant he was trying to sleep with her or had slept with her already. It was the only time he used it outside traffic court. We were briefly enveloped in a nervous silence, punctuated only by the ringing of the catamaran masts at the bay front, and then by the rasp of the woman's footsteps on the pebble driveway.

"Did you lock the door?" he asked.

"Of course I didn't lock the door!"

"Fuck. Can we get to the Dungeon?"

The Dungeon was Fusilli's makeshift bedroom most summers, a damp cellar beneath the widow's peak where he roomed with shelves full of canned goods and centipedes the size of small lobsters.

"What is she, a fucking assassin?"

There were footsteps on the porch, then knocking at the front door, more insistent this time. I slid my legs under the bed, tucking in beside him. Head and shoulders taller than his five-and-a-half feet, I had to curl on my side to fit. He did likewise, throwing his arm over my chest and spooning me.

"I'm glad you're here," he whispered in my ear. "We're again one in the ecstatic cahoots."

We held our breath as her silhouette worked the angles of the jalousie glass, trying and apparently failing to see inside. Would she have the gall to try the latch? After a few more half-hearted taps, her shadow disappeared. A car door slammed out back and was quickly followed by the asthmatic sputter of an aging exhaust.

Fusilli commando-crawled from our hiding place and scurried towards the back of the house. I followed, careful to stay low and wondering what the fuck he had gotten himself into this time. We crept through the kitchen and onto the back porch, which had been enclosed and turned into a mud room years earlier. Reaching the door, we peeked through the upper pane just in time to catch a compact car spinning its wheels in the sand and rocks, then fishtailing onto the asphalt and disappearing south.

Fusilli turned his back to the door and slid down onto his ass, sighing in relief and crossing his well-muscled arms across his chest. He turned his head, his dark eyes meeting mine as he tucked his chin-length, middle-parted hair behind his ears. He'd grown out of the quiffed look of our youth, but his dangerous smile persisted.

"Do I want to know who that was?" I asked.

"We were messing around on the beach. Thought I gave her the slip at Eddie's place."

"Is this the one who hit you with a pork chop?"

"That was years ago," he said. "But this one's just as nuts."

"Why are they always nuts?"

"Insanity means better sex."

"What kind of insane is she?"

"When we mess around, she talks crazy."

"Like, dirty?"

"Like *possessed*. It's gibberish."

Fusilli chuckled to himself as he stepped into the kitchen. The concentric ring bulbs on the ceiling flickered to life, illuminating walls covered in textured aquamarine wallpaper and a chipping Formica table thirty years out of date. It was surrounded by a variety of mismatched garage-sale chairs and an old deacon's bench on the far side, tucked into a recess in the wall. He pulled out the seat at the head of the table and fell into it. Behind him, the door to one of the bedrooms was open, the double bed made with corners tucked with military precision. A couple of suitcases lay in the corner. Had one of our elder cousins been down to go fishing? Grandpa was certainly in no condition.

I went for the '60s-era steel fridge, pulling the long horizontal lever. It opened with a satisfying *pop*, but revealed little more than a few bottles of Heineken, several condiments, and some ancient-looking pickles. I took a pair of beers and cracked the tops with an opener older than I was, its magnet still clinging stubbornly to the door and pinning the menu from the only pizzeria in town.

I passed Fusilli a bottle. A crucifix lay before him, crudely fashioned from popsicle sticks and bakery twine. An inscription penned on the horizontal piece read: "The Cross of Death." A fragment torn from a yellow sticky note was affixed to the top, reading "FUSILLI–DEAD!" It was not our grandfather's neat penmanship. I spun it on the tabletop so that the text faced him.

"Though death be poor," he intoned solemnly, summoning Shakespeare, "it ends a mortal woe."

Fusilli was a kind of savant; he remembered everything he read verbatim. Graduate school had only sharpened his mastery of obscure literature. He dropped quotes like an Ivy League professor who'd devolved into a trash-can preacher. He'd been unleashing this superpower on any woman within earshot since our adolescence. However, the emotional intelligence of the average Jersey barfly had improved over time. His act was wearing thin by the time we graduated college. In contrast, the cachet of my burgeoning medical career had improved my standing among women who would never have given me a second look. Of course, I didn't have it in me to trade on this. Mia and I had been together for six years, despite Fusilli's best efforts. And hers.

We clinked our green bottles in a wordless toast and headed back to the living room, falling onto the couch. A set of three small oil paintings my grandfather had done after the war hung above the mantle. Each depicted boats in the bay. In the first, a white rowboat overturned on the sand. In the second, a rowboat moored in the cove. In the third, a boat being rowed away by a lone sailor, Villabaia tiny in the background.

"How was your trip?"

"Took the train," I said. "The Torpedo finally died. The goddamn gas tank fell out of it in Newark."

"Peace be upon it," he said, clinking his bottle against mine again. "Mia couldn't drive you?"

"She's in DC." I shrugged. "New gig with the DEA."

"She's a narc on top of it?"

"Will you grow up? She's an attorney."

"Anyway," Fusilli smiled crookedly. "When the cat is away . . ."

"Her folks still have a place right up the street. She'll be here in a few days."

"You're a broken man. I blame myself for introducing you to her."

"We've been together for six years. We've invested a lot in each other."

"Dude. She's banging the New Haven Necromancer."

My alleged competition was her childhood friend Ian, an early-model finance bro in a North Face puffy vest. We'd first met him at Mia's sorority house in Georgetown. After hearing Fusilli's academic interests, Ian lectured us over red Solo cups on the findings of his Religion 101 paper. He'd discovered an "ancient human knowledge" by studying "forbidden Wiccan texts." He didn't know who he was dealing with: Fusilli was a theology major. Things got uncomfortable when Fusilli pointed out that the "religion of the ancestral peoples" was invented in the UK in the 1940s, and that its primary function was as a nontraditional treatment for anxiety, in essence giving people a sense of control over a random universe.

Irrespective of Ian's bullshittery, he made me anxious. I was forever waiting for the other shoe to drop, for Mia to end up with him. On the other hand, she'd had ample opportunity to trade me in. Mia and I had gone to different colleges, and he'd literally been across campus from her. If she'd wanted him, she could have had him easily. After graduation, he moved to Connecticut for a Yale MBA, and she stayed in DC. They'd barely seen each other in the last couple of years, mostly when they were home for the holidays. I needed to stop being so paranoid. They were just friends. Just. Friends.

I took a pull from my bottle. "That's an exaggeration, don't you think?"

Fusilli bugged his eyes at me. "I thought you were going to break the pattern of denial in this family."

"You're an archeologist, not a psychiatrist."

"Fair." He paused for a moment, studying my face. "So, are you going to marry her?"

I flapped my lips.

"After six years together, it's not that crazy a question."

"You think she's running around on me!"

"And *you* think sealing the deal will solve your problems. It won't."

Fusilli was probably right about that, but I didn't want to give him the satisfaction. Part of me hoped an engagement would indeed chase off Ian the Wiccan; my doubts about that were one of the things that kept me from pulling the trigger.

"What do you know about it?" I said. "I'm assuming you and Katie are 'on a break' again?"

We'd met Katie and her friends the summer before our freshman year of high school. They were part of a rotating crowd of Irish students and families that came to town for summer work. In the following years, Katie and Fusilli often got together when he went to visit his dad in the UK. They'd become a more serious item in college, making his dalliances less frequent. Twenty-minute crushes, he called them.

"I cannot be controlled or contained," Fusilli said, "and you know this better than most."

"When are you going to get your act together?"

"I'm comfortable in my own skin, Jack. You're the one looking for validation in our grandparents' ideals."

"What's wrong with them?"

"You see them through rose-colored glasses. I see them for what they really were."

"Fusilli, I'm just looking for a quiet, successful life. With a stable, normal woman."

Fusilli nodded and drained the remainder of his beer. "You're well on your way to both," he said, grimacing as he half-suppressed a burp. "So why are you so goddamn miserable?"

3

———

Misgivings and jealousy aside, I loved Mia. I was raised to. She straddled the line between my traditional Italian-Catholic upbringing and something more modern. We first met six years earlier, in the summer after our sophomore year of college. I was headed to meet my friends at the beach after dinner, a core group of about fifteen, each of us beneficiaries of grandparents with island properties. Free of the school cliques and class structures of our hometowns, we developed unique and strange friendships that would have been otherwise impossible. Their voices came into soft focus as I approached the crowd. Brian, the art-school dropout who dated a girl who ate raw meat and claimed to be a vampire; Portia, the coffee heiress with frightening sexual appetites; Jimmy Mumbles, a Korean kid the size of a professional wrestler who bounced at the only bar in town.

Mia stuck out immediately, the only face I didn't recognize. She was long-limbed and olive-skinned, pensive, and adrift at the edge of the melee. Fusilli was bending her ear with whatever nonsense he was freestyling that night. He spotted me from a few yards off and fell on me like a jackal in a babble of liquor and testosterone.

"Jack," he called out. "I want to introduce you to someone." He drew close, grasping my bicep with both his hands and lowering his voice. "She's a nice girl. Not my type but just your speed."

"So, you don't think you can get laid and want to split?"

Fusilli smoothed his hair, his dark eyes sparkling with delight. "Too tall," he said. "Her parents just bought Kiwi Herman's place. She's going to be a regular and I need to protect my reputation."

"What reputation is that?"

Fusilli chuckled as he guided me towards the object of his thwarted affection. A few inches shy of six feet, she was built like a dancer. Her shoulders overflowed with wavy, dirty-blond hair that poured down her back like a waterfall. Her features were angular; her cheeks and thin lips set in a nervous smile. Her most defining characteristic was her bright green eyes, the contrast with her skin tone reminiscent of the Afghan woman in the famous National Geographic cover photo. She wore a blue flowered sundress and white flip-flops, along with a thin gold necklace with a small cross.

"This is my cousin Jacques Frére," Fusilli enthused. "Metaphysician, gentleman, and scholar."

"Just . . . Jack," I said, sticking my hand out.

"That's some name," she said.

"What can I say? My mother likes shitty French romance novels."

"Mia," she said, taking my hand with an easy laugh. "You're the lifeguard on the block, right?"

"This week," I said. "They rotate us over the summer."

Fusilli gave us a pair of thumbs up and melted into the crowd.

We looked at each other for a moment, unsure what to do next. Mia finally broke the impasse.

"Who *is* that guy?"

"Honestly?" I said, looking over my shoulder. "The source of every insanity in my life."

Mia's face softened into a more genuine smile. "What's his name again?"

"He probably introduced himself as Don," I said. "But everyone calls him Fusilli."

"Like the pasta?"

"Yeah," I said. "The twisted one."

"Why does he talk like that?"

"He thinks he's a lot smarter than he is."

"That explains the accent."

"No, the accent is legit. Well, almost. His dad is British."

I liked Mia immediately. She was . . . kinetic. Her hands were in constant motion, like gulls in a variable crosswind. Laughing easily and often, her big green eyes gave the impression that she was always leaning towards me, hanging on each word and building my confidence as we talked. Her family was terminally Italian on both sides, providing the kind of cultural shorthand that allowed us to feel more familiar with each other than we otherwise might have. She had just finished her sophomore year at Georgetown and was looking for a summer job but wasn't thrilled at the idea of selling bathing suits or ice cream in town. After a while, we made our way to an empty bench under the gazebo and kept chatting.

"Where do you live?" she asked.

"The Cape Cod joint at bottom of the street," I said. "Oldest house on the island."

"The haunted mansion?" she gasped. "People *live* there?"

"Haunted mansion?"

"No . . . sorry. I'm just saying. It's got a *lighthouse*. Do you have a grizzled keeper, too?"

"Sorry, just Fusilli."

Mia threw her head back and laughed, giving me a backhand to the shoulder.

"It's a widow's peak, not a lighthouse." I said. "I'll take you up there sometime. Great view."

She sprang to her feet, eyebrows raised in expectation. "Can we go now?"

"I mean . . ." I paused for a moment, alarmed at the idea of bringing her anywhere near my reptilian siblings, then gave in. "Sure, why not?"

Mia glanced at what had been Kiwi Herman's house, so named because it was built by an eccentric architect from New Zealand. A modernist eyesore on the beachfront, it stood out from the surrounding bungalow and Victorian architecture. The roofline was a jagged collection of misshapen dormers, while the siding was stained the pale brown typical of 1980s condominiums. The second floor rose high above the dunes, its great picture windows affording spectacular views of the coast. The corner window was occupied by the silhouette of a broad-shouldered woman, her hands on her hips. She tapped her wrist, as if gesturing to a watch. Then, a shorter figure came into view, balancing on tiptoe and leaning side to side, perhaps checking different angles between the vertical blinds.

Mia took my hand and guided me out of the back of the gazebo, up the short flight of stairs and across the bridge that spanned the dunes. I was so surprised by the move that it took a moment to get my legs up to speed. Where was this headed?

"Don't get any ideas," she said, as if reading my mind. "We're just taking the scenic route."

"Why?"

"You ready to meet my mother? And grandmother? And sisters?"

We detoured north along the dunes and ducked through the next available passage west, emerging one block clear of the gazebo hubbub. The street was lit like a string of Christmas lights with mismatched bulbs. Some porches glowed pale yellow with the light meant to ward off mosquitoes, while others remained dark but were flanked by windows casting the tin glow of television tubes onto the sidewalk.

"It's different here," Mia said. "My dad sold our place in Wildwood to buy this one."

"This is a family town," I said. "Wildwood is . . . Babylon."

"It just kept getting seedier. And the rides are like, dangerous. I heard a girl got killed on the Crab Trap."

"You'll like it better here. Most people have roots a couple generations back. They want to keep it nice."

"You mean exclusive."

"Exclusive? With Fusilli on the loose?"

She laughed and followed me across the island's main thoroughfare. Turning left on the far side, we walked the verge of a tall wooden fence to the break that marked my driveway, then entered the sandy lot behind Villabaia. I led her along the juniper bushes on the side of the property to ensure we passed unnoticed in the shadows. The voices inside the house became clearer as we approached. It sounded like my siblings and cousins were arguing over a board game.

My brother Marco's voice surged above the chorus: "Suck. My. Balls."

My sister Aurora wasn't having it. "Read the rules, Marco!"

"Suck his balls," cousin Joe demanded.

"How many are you?" Mia asked.

"I'm the oldest of five. Two of my cousins live downstairs."

"I love them already."

"Total savages."

We circled the southern side of the house, then ducked through a small doorway and climbed the wrought-iron spiral staircase into the widow's peak. Built for small people, the low ceiling forced me to stoop to keep from peeling my scalp off on the ceiling. Mia did the same. There wasn't any glass in the windows, just a low railing to prevent a disastrous misstep. Mia was pressed up tight against my side. The heat of her sunburned arm felt good against mine, the contact accidental and unavoidable but somehow intimate.

A gentle westerly breeze stirred the American flag across the street, carrying the brackish smell of the bay. The moon shone bright on the water, edging Mia's features in silver. Citronella candles burned amber on the porch below us, revealing two pairs of legs jutting from under the eave. My grandparents often sat on the bench swing in the evening. I pointed and lifted a finger to my lips. She nodded.

"There's no light," she whispered, sounding disappointed.

"A fisherman built this place in the 1800s," I said, tapping the rusted iron hook that hung from the ceiling. "His wife would hang a lantern here to guide him home at night."

"How romantic."

I pointed out a flashing buoy in the distance. "That marks Dead Head Island. It's real shallow. Lots of rental boats wreck there. Way down to the left, you can see the fishing pier. The tennis complex beyond is where they do teen dances."

"Teen dances?"

"We went there to meet girls when we were kids," I said. "There was this Irish chick I used to sweat."

"You bring a lot of girls up here?"

I shook my head. "I never had my cousin's talent with women."

She gave me side eyes. "Hmm."

"What's *hmm*?"

"I'm trying to decide if I can trust you."

"Why?"

"I'm looking to have the summer of my life. I need a partner in crime."

"Something tells me you can get into plenty of trouble on your own."

"But who's gonna be the patsy?" She laughed, grasping my wrist and turning it to check the luminescent hands of my dive watch. "Come on, I'll let you walk me home."

We crept back the way we came and escaped through the yard. As we approached the boardwalk, there was a woman maybe ten years older than us waiting by the dune fence. Her striped dress was stretched tight over a heavily pregnant abdomen. She was just over five feet tall and had dark brown hair, the unruly mass gathered with a banana clip. She was wearing fishbowl glasses with gold frames a few years out of style. The woman crossed her arms judgmentally, waiting for us to come to her.

"Jesus," I said.

"Just follow my lead," Mia muttered, then called out. "Luna, this is Jack. I know him from school. We ran into each other at the boardwalk."

"Nice to meet you," I said.

Luna ignored me. "You were supposed to be home a half-hour ago, *Figlia del Postino*!" she said. "Now Nonna thinks you were taken by gypsies!"

"They call me the Postman's Daughter because I'm the tallest," Mia said.

"*And* the only blonde." Luna said. "Tita and I both had curfews until we got married. You're nothing special."

"I'm nineteen years old," Mia said, raising her eyebrows at me. "I was the first to go away to college."

"You were always Daddy's favorite."

"Exactly."

"*Vieni a casa, Mia! Non hai bisogno di passare del tempo con questo idiota!*"

"*Perché devi parlare così? Statazit!*"

"*Non capisce niente!*"

"*Io capisco tutto,*" I said, folding my arms and feigning insult.

Mia's jaw dropped, then she started to laugh and punched my shoulder. Luna's eyes widened at being caught out. She put a hand over her mouth, a diamond ring the size of a half-melted ice cube flashing under the streetlights.

"I'm sorry," she said between her splayed fingers. "Really sorry. It's been a long day with them, and I'm crazy with the hormones. No offense."

"*Nunca problema,*" I laughed. "My grandparents are Napoletan."

"Okay," Luna said. "So, you get it."

"I better go," Mia said. "Otherwise, they'll lock me in the basement or something."

Luna turned and started down the boardwalk, one hand over her belly, one hand in the small of her back. Mia put her arms around my neck.

"Thanks for playing along," she whispered before kissing me on the cheek. "I'll see you tomorrow."

The sisters mounted the back stairs to the second-floor deck. I felt her family's eyes on me as they stepped through the sliding-glass doors to a volley of rapid-fire Italian. The voices were cut short as the door slammed, the vertical blinds closing like prison bars.

Fusilli had been watching the scene from his vantage point at the gazebo and strolled over to meet me. "What was that all about?"

"I think I'm in deep shit with this one, Fusilli."

Mia was everything she seemed to be and more: quick, funny, and adventurous. My grandparents swooned when she spoke Italian, floating effortlessly between Roman, Sicilian, and Neapolitan dialects. She went out of her way to integrate with my sisters, once flying to New York spur of the moment to support the eldest after a bad breakup. Likewise, Mia's folks made me one of their own, which felt especially meaningful after my father's death and my mother's estrangement. Mia's dad came out for the father-son softball tournament at my college. He didn't correct people when they mistook him for my old man. In many ways, Mia and I grew into each other's lives organically.

In other ways, we'd slid off the tracks. Part of that was my jealousy over the Witchdoctor, and part of it was the old-neighborhood loyalty that kept her from cutting him loose. Part of it was the never-ending negotiation of professional and family responsibilities that kept us dancing between states. I wanted to recapture our initial energy, but it seemed fleeting, like boardwalk neon in the morning light. That desire was invariably followed by thoughts that grabbed me by the throat and told me to grow the fuck up, that all relationships cooled as they matured and this was the nature of adulthood.

It wasn't lost on me that I should have been more confident in Mia after six years. It was just hard to admit, even to myself.

4
_____

Owing to a combination of my long walk from the train station and a few too many Heinekens, Fusilli and I turned in early. Grandpa had prepared a two-page list of chores for us, some of which were going to be a real pain in the ass. I slept through most of the night untroubled. However, as dawn approached, I fell into a disjointed dreamscape.

My foot was stuck between the ties of a railroad track with a train fast approaching, the rumble rattling my teeth. Diesel and sand on my tongue, I cowered as the horn blasted. I awoke to find the sound was real and coming from a goateed lunatic with a bugle at the foot of my bed. I closed my eyes, disoriented and half-convinced I was still dreaming. When I opened them again, I was greeted by a vision Dante had not imagined in his worst delirium.

My Uncle Aldo, clad in dingy white briefs and what smelled like a half-bottle of tequila, was blaring a raspberry mishmash of "Reveille" and something that might have been "Ride of the Valkyries." The mirror on the wall behind him showed the sagging band of his underwear, the hairy crack of his ass lit in sharp relief by a floor lamp. When he saw my eyelids flutter, he took Grandpa's tarnished war horn from his mouth. Fusilli rose to a half-pushup on the pullout beside me. He offered Aldo a stare, equal parts venom and disbelief.

"What the fuck?" Fusilli said.

Aldo smiled, his mustache and goatee parting to reveal crooked teeth the color of tobacco and coffee. His voice sounded like he gargled with road salt. "Rise and shine, boys!" He pulled a cigarette from behind his ear, then grabbed a silver Zippo lighter from the mantle. He squinted at us as he lit it and blew smoke towards the ceiling, as if he was already disappointed at whatever our response would be.

Fusilli snorted and rolled over. Before he could close his eyes, Aldo snatched a broom from the corner, his lips tight around the butt of his cigarette. I jumped out of bed as the broom fell in my stead. Aldo's second swing was meant for Fusilli, the straw bristles just missing him. The handle split as it struck the bed frame. My cousin cursed and tumbled to the floor in a tangle of limbs.

"We start at oh-seven-hundred daily, and we finish when the bars open," Aldo said. "This morning, we're water-sealing the widow's peak. I don't give a shit what you do after. Work well, and I'll go easy on you. Screw around, and you'll suffer the Cross of Death."

Neither of us responded. Aldo eyed us a moment more and ran a hand over the day-old stubble on his shaved head. "Sloth will not be tolerated at Camp Uncle Aldo." He then turned on his heel, bringing the remains of the broomstick to his shoulder as he might a rifle and marching to the bedroom. He began banging through the dresser drawers with the performed frustration of a grounded adolescent, then came out wearing cutoff jean shorts, Chuck Taylors, and a red bandanna tied into a skullcap.

Fusilli turned to me, massaging the back of his head. "Cousin, I swear by all I hold sacred, we will avenge this."

"Goddamnit, Fusilli. You don't *hold* anything sacred."

"Be out front in ten," Aldo hollered over the slam of the back door.

I pulled on my shorts. "Just when the fuck were you going to mention Aldo?"

Fusilli began folding up the couch without making the bed, grimacing. "I didn't know how to tell you, man. I found him when I got here."

I had few memories of Aldo from my childhood, but two stood out, one involving him falling into a koi pond at a wedding, the other involving him tipping a boat off its trailer and flattening Fusilli's Honda hatchback when we were in high school. Both involved copious amounts of alcohol. My mother said he was a ne'er-do-well who went to Vietnam and never got over it, which was as good an explanation as any. Aldo was a professional fisherman by trade and had bounced between Seattle and Alaska for my entire life.

"Does Grandma know?" I asked.

"Yeah. Looks like he survived the winter here on booze and sardines. I think he burned some of the old furniture to keep warm."

"Did he come back because of Grandpa?"

"Not sure. Jerry Fitz got him a job, anyway. Bowling alley across the bay."

"The guy who owns the fish market?"

"He lost it years ago. Tax fraud."

"No offense man, but count me out. I don't need Aldo's bullshit."

"Come on," he said. "I'm offering you the best summer of your life. It's gonna be like the old days."

"We're twenty-six, Fusilli. Those days are over."

"That's what you think."

"What's that supposed to mean?"

He grinned. "Nora's back."

"Fuck off."

"Hand to God. She's in the Duffy's cottage."

"Holy shit."

Fusilli pulled an invisible microphone to his lips. "In this corner . . . from the Emerald Isle . . . weighing in at 150 pounds . . . the Killer from County Clare . . . Miss! Atomic! Bomb!"

Fusilli and Katie had introduced me to Nora under the Fourth of July fireworks the summer I turned fourteen. Nora's family was renting the place next door, and my grandparents all but adopted her. Our matching height and poor coordination made us fast friends. Despite her father's disapproval, Nora became my first summer girlfriend and by Labor Day, an ideal that no American girl could match. We evolved into pen pals when she went home but eventually lost touch. All of her letters were still in a trunk at my parents' house. My fingers twitched with the memory of her hair in my hands as we kissed, coarse like a horse's mane. Over the years, I'd fantasized about following Fusilli on one of his overseas trips. I imagined winning Nora back with a romantic gesture worthy of John Cusack, standing outside her window with a boom box playing Peter Gabriel or busking in a square on her way to school.

"If you're pulling my leg," I said, "I will strangle you."

ALDO WAS WAITING for us when we got outside. "You look like hammered dog shit," he began.

"I'm paying for my sins of last night," Fusilli said, squinting against his hangover and the climbing sun. "Villabaia is the ninth level of hell and you're Satan incarnate."

Aldo motioned for me to help him with the ladder, grunting as we manhandled it against the building. He then presented me with a bucket filled with a milky substance. I hadn't yet had my coffee, but Aldo was looking surly, and it seemed like less hassle to cooperate. The ladder was probably older than the sum of our ages at the time and had an unsettling bounce. My foot cracked a rung at the halfway point, the maple stringers creaking forebodingly at the insult.

"This is fucking stupid," I said.

"Higher," Aldo said. "The ladder is fine."

The final rung still bore the faded yellow and black inscription: NO STEP. I hung the bucket from the top of the right stringer, then began slathering a thick coat of the stuff on the siding. The ladder rocked perilously with each swing of my arm.

I was nearly finished when an Irish voice rang out. "Just what are you gobshites up to now?"

I craned my neck to see a lanky redhead wheeling up on a blue beach cruiser. She wore oval sunglasses a size too large for her elfin features, her cinnamon-freckled skin a fair match for beach sand in the sun. She was more than a decade older than when I'd last seen her, but it was unmistakably Nora. A hundred yards behind her lay the catamaran we'd first kissed beneath, the fiberglass hull a fading facsimile of its original brilliant blue. The sprig of hope Fusilli had planted began to take root in the space resignation had long occupied.

"Hey Nora!" Aldo hollered before releasing a mighty cough. "Painting today."

"And who's the poor bastard up top?"

"My nephew Jack."

I waved, a grin plastered across my face. "You've grown up, Jack! Take care, won't you? My first-aid skills are a bit rusty."

I started to reply, but was cut off by Aldo, who let go of the ladder to use his hands to emphasize whatever he was about to say. Fusilli wasn't paying enough attention, nor was he strong enough to stop the ladder tipping off to the right. I dropped my brush and grabbed the iron railing above me, knocking the bucket of sealant over and showering both Fusilli and my uncle with the stuff as the ladder smashed into the El Camino's hood.

For a moment, things seemed as though they would be all right. Then, the rusted bolts that secured the top of the railing sheared off, the wrought iron frame bending out horizontally. For an instant, I was suspended inches from the wall and about a story and a half up. I tried to throw myself towards the window below me, but my weight shift caused the railing to part entirely from its moorings, and I swung into the wall. My feet hit the windowsill below, breaking my fall as the rail fell past me. Momentarily balanced, I struggled to grab onto something, but the siding offered little purchase. I fell backward to the pebbled lawn, my shoulders taking the brunt of the impact, the sound in my head like that of a bag of marbles hitting a tile floor.

I lay semiconscious for a few moments. When my eyes came into focus, Nora was hovering above me, her auburn curls framing friendly dimples. She peeled off her sunglasses, revealing the crisp blue of her eyes.

"Christ, Jack!" she said. "'Twas quite a fall!"

Fusilli poked his head into my field of view. I grabbed him by the shirt collar and drew him close. His breath was foul.

"We're going to die here, you know," I said.

He and Nora grasped my arms and helped me to my feet. Fusilli offered a jowly Churchillian accent. "Some may make the ultimate sacrifice in service of the mission," he agreed.

"You're fucking mental," Nora said. "The lot of you."

IT TOOK a couple of expired aspirin and a nap to settle my headache. I woke in a better mood, which improved further after seeing neither of my esteemed relatives were around.

Standing in the kitchen over the old propane range, I loaded my grandfather's ailing moka pot with espresso grounds and water, then awaited the familiar burble and hiss. The thing had always seemed vaguely dangerous, as though it could detonate like a grenade despite the tiny brass pressure-relief valve. When it was finished, I poured the thick brew into his favorite blue-plaid mug. It had been repaired several times over the years, the surface crazing like a museum vase. The taste was bitter but comforting. I was about to sit when fragments of Nora's voice drifted in from the front of the house. Peering out of the living room window, I found her straddling our porch railing, emptying a bag of potting soil into one of the rectangular planters atop it. She had a cell phone cradled between her cheek and her shoulder.

Getting a look at the state of my bedhead in the mirror, I dove into my old dresser drawer, finding my swimsuits and sun-bleached desert camo boonie hat. Beneath them lay my Luminox dive watch, the black steel case and crystal mauled by years of shore-break bodysurfing. I hadn't worn it or the hat since my days in the lifeguard chair. The battery having died long ago, the hands were stuck at 5:33 p.m. on the third of some forgotten month. The thick rubber strap showed considerable dry rot. I glanced at the polished titanium Citizen on my wrist, the Blue Angels flight model. It had been a graduation gift from Mia. I'd asked for it because the aeronautical slide rule on the bezel appealed to the nerd in me. It allowed estimation of fuel consumption or arrival time. It was classy, the kind of thing I ought to be wearing now that I was a doctor. However, it felt like gaudy costume jewelry. I was tempted to swap it for the Luminox. I could get a battery in town, but then there was the risk of intramural warfare with an offended Mia. I didn't need to resurrect an old watch. I needed to grow into my new identity.

I grabbed the hat and stuffed my mop of brown hair under

it, then stepped out into the afternoon. The bag of soil was now crumpled at Nora's feet. She smiled and gestured with a finger to indicate she would be only a moment longer. I was excited in a way I hadn't been since my teenage years. Nora was back. This could only mean good things.

"Yes, mother," she sighed, rolling her eyes at me. "Christ, mum! It's only a month or two. Speak soon. Bye-bye."

She clicked the phone off. "Time for a proper hello!" she said, jumping to her feet and throwing her arms around me. "So good to see you!"

"You too, Nora," I said, returning the embrace.

"I feel a bit responsible for your tumble. How're you keeping?"

"Could be worse."

"Worse than living with those daft bastards?"

I considered this for a moment. "If I leave tonight, will you come with me?"

She raised an eyebrow, then just shook her head and laughed. I gestured at a small tray of blooms that were resting on the railing behind her. "You have a green thumb?"

She sat down on the rail again and swiveled to grasp the tray, balancing it in her left hand and digging small divots in the fresh soil with her right. "I hope it's not too presumptuous, but nothing proper grows in the sand. I miss the flowers back home."

Nora began removing the plants and placing them into the holes like puzzle pieces. My grandfather would have appreciated the blaze of the marigolds. Gardening was his only hobby, and he defended his flower beds and vegetables as he had his wartime field hospital in the South Pacific. "We need the help, as you can see. Grandpa hasn't been down to do the planting."

"He was so good to me when we were kids," she said. "My dad loved going to the pub with him."

"They aren't making them like Grandpa anymore, that's for

sure," I said, trying to scrub the sadness from my voice. Grandpa had survived a childhood in the coal mines of Pennsylvania, a stint in a Philadelphia orphanage, and Hirohito's worst in the jungles of the South Pacific. It was hard to believe he might be taken down by bowel cancer in the armpit of New Jersey.

"You here with your folks?" I asked, trying to change the subject.

She flicked her head towards the house beyond the hedge that ran north–south between our property and the neighbors. "Just me," she said. "The Duffy's were kind enough to have me back. The missus went to uni with my Da."

"You must get a lot of vacation!"

"Between jobs," she said. "How're your sisters? How's Marco?"

My family was something to see back in the day, before my father died. He spent most of the summer working back home in New York, leaving my mother to lead a wagon train of five children to the beach daily. Over time, my sisters had grown from a teenage annoyance to a Greek chorus bent on analyzing my life. The worst part was that their pronouncements were typically right on target. My brother Marco was another story. He'd gotten hooked on opiates in high school. Marco was fresh out of rehab again but was doing better, according to the girls. I didn't want to get into it with Nora.

"The girls continue to haunt me," I said. "But I've gotten better at avoiding them. My brother partied a little too hard for a few years, so he's getting his act together."

"No harm," she said. "Life isn't always straightforward, is it?"

Before I could respond, her phone rang again. My heart sank at the sight of her silver Claddagh ring as it flashed in a beam of sunlight. That reflexive, subconscious pang gave me pause. The idea of Nora's partner shouldn't have meant anything to me. I was in a committed relationship with Mia, and we were talking about getting married.

"Hell. This is Daniel. Catch up later?"

She smiled as I nodded, then passed me the half-empty tray of flowers before heading off. "Make your gran-da proud, Jack."

There was nothing I wanted more than to make my grandfather proud. He was the family patriarch and my male connection to an era I had romanticized beyond any connection to reality: I knew he'd belonged to the greatest generation before the term had even been coined. He lacked the baby-boomer need for self-actualization that had ruined my parents and was impatient with the navel-gazing of my generation. I'd done everything I could to fashion myself in his image. He believed in commitment and loyalty and would definitely not approve of my sweating Nora instead of shopping for Mia's engagement ring. The idea of disappointing him was anathema. I needed to wise up before I found myself in a bad situation.

5

Fusilli became a night owl in our teens and loved company during the dark hours: female, ideally, but I would do in a pinch. This arrangement was apparently continuing in our twenties. He woke me at a little past two in the morning, straddling my chest and shaking my shoulders.

"Arise, man!" he called like a medieval town crier. "Today is the day when knights in splendid armor ride mighty steeds to glory!"

Aldo pounded on a bedroom wall, his voice muffled by the plaster between us. "Shut the fuck up, you two!"

Fusilli leaned in close, his alcohol-laden breath pouring across my face. "Our master is the devil," he whispered.

"Goddamnit, Fusilli," I said. "Please just go to sleep."

"We have a mission. We must venture to Castle White, where we will find provisions and men sympathetic to our cause."

"Christ almighty."

"Spare me your blasphemy, cousin. I love you more than Jesus."

Fusilli was staging a full-scale regression into his teenage persona. Nothing would shut him up when he was drunk and hungry save a pile of sliders. I disentangled myself from the sheets, then followed him out into the night in my boxers and T-shirt. Fusilli's black 1970 Chevelle lay in a pool of streetlight by the mailbox. He threw the keys to me as I circled around the far side. Had I been on top of my game, I would have checked the upholstery before falling in behind the wheel. The seat squished and foamed like a dirty kitchen sponge as my ass met the sodden cushion. The scent of mildew rose up like a cloud of mustard gas.

"Fusilli!"

The passenger side window filled with his gap-toothed smile, which melted into an apologetic grimace when he saw the darkening seat of my shorts. "Sorry, man. I forgot to put down fresh plastic."

I groaned and reached down to pick up a wad of wet garbage bags and duct tape the size of a basketball, tossing it at him. He swatted it aside. The convertible top leaked in the rain, amounting to medieval water torture for anyone in the cabin.

The engine roared as I turned the key, then settled into a familiar percolation at idle. I jammed the stick shift into first and pulled onto the boulevard, swearing at the tuberculoid grind of the gears. However, the janky transmission was at least partly my doing. I had never learned to properly drive standard. Fusilli had been my sole (and usually, drunk) instructor over the years. Still, she had been a serious machine in her day. Custom work gave it 500 horsepower on regular gas, and then there was the methanol boost we'd installed ourselves. There were few modern cars that could match it. We'd never lost a race with Fusilli behind the wheel, a youthful Han Solo steering us towards certain doom while I clung to the *oh shit!* handle, howling prayers for deliverance like a terrified Wookie.

"Where have you been all night?" I asked.

"Went by Brown's place. His kid brother is back from Gettysburg for a few weeks."

"A few weeks?"

"Five-year plan. He didn't graduate on time."

"That kid must have smoked his weight in pot over the years."

"Don't be such a drag," he said. "Where has responsibility gotten *you*?"

"Medical degree? Good residency? Steady girlfriend?"

"A mountain of debt? An anxiety disorder? Whatever social disease Mia caught from the Witchdoctor?"

"Wiccan," I said. "That fucker's gonna sacrifice her dog. Wait and see."

Fusilli cackled in delight.

White Castle was just across the bridge to the mainland. Given the typical late-night denizens of the joint, it was hard to believe that a drunken jackass and his boxer-clad chauffeur were that far out of the ordinary for the acne-addled clerk. Nevertheless, he looked at us like we were men possessed as we strode through the doors, our entrance heralded by the chintzy bells on the jamb. Fusilli gazed at the clerk as though he was Saint Peter, guarding a fast-food paradise veiled by steam-grilled onions and whatever West-African dialect the cooks were shouting over the sizzle.

"Brother!" Fusilli called out, raising a fistful of cash. "We are messengers from God. We have come forth, that you might . . ."

The cashier began to reach for the phone but stopped as I clamped my hand over Fusilli's mouth. "Just give us twenty sliders with cheese and some Cokes and promise not to call the cops on this asshole."

We had a few moments of peace once we were seated at a booth, a tray full of burgers between us. However, our quiet gluttony was soon interrupted by the jingle of the doors behind me. Fusilli's eyes widened, then he slid beneath the table like an anaconda. I turned to see a brunette a few years younger than us strutting through a cloud of cigarette smoke. Her face was a carnival of greasy eye shadow and fire-engine lipstick, applied with the finesse of a stonemason. Her perm could have landed her in a Mötley Crüe video, as could her tasseled leather halter top and matching concho-belted miniskirt.

"I'm Candy," she started. "Don's girlfriend. And you are?"

"Fucking tired," I replied, glancing downward at the whites of Fusilli's eyes.

"Why is he under there?"

"We're having a little family time."

She reached beneath the table, grasped Fusilli by the arm, and pulled him from his hiding place. He fell into the bench seat like a rag doll. "Why didn't you wait for me?"

"Sorry," he slurred. "My cousin took me to get some food."

"I didn't see you at the party," she said, looking me up and down.

"No, lover boy here got me out of bed."

Her eyes narrowed as she looked back to him. "So, you ditched me."

Fusilli swallowed heavily, as though he had just puked in his mouth. His eyes darted to mine.

"How did you find us?" I asked.

"The Lord makes my lamp bright and my path straight," she said, her eyes taking on a strange gloss.

"Holy shit," Fusilli said.

"This was great, but we gotta go," I said, half-dragging Fusilli from the booth and sending the few remaining burgers flying. My cousin was too drunk to walk properly, so I threw him over my shoulder like a sack of potatoes and burst through the door. I stuffed him feet-first through the open window on the passenger side, the report of Candy's hooker heels against the pavement like gunfire close behind.

"You bastard!" she shouted after us. "You'd better call me!"

The tires squealed as I dumped the clutch, mashing the accelerator to avoid a stall as we exited the lot. "I know you like nutjobs," I shouted over the engine. "But never screw anyone crazier than you."

"Cousin," he said, suddenly lucid. "There are seven basic truths of the universe, six of which were yet to be discovered. You'll be credited with this insight."

"What was the first?"

"Never bet your own money on a sure thing."

We took a jughandle and went back towards the bay bridge. Fusilli fiddled with the radio for a bit, then reached up and tried to open the convertible top. The sorry mess of vinyl and metal peeled back like a beach umbrella in a thunderstorm, popping several rivets and nearly tearing free of the car. Fusilli met my eyes for a moment and shrugged, then stood up on his seat, dropped his shorts, and unceremoniously tried to urinate over the side. The headwind and angle ensured that he peed all over himself.

Lights and sirens erupted from the darkness as a cop car raced up behind us. I grabbed Fusilli by the arm and yanked him into his seat. "The third basic truth of the universe is don't piss into the wind!"

I flicked the switch for the hazard lights and pulled over, trying to imagine what the cop was going to say when he saw me in my underwear and Fusilli with his pants around his ankles, drenched in his own urine. I didn't have to wait long. Blinded by the spotlight in my mirrors, the only warning of the trooper's approach was his keys and handcuffs jangling like Christmas.

"Son," he sighed, thumbs hooked on the gun belt that hung at my eye level. "Do I *really* need to explain why I stopped you?"

"No sir," I said.

"Wanna give me one good reason why I shouldn't throw both your asses in the hoosegow?"

Fusilli tugged his shorts up over his bare ass. "There are human qualities still to be discovered?"

"Officer, I apologize," I said. "He's had a lot to drink."

"No shit," the cop said, adjusting his broad-brimmed hat.

"I'm just trying to get him home safely."

"In your skivvies?"

"Yessir. I didn't have time to get dressed. I heard him start his car and ran out to stop him."

"I don't suppose you have your license on you?"

"No, sir," I said. "I'm an ER doc up at Saint Sebastian. I was just imagining him killing someone on the road."

The trooper seemed to think this over for a moment. "I'll let it slide, since you're doing us all a favor here, Doc." He paused and gestured at Fusilli with his pad. "But I'm writing you a ticket for urination in public."

Fusilli forked over his wallet, shrugging apologetically even as he continued to mumble incoherently to himself. The cop headed back to his cruiser to take down whatever pertinent information cops take. I was surprised my cousin still had a license, given the number of violations on his record. By the time the cop returned, Fusilli appeared blissfully unconscious. The officer regarded him with some measure of pity, shaking his head and handing me the wallet and ticket.

"Drive safely, son."

I waited for the cop to pull out and accelerate away, then reached over to check Fusilli's breathing. He slapped my hand and sat up.

"I trained you well, my young apprentice," he said.

"Goddamnit," I said. "You were playing possum."

"You've always been the respectable one."

"He could have arrested us, man! This kind of shit doesn't fly anymore."

"You used to be more fun, Jack."

"I grew up. You should try it."

Fusilli flapped his lips and reached over, snatching the ticket from me. "$175? I didn't even get to finish!"

"Serves you right."

"For the same price, I could have . . ." He ran his finger down the list of infractions on the back of the paper. "Driven on the sidewalk. And littered. Without a life jacket."

"There's always tomorrow, you fucking sociopath."

WE SPENT the following morning patching the concrete around the outside shower, Fusilli intermittently puking in the bushes. I put him to bed after lunch and did some fishing to calm my nerves. I couldn't decide whether I ought to pack my stuff and catch the next train or just murder my housemates and live in peace until someone discovered the bodies. Maybe I could wall them up in the Dungeon, Edgar Allan Poe style.

When I returned to Villabaia for dinner, Nora caught me as I climbed the back stairs. "How's the head, Jack?"

Nora was radiant against the dark-stained wood shingles that sided the cottage. She was balancing a wicker-clothes basket on one hip and was tossing some T-shirts over the clothesline with the opposite hand. I imagined her doing something similar under broken gray clouds behind a stone house on the Irish coast. Coming home from my shift in the little country hospital, I would steal up behind her and bury my nose in her hair. I would take her inside, and we would do unspeakable things in front of the fire. We would have dinner when our children got home from school, and I would not waste a single thought on my crazy family back home.

"Better," I said, gesturing with my fishing rod back towards the bay. "Nothing biting today."

"Best left to professionals, I'd say. Fancy a cuppa later?"

"I'd like that."

"Stop by this evening," she said, making for the door.

"Jack?" Fusilli called from the kitchen. "I need you."

Nora laughed and flipped her hair to the side as she looked over her shoulder. "Feel free to bring the lovely Fusilli, if you like."

I went inside to find my cousin at the kitchen table, head in hands. He was pale and sweaty, enough so that I guessed it was something more than just his hangover at work.

"You all right, man?" I asked.

"Dark forces stalk me," he said.

"What does that even mean?"

"Kerry came by."

"Candy."

"Whatever, man. We got it on."

"Dude. On the couch?"

"No, in the Dungeon."

"Classy," I sighed.

Fusilli stood up and spun around, revealing scratch marks in his back in various stages of oozing or clotting.

"Jesus."

"Is it bad?"

"I've only been a doctor a few weeks, but it ain't good."

"I think she was speaking in tongues." He paused for a moment, then raised his eyebrows. "What do you know about exorcisms?"

"You're the archeologist."

"What if she's wolfen?"

"What if we tried an old-fashioned breakup before resorting to the dark arts?"

"Okay. We can handle Candy later."

"What's this *we* shit?"

"A mission," he said.

"Not tonight. I'm hanging with Nora," I said.

Fusilli's chest swelled, his eyes widening. "The burning bush will speak to you, as it did Moses."

"I've got a girlfriend, dude."

"Here," Fusilli said, flinging an envelope at me. "Let me help you with that."

My name was on the front, written in Mia's hand on an official DEA envelope. There was no postage.

"Where'd you get this?"

"Mia stopped by to surprise you on her way from DC. She couldn't wait around, though."

She'd added a good two hours to her trip with a detour to the beach. What was so important that she couldn't wait? An anxious suspicion seeped into my chest, same as it did when she cancelled plans at the last minute or when I couldn't get her on the phone. The note was an unexpected apology. She was sorry for "letting it be weird" with Ian and didn't want a childhood friendship to get in the way of our building a life together. She loved me, and she wasn't going to see him again. Her parents had gotten us tickets to see *Phantom of the Opera* in a few days. We could get together and talk more about the future then.

I should have been happy about this, or at least relieved, and part of me was. There was another part of me that felt she'd shown too little concern for my feelings for too long. At the end of the day, I was supposed to be Mia's partner. Ian was just some pentagram-scrawling weirdo she'd known since grade school.

Except, he wasn't. That's just what I told myself and what Fusilli and I told each other to temper my insecurities. Ian was decent-looking and wealthy. His résumé was impeccable, and he was vying for a position as one of the financial masters of

the universe. His family traded commercial real estate like
baseball cards. Even before he was working at the stock
exchange, his father was leasing him a new BMW every other
year and filling the trunk with the latest overpriced shit from
Nordstrom. I was going to be making subsistence-level wages
until I finished my internship and residency. On paper, he was
the better bet if you wanted to start a yuppie life, and Mia very
much wanted that life.

"Well?" Fusilli asked.

"She's sorry about the thing with the Witchdoctor."

"Wiccan," Fusilli corrected, taking a swig of his beer. "He
practices Wicca."

"He went to Yale, for God's sake."

"Where he studied the ancient wisdom."

"The fucker cooks books at the Stock Exchange!"

Fusilli and I looked at each other and broke up laughing.
The whole thing was ridiculous; I was competing with a white-
collar criminal who'd shown a passing interest in black magic.
It was nonsensical on its face. I needed to chill out.

"There's something else," Fusilli said.

"What's that?"

"Candy is a waitress in town. She thought she recognized
Mia from a few weeks back."

I rolled my eyes at him. Mia hadn't been down since the
previous summer. I was about to dismiss Candy as a flake when
we were interrupted by the sound of Aldo's El Camino sham-
bling into the drive, then the slam of the door. My uncle poured
himself into the chair my father once occupied at the head of
the table. It had been six years since Dad's passing, but his
chair was still the last to be filled at any meal. Aldo fished a
nearly empty pack of Camels from his T-shirt pocket and
nodded his thanks when Fusilli passed him a clamshell
ashtray.

Aldo coughed as he took a drag, then looked me over as he gestured towards the letter with his cigarette. "Who from?"

"My girlfriend," I said, crumpling the note and throwing it towards the trash. It bounced off the rim.

"Not good?"

I shrugged. "Whatever."

"He's gonna bang Nora," Fusilli said.

"I'm not going to bang Nora. I don't roll like that." I wasn't going to sleep with Nora, but goddamnit, I wanted to. I deserved it. *Mia* fucking deserved it. The one person who didn't deserve it was Nora. I needed to keep that last part centered in my mind. I wasn't going to pull a Fusilli on her.

"When I was younger than you, Uncle Antonio would deliver the bread when my parents were away," Aldo said. "I used to ride along and watch the truck while he got blowjobs from the lady on Guido Street. Then we'd go back home and have lunch with Aunt Marian."

"What's your point?" I asked.

"Commitment is a delusion," Aldo said.

"To thine own self be true," Fusilli added, putting on his most Shakespearean accent.

"Jesus Christ," I said.

"For fuck's sake, will you just live a little?" Fusilli said. "You're not married. You're not even engaged. You always hoped Nora would come back someday, and now she's *right fucking here.*"

"So, I get down with her and then lie about it?"

"No, you keep it to yourself," Fusilli said. "Just like Mia does."

I actively avoided thinking the way Fusilli did, because it ate away at any remaining trust I had in Mia. I loved her, and I wanted to believe in her, but she also might be on her way to Ian's, and I would be none the wiser.

"And what about loyalty?" I finally asked.

Fusilli tapped Aldo on the arm and pointed at me as if to say, "get a load of him."

Aldo rolled his eyes, his chair creaking as he rose to his feet and made for the front door. "Antonio and Marian are still married after fifty years."

As the screen door slammed behind Aldo, Fusilli began to laugh. "Goddamnit, Jack. He's starting to grow on me!"

"Fuck that guy," I spat.

6

Ducking through the gap in the hedge, I stood behind the Duffy's cottage for the first time in many years. They'd long cultivated the rustic coastal architecture. The siding was deeply weathered, the uniformity of the dark-stained shingle pattern broken by a few windows with large, white-framed jalousie glass panes. Nora stepped out onto the tiny back porch as I approached, clad in cutoff jean shorts and a baggy blue flannel with the sleeves rolled back. Her loose shirttail fluttered in a breeze presaging the squall line across the bay. She worked her fingers into her hair in a vain effort to disentangle her curls, which fell to her shoulders with the volume of a lion's mane.

"I think you were standing right there the last time I saw you," I said.

She winked at me. "Fusilli all right, then?"

"Fusilli is . . . not well."

"The inmates run the asylum, I reckon," she laughed. "What did he used to call me?"

"Miss Atomic Bomb," I said. "You earned it with the right hook you dropped on Brad."

"He shouldn't have grabbed my arse," she laughed. "I remember you two swooped in like Batman and Robin when he tried to get up."

"You didn't need us," I said, pantomiming her swing and the jerk of Brad's head. "Pow!"

Nora's dad had been an amateur boxer, and the apple hadn't fallen far from the tree. She put up her fists. "*Éirinn go Brách,* mate."

I raised my hands in surrender. Nora smiled and bounced down the two steps with confidence. I was surprised when she took my arm and pointed us towards the street. There was a hint of booze on her breath. "Let's go check out the sea. I bet it's in a state."

We passed rafts of darkened houses, their pebble lawns weedy and unkempt with the off-season, their yards missing the familiar dogpiles of beach cruisers. Salt mist hung heavy on the dunes beyond the boardwalk, outlining streetlamps and turning the distant southern amusement pier into a neon orange smear. Climbing the dune bridge, I imagined walking with Nora along the Cliffs of Moher, the carnival replaced by the twinkling lights of Galway. Did the ocean smell the same in Ireland? Would her saltwater kisses taste the way they did when we were young?

My escapist fantasy was interrupted by the sight of Mia's house on the next block. The excitement of possibility was replaced with guilt, as though I was a kid eating forbidden chocolate from my mother's baking closet, the kind that invariably tasted like shit. Was this how Fusilli felt during his shenanigans? I told myself we'd be unrecognizable from Mia's place, but that only made me feel worse. My guilt wasn't over the possibility of discovery but the realization that I was behaving dishonorably.

"So, Jack," Nora chirped. "What have you been up to the last few years?"

"You know, college and all that. I just finished medical school."

"Look at you! Your gran must be proud."

"You?"

"I studied journalism. Was writing for the local paper, but I got sacked."

"Ugh. Sorry."

"Fodder for my autobiography someday." She shrugged. "They'll say they knew me when."

"Are you still writing?"

"A bit," she said. "I'm a barmaid at Captain Kidd's for now. Prolly work for the Da when I get home until I figure things out."

"He had a grocery store, right?"

"Produce distributor."

I nodded, then looked back over my shoulder at a staggered flash of chain lightning over the bay. "I'm worried we're gonna get caught out here."

"Ye won't melt, will ye?"

I shrugged. "Your call."

"It's always raining back home," she said. "Nice soft days, we call them."

"I would love to see Ireland."

"You were always welcome."

"Your dad would beg to differ."

"His bark is worse than his bite."

I broke the deadlock, leading Nora onto the beach and away from Mia's house, as if physical distance might translate into its emotional equivalent.

"We had a lot of adventures in the old days, you and I," Nora said. "Learning to surf, going to the boardwalk." She poked me in the ribs playfully. "Shifting you under the boats."

Nora's breasts were the first I'd ever touched, the skin

perfectly smooth, the hollow between them firm and angular. In my inexperience, I'd expected them to be soft.

"Hard times to forget," I smiled. "Maybe that's the story you should write."

"It was the best summer of my life," she said, her eyes focusing on some invisible point in the middle distance. "Everything feels so intense when you're young."

"What brought you back?"

"I just needed a break, really. Lots of pressure the last few months."

I gestured to the Claddagh ring on her left hand, which was still wrapped around my arm. "From him?"

Nora let go, making me immediately regret the comment. Her cheeks turned more purple than red in the darkness. A bouquet of reflected lightning bloomed in her eyes.

"Em . . . yes." She paused. "Among others."

My stomach tightened. I lacked even the most basic instincts when it came to women. It was how I found myself wondering if my girlfriend was screwing someone else when the answer should have been obvious.

"Fuck. Sorry if that's a bad subject."

"It's all very confused at the moment," she said. "Let's leave it there, okay?"

"Fair enough."

She reached out and squeezed my shoulder. A moment later, there was a more violent peal of thunder, and it started to rain in steady, fat drops.

"For fuck's sake," she sighed, grasping my hand and pulling me towards the nearest passage through the dunes. "This isn't soft rain."

The rain increased to a steady downpour as we hurried back, our clothes soaking through by the time we got to the cottage. It was hard to pull my eyes from where her shirt was clinging to her hips and chest as she fiddled with her keys. She noticed my poorly veiled glances and grabbed a heavy woolen sweater as we entered. As its formless bulk swallowed her curves, she seemed to rethink the move. Her darkened eyes dared me to keep gawking as she left the top of the sweater unbuttoned, then tied the sash tight above her waist. She tried the lights, but the power was out.

"Dreadful," she sighed, ducking into the bathroom and returning with a pair of towels, throwing one my way.

I put it over my head and rubbed vigorously, then peered out from under it and broke into my best Irish brogue. *"Ye won't melt, will ye?"*

"Your accent is still shite," she laughed, pitching her towel back through the open bathroom door. She turned on her heel and slid into a narrow hallway that led towards the back of the cottage. "Will you have tea?"

"Sure." I followed her across hardwood floors that had been gently warped by the incessant humidity, the varnish worn away from generations of sandy feet. Entering the kitchen, she produced a hurricane lamp from the cupboard. My nose registered the oily smell of the fuel, followed by the sting of sulfur as she struck a match. She placed it on the small table against the western wall and adjusted the burner. The liquid in the lower vessel swirled gently beneath the flame, the glass upper curving like her hips into her waist, then flaring towards her chest.

"It's not like I remember it, Jack," she said, moving to the old enamel sink and filling a silver teapot. "Nobody lives here, really."

"It'll get busier after Memorial Day," I said. "Why did you come alone?"

"I wanted some time to think."

"About?"

"Ah, you know. Life's too fast, like."

I cracked a half-smile. "I remember you being much more . .
. direct, Nora."

"Look who's talking," she said, lifting an eyebrow. "You
didn't move into a flat with those nutters for a holiday, did you?
Where's the rest of your family?"

The thunder had grown so loud that each clap felt like a
safe landing on the roof, rattling glasses in the cupboards. I
lowered myself into one of the two chairs at the small table,
offering a sad chuckle. I thought about editing my story for her
and then decided not to bother. She would be gone in a matter
of weeks, and it might be good for me to unburden myself to
someone uninvolved.

"My family is a wreck, honestly," I said. "This whole scandal
with child abuse in the church? My brother was one of the
victims. That's how he got messed up on drugs."

"I'm sorry to hear it, Jack," Nora said, her eyes falling. "Ireland's no better."

"My parents worked in the parish and missed the signs,
until it was too late. Same as most other people. We stopped
talking when it got ugly. My dad died a couple years later."

"So, are you running away from something or towards
something?"

"A little of both, I figure."

"Maybe we know each other better than we think."

"I'm happy to listen, Nora."

"Ah, fuck it." She switched off the gas and stood there with
her hands on her hips for a moment. Then, she opened a
cabinet beneath the countertop, producing a half-empty bottle
of Irish whiskey and a pair of shot glasses. "We need something
stronger than tea for this conversation."

"I don't mean to pry."

"We're old friends, right?" she said, sitting on her knees on
the chair across from me. She cracked the bottle and poured us

both a shot. "I'm supposed to marry a lad I've known since I was a child."

"Daniel?" I asked.

She nodded.

"Congratulations," I said quietly, my heart deflating.

"We're drinking whiskey, Jack. Not champagne."

We locked eyes and slurped down our drinks. She poured another pair of shots. She sipped at this one, and I did likewise.

"You don't want to get married?"

"I'm the oldest girl. There are expectations." She ran a finger around the rim of her glass. "You remember Mum and the Da."

"Yeah." I reached for her hand, and she took it with a squeeze and a smile that seemed grateful. The last time I had seen her father was when Nora and I had kissed goodbye on Labor Day, 1989. Her mother had to keep him from beating the living Jesus out of me. Nora later wrote that he dragged her to confession the morning they landed in Dublin.

"I'm just not ready to be someone's live-in maid and child-minder."

"It's not the 1950s anymore."

"Closer than you think in County Clare," she said softly. She paused for a beat, then rapped her glass on the table like a gavel. "Right, you must be the most eligible bachelor in town by now, Doctor. Do you have someone?"

"Sort of," I lied. I was surprised at how easily the words escaped my lips. This wasn't like me at all. I'd always tried to talk Mia up. Georgetown. Salutatorian. Law School. Working for the DEA.

She raised an eyebrow.

"It was long distance for years and became kind of a mess."

"How so?"

"I think there's someone else."

"Ah," she nodded. "So, what's next?"

"I need to have a real talk with her. I've needed to for a while."

"You either do a thing," she said firmly, meeting my eyes, "or not."

"That's your mother talking."

"Maybe."

I drained what remained of my shot, my stomach warm and my head beginning to swim from the first. I'd never been much of a drinker, mostly beer in college and much less of it in medical school. Nora poured me another.

"We put a lot of pressure on ourselves," I said. "Firstborn and trying to live up to expectations. We should have freedom to explore."

She raised an eyebrow at me, her lips perched in a Cheshire half-smile, ready to pounce.

"*We?*"

I felt my cheeks flush and looked away. "You know, we. Like, the royal we."

"Right," she said, her voice alive with barely restrained laughter. She leaned forward, her hair spilling over her face like a veil. She sat back up and finished her drink before pulling a hair tie from her wrist and bundling her mane into a poorly controlled ponytail.

"I apologize," I said, clamping my eyes shut for a moment. "I don't even know what I'm saying. Ignore me."

The light danced yellow orange across Nora's brow and nose, leaving her face half in shadow. She pushed the lamp aside, then leaned across the table and gathered my hands in hers. My guts weightless, I leaned in awkwardly to kiss her. First our lips, gentle and soft, then our tongues slick with whiskey, and then a sigh as I ran a hand up her neck and into the mass of damp curls behind her ear. I was a teenager again, reliving one of my most intense experiences. Then, my conscience began reeling in my libido.

I pulled back slowly, but only by a half-measure. "I should probably go," I whispered, my chest filled with equal parts excitement and self-loathing.

"Like my Gran used to say," she chuckled, leaning back and cradling her chin in her hands. "If it's drownin' you're after, don't torment yourself with shallow water."

"I'm going to write that one down."

"So, what's she like?" Nora asked, her tone adrift between suspicious and playful. "This girlie of yours."

"It's a long story."

"We've got all night, Jack."

7
———

It wasn't always fraught between Mia and me, but it wasn't always clear that it was going to work out, either. Labor Day hit like a heavyweight that first summer we were together. On the Sunday night before the holiday, Mia and I crawled under the overturned lifeguard boat for the last time before our junior year of college. We'd only been sleeping together a month or so but had figured out each other's rhythms quickly after the initial awkwardness. Her body rose again and again to meet me until we were both spent, until she broke down and her tears mingled with the sweat pouring off my face.

"It has to end," she whispered, thumping a fist against my chest. "It has to end, but I don't want it to."

"It's a long way from Washington to Albany."

"It still feels like shit."

The surf peeled softly across the sandbar in the distance. I didn't want it to be over either, but I also didn't want to get tied into a relationship that was doomed to long-distance failure. I knew a half-dozen people who'd been heartbroken when their high-school love found someone new at college. I had to believe the statistics for Jersey Shore romances were even bleaker.

"You said you wanted the summer of your life," I said. "Did it deliver?"

"Yeah, but falling in love with you wasn't part of the plan."

"No?"

"You were supposed to be the patsy, remember?" She pushed me off to the side and tucked against me like a spoon. "The summer fling before I started studying for LSATs."

"The MCATs won't be any picnic, either," I said. "But you've been a great distraction."

She elbowed me in the ribs. "So, now what am I supposed to do, wise guy?"

"We'll keep in touch."

"That's going to make it worse, not better."

"How about this," I offered, kissing her ear and hugging her close. "If you still love me come October, maybe I'm more than a summer fling, and we'll figure something out."

That fall, I was registered for the 2 p.m. showing of the Admiral's European History Hour. The Admiral was Dr. Ken Donaldson, a short tree trunk of a man with Popeye forearms. His voice was deep, militaristic, and loud to the point that we all assumed he must be half-deaf from wrestling steam pipes in the bowels of a diesel-powered destroyer. In truth, I didn't have any idea what his duties or rank had been. I only knew he had served for the better part of thirty years in the US Navy before retiring to academia. Everyone called him "sir" after one of the ROTC kids set the precedent on the first day of class.

The Admiral's course consisted primarily of lecture, or rather, of his hollering at us about military strategy and dates. On the first Thursday in October, it had grown unseasonably warm with a tropical system that had moved north from the Carolinas. The humidity and honeyed light of autumn pouring through the open windows made me think of the beach and of

Mia. I imagined sitting in the shadows of the gazebo at the top of the street, watching her brush her hair in her distant bedroom mirror. I would wait a half-hour after her lights went out before creeping up to her window and levering the screen open. She would lean out and kiss me sweetly before we stole off into the night.

I regretted not telling Mia I loved her, regretted not making a plan before we left the safety of the beach and retreated to our winter lives on campus. We'd discovered something new and precious in each other and were going to squander it over concerns of standardized tests, grades, and careers. I'd lost my high school girlfriend, Mae, after not following her to California. Geography seemingly had it in for me again.

My moment of self-flagellation was badly timed because the Admiral was on a tear.

"And Hitler," Donaldson yelled, his voice booming off the painted block walls, his fist pounding the podium with each emphasized word. "A rank *corporal* chose to discount the advice of his generals, who were some of the best military minds in history."

He paused for a moment before shouting, "Frére!"

My heart stopped as I looked up to meet the Admiral's glare. "Yessir?"

"What do you think about that?"

"Crazy, sir!" I barked. "But unsurprising from a fascist who demanded fealty rather than the advice of an apolitical military."

The Admiral held his tongue a moment and then offered a cockeyed grin. "Good man," he said, clearly amused at having nearly caught me out. He gestured towards the window. "Don't get too distracted by your friend out there."

My eyes found her feet first, the gathering maple leaves burning red and orange and rippling around her ankles. The hem of her little flowered sundress clung tight to one leg and flowed freely from the other. Her arms were crossed just below the curve of her breasts. Mia's eyes wrinkled as she smiled and offered the smallest wave. It took me a moment to process the scene, to understand that I was witnessing reality and that I had a part to play in it. Before I knew what I was doing, I'd swung my legs over the radiator and ducked through the window, heading for Mia on a dead run like the money shot of a shitty '80s rom-com. I gathered her up in my arms.

"Surprise!" she squealed.

"How?"

"I flew," she said, grabbing my face and kissing me. "It wasn't that expensive. I bought some extra textbooks on my dad's credit card, then said I lost the card and returned them for cash."

"You're unbelievable."

"Believe it," she said. "It's October third, and I'm still in love with you. That was the deal."

I'd helped my roommate rebuild an old Harley sophomore year and called in the favor when we got back to the dorm. Stuffing some camping gear into the saddlebags, Mia and I disappeared into the warm twilight of the New England fall. I was grateful for the feeling of her arms tied around me as we wound towards Vermont, for the second chance I didn't feel I deserved. She'd never been on a bike before, but her knees clamped tight to my hips, and her laughter in my ear urged me to crack the throttle wider out of each successive turn.

By sunset, we found ourselves on a secluded quarry lake, in a sweet-smelling stand of pines. Our footfalls were soft on the browning needles as we made our way through the trees, towards the campsite at the far edge of the granite pool.

I built us a fire and put out a tarp and our blankets so that we could lie under the stars, the way we had on the beach all summer. Beneath the protection of Orion's sword, we undressed each other slowly as the crackling of the logs kept time beside us.

"I was expecting a charming country inn," Mia said as we slipped beneath the covers. "My idea of roughing it is a hotel with room service only until midnight."

"Champagne taste and beer money," I said. "But look, we've got nowhere to go but up."

"I'm going to hold you to that when we graduate from professional school."

"You planning on hanging around that long?"

She slid her hands down my stomach and took hold of me. "I've gotten attached."

"I love you, Mia. I shouldn't have let you go the way I did."

She smiled against my cheek, then kissed my neck. "How about this," she said. "If you still love me in November, then maybe this is more than a fall fling, and I'll let you come over for Thanksgiving."

My lips found hers, and my lungs filled with the familiar warmth of her skin, and I was the happiest I had ever been. Six years later, the memories of that weekend were as vivid to me as the moment I'd made them. I learned that Mia had a way of calming my mind, of narrowing my focus and blurring the edges until all that remained was the moment I was sharing with her. It was hard to let go of that. Part of me wanted to believe she still felt the same way. That we could still be the same way. That there was some way of turning back the clock and resurrecting those early feelings, but each sweet memory I tried to summon seemed contaminated. Part of it was what I feared she'd done with Ian, but part of it was the game I was playing with Nora.

$$8$$

Morning found me flipping my pillow repeatedly, looking for a cool spot to rest my cheek. Each turn left me slightly more surprised that Aldo had not yet rousted us. I got up around noon and made a quick survey of the premises, finding no evidence that my uncle had returned the night before. I made some coffee, which eventually attracted Fusilli like a shark following a chum line. When the moka pot finished its bubbling, I poured us each a half mug. He raised the cup to his lips, then made a face and went for the sugar bowl, its contents petrified with age and humidity. Fusilli broke off a chunk the size of a walnut and dropped it into his cup.

I went to the front porch and straddled the railing, the sun heavy on my face, same as it once felt from my lifeguard chair. Closing my eyes, I inhaled the dry perfume of the dune grass and knapweed and tried to access my younger self. In the old days, my life revolved around the tides and weather forecast. My grandparents were young for their age rather than ailing. Fusilli was more circus sideshow than agent of chaos. Lord, take me back to the time of sneaking under catamarans with Nora.

"So," Fusilli asked, allowing the door to slam behind him. "How were your negotiations with the Irish?"

"We had a nice visit. She's working at Kidd's. Has a fiancé back in Ireland."

"Let's try this again. How did it go with Nora?"

"I didn't sleep with her, if that's what you mean."

"Not yet."

"Give me a break, man."

"I just want you to live a little."

"You want to live vicariously through me."

"I am understandably curious," he said, eyebrow raised. "Red is nature's danger signal."

"Danger signal?"

Fusilli shrugged. "Katie says she's pretty wild."

"Whatever."

I put my mug down and leaned back on the railing, the heat of the day radiating into my spine. Nora *had* put away an impressive amount of whiskey, and for a woman betrothed, had been awfully eager to make out. Warning signs, or exuberance at breathing free American air? I wasn't about to debate it with my cousin, but Nora might not be the kind of woman I should risk my relationship with Mia and her family for.

"Is your place in Italy all set?" I asked.

"Yeah," he said. "Same place I crashed in the spring. The university rents it."

"The idea of you in the Vatican Library blows my mind."

"The wily Fusilli can adapt to a variety of habitats," he said, approximating David Attenborough. "Known as the Happy Genius, Fusilli thrives in dank crypts, musty libraries, and Syrian whorehouses perfumed with frankincense and myrrh."

Fusilli was no genius, but he was both a little too smart for his own good and had a knack for stepping in shit. During his master's work, he'd been assigned to a dig in Israel. He was part of a team that uncovered an ancient Zealot antechamber and, within it, a number of well-preserved writings. After their initial study, Fusilli's thesis advisor believed there was evidence that Christ and his followers had revolutionary political leanings. The text told a decidedly different story than what the church had cultivated for two millennia. This would be the subject of Fusilli's PhD work. This would have been a coup under any circumstances, but there was more. Fusilli's inarguable good looks and ability to wax poetic got him an interview on the then-nascent National Geographic Channel. He got more airtime than his boss. I thought there was a decent chance he'd become a talking head in their regular programming.

"You'll have to come visit," Fusilli said. "Italian women are something."

"I already have one."

He flapped his lips. "Mia is Italian-American. You can do better."

"Have you?"

He winked. "I don't kiss and tell, *Dottore.*"

"Yeah, sure. When was the last time you saw Katie?"

"We had a nice visit at Easter. It's just hard, traveling so much."

It had been years since I'd seen Katie in anything other than a photograph. She'd been over for Christmas break a couple of times and seemed to have been growing up into a sensible woman. I couldn't imagine what she was still doing with my cousin.

"Would she be willing to join you in Italy?" I asked.

"Not necessary. I'm going to try to keep my Italy trips short and do most of my writing at Trinity."

I raised an eyebrow.

"Her idea," he said with a shrug, "not mine. You can ask her yourself when she gets here."

"She gonna crash with Nora?"

"The Villabaia Refuge for the Mentally Deficient seems beneath her, don't you think?"

"You're still hiding the true nature of this family from her?"

"Wouldn't you?" He laughed. "Speaking of which, when's the invasion of your siblings expected?"

"I'm not sure it is. Aurora's finally working. Lidia is applying to graduate programs. Gabriella is . . . being Gabriella. But it would be good to get Marco down here and away from his druggie friends."

"You're not responsible for his shit, man. I hope you know that."

I'd gone to my parents when our parish priest started acting weird with me but allowed them to half-convince me that I was misinterpreting his behavior. In the meantime, he was already abusing my brother and introducing him to the opiates that would derail his life. I was an Eagle Scout and my dad was a pillar of the community. The authorities might have believed me had I gone to them earlier. Marco blamed me for not rescuing him and, in my darker moments, I thought he might be right.

"It would be nice if *he* knew that," I said. "But I appreciate the sentiment."

We were interrupted by the jangle of the old rotary telephone in the kitchen. I moved to stand, but Fusilli waved dismissively and disappeared through the screen door. He reappeared a few moments later. "Grandma and Grandpa are coming down," he said.

I raised my eyebrows.

"He wants to go crabbing," he continued.

"Maybe he's feeling better?"

"I guess we'll see."

I took the premed track as an undergraduate, but my first love was physics. Grandpa was the person who first recognized my aptitude and nurtured it like one of the tomato plants in his garden. When I was five or six, he caught me with a pair of old binoculars on the front porch. Perched on the railing in my Luke Skywalker Underoos, I was scanning the sky for spacecraft, hoping for the imminent arrival of X-wing fighters. The next day, Grandpa ordered a six-inch reflector telescope out of the back of an astronomy magazine he found at the drugstore in town. He assembled it later that week and, in so doing, changed my life forever.

Grandpa led me to the park across the street. I trailed behind him with a large bucket. Setting up near the edge of the bay, beyond the merry-go-round and monkey bars, he brought Jupiter and its moons into focus and stepped aside. I climbed atop my overturned pail and peeked into the eyepiece. Jupiter was a swirling pink and peach marble, set like the central pearl in my mother's favorite necklace, strung within a line of tiny Galilean moons that shone like diamonds. Dumbfounded, I turned to look over my shoulder at the full moon rising behind us. My grandfather peered at me over his bifocals and asked what I was thinking.

"Is there someone on Jupiter looking at our moon?"

"I don't know," he asked. "How could we find out?"

"Let's wait until it's nighttime there and look for streetlights."

"Good idea."

Grandpa adjusted the equatorial mount as the stars marched across the night. I checked Jupiter again and again until I finally fell asleep with my head in his lap, dreaming that I could leap into the sky. My future as a scientist was written. When I got to college, I had access to extraordinary optics that could track celestial bodies with surgical precision. Their crisp resolution was a technical marvel, but the subjective experience was always lacking. It felt meaningless when compared against the memory of seeing the planets first-hand at age six, my grandfather's hand patiently turning the knobs to keep Jupiter squarely in my field of view.

I made a mental note to get the telescope back from Mia's place as Grandpa pulled into the driveway, the sand crackling under the wheels of his old cat-shit green Plymouth Duster. The creak of the parking brake was followed by the two taps of the horn that always heralded his arrival. I hurried to the back door as I had every weekend of my childhood. Grandpa exited the door quickly and closed it firmly, but his white T-shirt and houndstooth baker's pants hung loose on his limbs, as though he was cosplaying a geriatric skate rat. He'd lost more weight in the few weeks since I'd last seen him. Grandpa made his way to the trunk slowly, then sprung the latch and reached inside, producing a cardboard box full of fresh bread from the family bakery and vegetables from the stand in town.

Grandma came around the opposite side of the car. She was a little slower since her knee replacements. The surgeon who'd done the work didn't believe in physical therapy, which meant she never got her full range of motion back. Orthopedic surgeons made me tired. The joke about them protecting their hands by stopping elevator doors with their heads was right on. She wrestled a great pot of tomato sauce from the trunk, then balanced it on the bumper as she closed the lid.

I sprung the latch on the screen door and offered to take the box from my grandfather, but he shook his head at me as he squeezed past, unwilling to yield to disease or time. My grandmother had no such reservations and passed her pot of sauce to me, the aluminum shell dented and scratched from decades of Sunday dinners. It had originally belonged to her mother.

"Take this a minute, would you, sweetheart?" she said.

I nodded as I accepted the weight, as surprised as I ever was that she was able to move it around.

Grandpa dropped his box on the table with a thump. "Crabs biting?" Grandpa asked over his shoulder. "We should catch a few to throw in the sauce."

"Francesco," Grandma said. "We need to start saving them for Christmas."

"Breathe through your mouth, Elena," he said, smoothing the shock of white hair that continued to defy his chemotherapy. "Plenty to go around."

Grandma followed me and toddled towards the refrigerator. Her close-cropped, half-gray hair and minimal wrinkles belied her age. She could have easily passed for a woman in her late sixties despite having eighty-two years on the odometer. Her approach to life was relentless, her daily routine of cooking, cleaning, and volunteer work a strange fountain of youth that kept her body strong and her mind sharp. There were no measurements when she was in front of the stove. She judged by eye as her mother had and her grandmother before. For Grandma, cooking was her expression of love for us. She never looked happier than when I came home from the beach early and squished a couple of her meatballs between slabs of Italian bread. "*Mangia e fatta grossa,*" she would say.

There was a quick knock at the back door as we unpacked the groceries, then the sandy metallic grind of its skirt against the threshold.

"Uncle Francesco? Auntie Elena?" Nora called as she stepped in, pulling her curls away from her face and tying them back with an elastic from her wrist. "Is that you?"

Grandpa raised his bushy eyebrows and turned, his features softening. "Nora girl?" he said. "You're all growed up!"

"Surprise!" I said.

"Been a few years, hasn't it?" she said as she hurried towards Grandpa. "You're looking fit, aren't you?"

"They haven't put me out to pasture yet," he said. "How's the family? How's your father?"

She waved a hand dismissively, then leaned down to kiss him on the cheek. "Wondering what I'm doing here at the beach instead of helping at the warehouse, I suppose."

"Tell him I'll give him a good price on my tomatoes."

"Sweetheart," my grandmother said, tears forming in the corner of her eyes as she wrapped her arms around Nora's waist. "Look how beautiful. Your mother's Christmas cards don't do you justice."

"Oh, g'way outta that!"

"What brings you back?" Grandma asked.

"You know," Nora said, sending a wink and thumb in my direction. "I'm between jobs and thought I should come keep this lot out of trouble."

"You've got your work cut out for you," Grandpa laughed. He turned to me and shook a threatening fist. "You and your knucklehead cousin behave yourselves. She's a nice girl!"

"She's a *good* girl," Grandma corrected. "My mother always said, 'there are *good* girls and there are *nice* girls. Know the difference'."

"My gran was much more direct with my brothers," Nora laughed.

"Oh?" Grandma said.

"*Stiúradh saor ó claitseach*," Nora said. "Steer clear of sluts."

Grandma belly laughed. "The old timers are always worried about the family name."

"The Italians and the Irish aren't so different," Nora said.

Grandma's expression grew wistful and distant. "When I first got my period, I thought I was sick. I went to my mother, and she slapped me across the face and said, 'Never let a man touch you!'" She laughed. "I had no idea what she meant!"

"Not exactly proper sex ed, is it?" Nora said.

"'Better I cry at your grave than you bring dishonor to our

family', she would say," Grandma continued, shaking a crooked finger at us. "I was scared of my mother. I tried to do better with my children." She pulled me down by the arm and kissed my cheek. "And grandchildren."

"You occasionally succeeded," Grandpa said.

What would my grandparents think if they learned I'd been making out with Nora? That I was aspiring to be a philandering jerk like my cousin and uncles? I wasn't going to sleep with Nora. I wasn't. Yeah, we made out a little. I was just enjoying time spent with someone from the old days, someone who knew me before I was an anxious mess and saddled with nearly a half-million dollars in student loan debt. Mia and I had history, and she came from money. It's not that I would have married for money, but a future with Mia made sense for lots of reasons. If she really wanted the Witchdoctor, she would have left me for him by now. I wasn't seriously going to risk everything for a decade-old childhood crush. That was crazy talk. Nora would go back to Ireland in a few weeks, and all of this would be a brief, harmless detour.

GRANDPA STRAPPED on a pair of old sneakers from the bucket we kept under the back porch, then waded into the shallows. Fusilli and I did likewise. You didn't enter the bay barefoot, lest you step on the remains of a beer bottle or kick a cinder block mooring. The old boat bobbed ahead of us, a sixteen-foot Ray Hunt design with a closed bow, small windshield, and seating for six. The aquamarine paint was peeling in the places it hadn't worn away completely, while the original registration numbers on the bow had been replaced by reflective mailbox sticker lettering. The stern hung lower than it should have under the weight of an outboard motor long past its prime. It was only sixty-five horsepower but took a few people to lift.

Someone had once tried to steal the damn thing off the transom and gave up after dragging it ten feet across the sand. It took us weeks to clean it out and get it running again.

Grandpa opened the canvas cover, then heaved himself over the stern with surprising agility. Maybe he wasn't as sick as I'd thought? Fusilli and I followed, then made our way forward on opposite sides to finish opening and stowing the cover, the report of each snap like popcorn. Grandpa reconnected the battery and fuel lines and started the engine. The stern settled lower as he dropped the prop, the clatter of the pistons finding the low rhythm of my childhood. As Fusilli disconnected the mooring line and Grandpa pointed us towards the channel, I wondered how many more of these rides we'd have together. The thought was cut short as Grandpa jammed the throttle against the stop, throwing us headlong into the mildewed rear seats. He laughed over his shoulder as we sped towards deeper water.

It was a fifteen-minute ride around the back side of Dead Head Island to the grassy flats. Halfway across the bay, the brackish salt breeze began to mix with the manure of the horse farms on the far side. The water was quiet and not much more than chest deep. Grandpa killed the throttle, allowing us to coast to a stop as our wake overtook us. He used the wheel to pull himself upright but paused at three-quarter height, grimacing and reaching a hand behind his back. I wondered if the disease was spreading to his bones. It was a rare complication of his cancer and usually a poor prognostic indicator.

"You okay?" I asked.

"My back," he grunted. "Just the usual."

Fusilli and I exchanged a glance as Grandpa reached into his old wicker creel and produced a handful of drop lines, weighted bait clips wrapped in a long length of twine. You stuck the pointy end through a piece of fish, usually moss bunker, clipped it tight, and then dropped it over the side.

When a crab started walking away with it, you retrieved the bait slowly, finger over finger, then netted both the remaining bait and your quarry. With any luck, you had dinner in a few hours.

Fusilli began unrolling the drop lines as I pulled the bag of defrosting moss bunker out of the bushel basket. Using a bait knife, I began cutting the fish into thirds: head, midsection, and tails. I was careful as I worked. The oily reek of bunker was impossible to get out of contaminated clothing, defying the most powerful laundry detergent and following the unfortunate sportsman like a voodoo curse. Fusilli helped bait the lines with equal care and tossed them over the stern as Grandpa perched himself on the back of the driver's seat. He began casting off the starboard side with a lightweight rod. Line buzzed from the reel as his lure arced towards the deeper water of the channel, then spiraled back through the bronze guides as he began the retrieve. The rod was a classic from the Leonard Company, hewn from bamboo and coated with a thick yellow varnish. Originally meant for fly fishing, it had silk wrappings and cork grips, both of which had seen better days. In fairness, the thing probably belonged in a museum. I'd once looked it up in the library. The stamp on the reel seat suggested manufacture in the early 1920s.

"Maybe we ought to get you a new pole this summer," I said.

"Nah," Grandpa said. "This one still works. I got it off Joe Ellsworth during the war. He taught me how to cast flies in a rice paddy."

"Did you guys keep in touch?"

"He never made it back."

"Ugh," I said. "Sorry."

My grandfather rarely talked about the war, at least not the real war. He told stories about working in the hospital, about the guy he'd put in a body cast for the trip home after driving a

Jeep off a cliff, about passing instruments to surgeons of super-human skill. He sometimes laughed about shooting primitive antibiotics into the asses of soldiers who'd gotten venereal diseases, a legacy I'd once honored by treating my cousin for the same. Grandpa talked about how he got so drunk on VJ Day that his friends carried him out of the officer's club and put him in a cot in the nurse's showers. However, Grandpa never spoke of death, of fearing a Japanese advance, of standing on deck on a troop transport in the middle of the ocean, wondering if a whitecap was actually an oncoming torpedo that would blow him to kingdom come. What was it like to be a kid from the mines of Pennsylvania and suddenly find yourself in the South Pacific, checking your bunk for snakes or your shoes for scorpions?

I started threading a bunker head onto a clip and Grandpa waved, putting his pole aside. He squatted down next to me, relieving me of the knife. "This is how I learned to do it in China," he said. He hadn't been to China so far as I knew but had used the line a million times when we were kids, anytime he meant to teach us something. My dad once tried to appro-priate the catchphrase, but my sister Aurora set him straight.

"No, Daddy," she said. "Only Grandpa went to China."

Grandpa spun the knife in his hand, then used the point of the blade to pop the eyes from the fish head and fling them over the side the way a Vegas dealer might throw cards. He then put the tip of the bait clip through the empty sockets.

"The eyes scare the crabs away," Grandpa explained.

"I thought that was an old wives' tale," I said. Grandpa just winked at me.

I moved to drop the bait, tying the end of the line to one of the cleats on the port side. Fusilli had already put the other lines in the water off the stern, and one of them was taut.

"Fusilli," I said. "Get the net."

I started bringing the line up slowly, the edge of the

gunwale digging into my ribs. The weight of the crab and the intermittent tug as he tried to swim off with the bait were thrilling. I was ten years old again and in my element. As the crab materialized from the ochre gloom, Fusilli stabbed with his net and swept the hoop under our prey, snaring it and pulling it from the water, legs flailing and claws snapping at the air.

"All right!" Grandpa enthused, pushing the old wicker bushel basket towards us. "One down. Scoop up some weed to put in the basket to keep him from drying out."

Fusilli inverted the net over the basket, dumping the crab. It skittered across the staves in a vain effort to climb out. I turned my attention back to my line. The crab had done a number on my bait, pulling most of the remaining entrails from the hollow in the center of the fish. As I tried to reposition the bait clip for better purchase, the fish slipped from my grasp and into the water.

"Shit," I spat.

Fusilli wasn't quick enough with the net. A decent-sized bluefish flashed beneath us, snagging the bait in his mouth and disappearing into the glare of the rising sun.

"Shit," I repeated.

"It's like when you're making time with a chippie at the bar," Grandpa said. "You buy her a few drinks, then you turn your back for a minute, and someone takes off with her. Fattening frogs for snakes, Ellsworth used to call it."

"They never got away with our bait back in the day," Fusilli said. "I was the Master Baiter."

"You, uh, might want to rethink that title, buddy," Grandpa said.

The three of us exchanged looks and started laughing. My grandfather loved to laugh. You couldn't have paid him to watch a drama or war movie, but he'd watch *Looney Tunes* with us for hours. His favorites were the Wile E. Coyote sketches, particularly the one where he refers to himself as a super genius while Bugs Bunny repeatedly outwits him. If it wasn't *Looney Tunes* on Saturday, it was Abbott and Costello on Sunday while my grandmother was making the sauce. Grandpa's older brother, Chris, worked as a bartender in comedian Jack Benny's restaurant. When Grandpa went to visit Chris after the war, he'd sneak Grandpa into the joint after hours to hear Benny entertain the staff. Grandpa always said Benny was a good guy who never put on airs and always had kind words for his people. I would have given anything to go back in time and see my grandfather as a young man in the back of the bar, tossing back a beer and laughing his head off.

Not getting any action, Grandpa reeled up his line a final time and changed his spoon for a surface popper. Tying on the new lure, he asked, "How's that Irish lass of yours, Don?"

A strange look crossed Fusilli's face, like a cat trying to decide if he was going to knock a plant from a high shelf. He thought better of whatever he was about to say, then offered a curt, "Okay, I guess."

"Trouble in paradise?" Grandpa asked. "Your grandmother says she's coming over for a visit."

"Things are good," Fusilli said. "You know how it is. A lot of travel, not a lot of time together."

"I understand," Grandpa said. "I was overseas for four years in the war, exchanging letters with your grandmother."

"Was that hard on you?" I asked. "You were engaged then, right?"

"Yeah, engaged," he said. "But there weren't a lot of options in the South Pacific, anyway. Especially New Guinea. There were the nurses, of course, but you didn't risk fraternizing. Then, there were the Ubangis."

"Ubangis?" Fusilli asked.

"The natives," he said. "Some of the fellas would go down to the paddies and have fun with them. But I didn't want to have to tell the priest in confession, so I kept my whistle clean."

Fusilli and I laughed.

"Your whistle?" I said. "I'm gonna have to remember that one."

Grandpa peered at Fusilli over his bifocals. "Maybe consider it a little bit of free advice."

"Huh?" Fusilli asked.

"It's fun getting your oil changed," Grandpa said. "But mind the consequences."

"Yeah," Fusilli said, his eyes falling. "Consequences."

"You make your choices, and then you live with them," Grandpa said, winding up for another cast. "That's the name of the game."

Although he couched his values non-confrontationally, our grandfather had a deep-rooted sense of personal responsibility. The youngest of six children, his father had worked in the coal mines of Pennsylvania while his mother farmed a small plot of land and raised chickens. He often told stories about gathering eggs before school and of dodging the falling debris that killed a boyhood friend collecting errant coal from the slag pile. It was hard for me to imagine chipping away at rocks to ensure your family had heat or being so hungry that you ate fruit and vegetable peels. I wasn't cut out for depression living, but part of me felt that history in my blood. It was how I survived the delayed gratification of endless schooling, of living loan check to loan check, of subsisting on ramen noodles and Grandma's leftovers.

Grandpa's parents died just after his seventh birthday. He and his twin brother ended up in a Catholic orphanage in Philadelphia. It was clear the nuns had been hard taskmasters. Grandpa once said that the discipline of the army was easy compared to the day-to-day at St. Joseph's House for Homeless and Industrious Boys. Despite his hard upbringing, or perhaps because of it, my grandfather was relentlessly positive and had an unparalleled work ethic. He was a formidable role model. He insisted we do things *because* they were difficult and framed setbacks as backhanded encouragement. If I complained about a challenging exam or patient, he always offered the same response: Would you want to be called Doctor if it were easy?

Grandpa opened the bail on his reel and cast his line out over the bow. The lure crossed the sky like a meteor, then fell to the water some twenty yards away. He began his retrieve in a series of sharp tugs that caused the popper to splash like a struggling baitfish.

"Do you think it was easier in your day?" Fusilli asked.

"In a way," Grandpa said. "The Depression was hard, but the choices were simple. We didn't expect to be happy. You worked, or you died. You fellas have so many opportunities, you don't know whether to shit or go blind."

We laughed as he continued. "But I think if you stick to your principles, you'll do all right. Take your big cousin over there. He's got it figured out."

My stomach tightened. I didn't want to be held up as an example.

"I think I'll keep my own counsel on this one," Fusilli said with a crooked smile.

It took us a couple of hours to fill the bushel basket and return to the mooring. Once we came ashore, we set about dispatching the crabs. Grandpa used the pole of the dip net to fling a crab onto the sand, then pinned it in place by putting the pole across its claws. He grabbed the point of the carapace and, with a cheerful "so long, Charlie . . ." pulled it off, separating the brain from the body and revealing the crab's innards. Grandpa handed the bodies over to us for further processing. We pulled out the guts and gills and rinsed the bodies clean in the bay, Fusilli singing "Another One Bites the Dust" over the chattering of the gulls. It all felt remarkably normal. Like

Grandpa wasn't dying. Like I wasn't sleepwalking into an illicit affair akin to the one my cousin was embroiled in.

THE WESTING SUN sharpened the contrast between the black-iron framed windows and the bone white shingles as we approached Villabaia. It would have been a peaceful scene if not for the escalating battle royale within. The commotion sounded like it was coming from the kitchen. Grandpa, Fusilli, and I exchanged uncomfortable glances at the sound of Grandma's voice carrying through the curtains as we walked up the pebble drive.

"Aldo," she said, her voice equal parts angry and confused. "What are you doing with this stuff? You're not a kid anymore."

"Don't worry about it," he said.

"Yeah, 'don't worry about it' . . ." she said, mimicking his inflection. "You need to straighten out."

"It's not mine," he said. "I keep it here for Jerry Fitz. So his kids don't get into it."

"And what about your nieces and nephews? What about when they get here next month?

"I'll worry about it then. It's just a little grass."

"Your father isn't going to be around forever, Aldo," she said. "At some point, you're going to be the head of this family. You need to set the example for the next generation."

"Some things skip a generation, Ma. I didn't ask for the job, and I'm not taking it."

We circled around the back of the house. My grandfather sighed, propped his fishing pole up against the old Plymouth, then leaned into the car, resting his butt against the driver's door. His white T-shirt was laden with sweat and hanging from his shoulders, the underarms slightly discolored with antiperspirant. He looked tired, perhaps from the day on the boat and his cancer, but maybe also from trying and failing to reach his son for the better part of fifty years. Grandpa took his black plastic comb from his pocket and smoothed his hair back.

"That's Aldo," Grandpa muttered.

Fusilli and I started towards the stairs.

"Hold up," Grandpa said. "Let them hash it out. Pretty soon, I won't be here to referee."

My cousin and I exchanged a look. We would have all liked it if Aldo and Grandma could learn how to deal with each other. I didn't see it in the cards. They had been at odds since his birth. According to my mom, it was at least seventy-five percent of the reason Aldo had moved to Alaska in the first place. My grandfather was the eternal optimist, but he was wrong here. This was only going to get worse after his moderating influence was gone.

Aldo continued his tirade. "When exactly did I become leadership material, Ma? When the nuns used to keep me for detention four days out of five? When Uncle Pietro would grab my balls when I walked past?"

"Your father handled Pietro. Why do you always bring up the past?"

Grandpa crossed his arms. "Pietro was no good. He got what was coming to him."

Fusilli and I exchanged uncomfortable glances. Uncle Pietro had a bad reputation among the older generations in my family. They only mentioned him in passing and only in Italian. He might have spent some time in prison and died unexpectedly in the early sixties. I didn't want to know what misfortune had befallen him.

Inside, Aldo kept pushing.

"Maybe . . ." Aldo said. "Maybe it was when I got Wendy O'Donnell pregnant, and we went to Harlem for the abortion."

Fusilli's expression said he knew as little about this as I did. Time seemed to slow as we looked at Grandpa. Grandpa stretched his arms behind him, gripping the edge of the car roof and looking every bit like Jesus on the cross. A bead of sweat rolled down his nose and fell to the sand, making a tiny dark spot that could have been mistaken for blood.

"We don't talk about Wendy like that," Grandma said.

"I loved her!" Aldo shouted. "They sent her away like trash!"

"She couldn't have children after what happened," Grandpa said. "She got septic and lost some . . . organs. She took her vows and joined the convent."

Fusilli looked over his shoulder and then dragged a toe through the sand slowly, purposefully. Was he considering his own experiences? Were there decisions that kept him up at night?

"You make your choices," Fusilli murmured, repeating Grandpa's earlier words. "And then you live with them."

Grandma and Aldo weren't letting up in the kitchen.

"It was tragic," Grandma said. "What happened to her was a terrible thing."

"If we don't talk about it, it never happened, right? Like the gooks I burned in 'Nam!"

"It was war," Grandma said, her voice softening. "Your father dealt with shell shock, too. He wasn't right for a long time. You should ask him sometime."

Aldo flapped his lips. "He worked in a goddamn hospital."

"You don't know what you're talking about."

"What's that supposed to mean?"

"Your father fought in China," she said. "He doesn't talk about it, but he did. He only worked in the hospital later."

"What?"

"His whole unit was killed in action. That's why he was reassigned to the hospital. That's why he never went back into combat. His brother was in the South Pacific, and they thought it would be good for your father to be with family. So, they transferred him to the medical corps."

A soft breeze stirred in the dried juniper leaves at the edge of the property, leaving them swirling in tiny dust devils. I'd never heard this part of my grandfather's history. As far as I knew, he'd been attached to a station hospital in the Pacific. He also spent some time in Australia, but I didn't realize he'd seen action before that. The pained look on Grandpa's face told me Grandma's account was accurate. He had probably planned on taking all of this to the grave with him.

"Twenty-Second Reconnaissance unit," Grandpa said. "We were there to keep tabs on the Japs and to organize the resistance."

"All of them died?" I asked.

"If I hadn't been on patrol," Grandpa said. "I would have been strung up with the rest of them."

"Jesus," Fusilli said.

"The Japs couldn't shoot for shit," Grandpa said. "They used bayonets."

"So, when you used to say I learned this in China…" I said.

Grandpa reached for the knife on his hip, popping the snap on the scabbard. It was thin, perhaps six inches long, with a leather-wrapped handle. He spun the blade expertly in his hand, then fired it twenty feet across the yard with a flick of the wrist. He buried the point in one of the four–by–four timbers supporting the staircase with a muted *thunk*.

"When I said I learned this in China," he said. "I wasn't always kidding."

Grandma and Aldo kept at each other for a few more minutes, until he burst out of the house and saw us. His bald head slick with sweat, he snapped to attention and saluted Grandpa, then fished his keys from the pocket of his cut-off shorts and stormed down the steps. The slam of his car door out front was followed by the junkyard rumble of the engine turning over, then the spin of his tires in the sand as he blasted onto the boulevard.

My grandfather took a deep breath. "Aldo wasn't an easy kid," he said. "But it was a whole 'nother thing when he came back from Vietnam. It was like we didn't know him anymore."

"That guy is ..." I started.

Grandpa silenced me with a raised hand. "*Xiǎoxīn nǐ suǒ shuō dehuà,*" he said quietly, in what must have been Chinese. "Careful what you say."

9

———————

Nora's weakness for donuts led me to Ocean Bakery shortly after they opened the following day. It was a simple storefront on the main drag in town. Clean and well-lighted, the glass counter and racks behind were filled with a variety of cakes, donuts, and pastries. A half-dozen high-school and college-age girls peered over the top of the cases, the rings beneath their eyes and haphazard hair betraying their late-night antics. My summer love interests had looked the same a decade earlier.

There was nowhere to sit and barely anywhere to stand in the sea of bodies looking for the fresh crumb cake and cinnamon bread that perfumed the air. The creaking gears of the mechanical counter above the single register marked time like a broken metronome. The wait wasn't terrible; in my childhood, the line stretched around the block, and its shortening was the first harbinger of the end of my youth at the shore. As the old timers died off and their offspring were priced out of summertime island living, the *nouveau riche* were more apt to seek out a Dunkin' Donuts or Starbucks.

I got a couple of boxes of donuts and crumb cake, along

with a loaf of cinnamon bread that my grandfather would duti-fully toast until our bellies were full. I dropped most of it at the house but took a small portion of the hoard over to Nora's. Her face appeared between the curtains, her eyes tracing the red and white baker's twine like the lines on a map. Her cheeks melted into glee as she yanked the door open, the edge nearly clipping her nose and forcing her to feint like a boxer.

"Is that what I think it is?" she asked, stepping aside.

"I've come to fatten you up so this Irish guy won't want you anymore."

"This is quite a strategy, Jack," Nora laughed. "I see the hand of Fusilli." She leaned in and kissed me, then turned on a heel and led me to the kitchen, the well-worn floorboards creaking like approaching fate. I followed her to the kitchen, where she slid into a seat on the far side and folded a leg under her bottom, propping her higher than she otherwise would have been.

"This is one-hundred percent Jack Frére," I said, peeling away the twine and offering her first choice of the goodies.

"I think I prefer *Frieri*," she said, the free-air-ay pronuncia-tion comical with her accent. "That's how it was originally, your gran said."

"You can blame my dad's folks," I said. "They changed the family name when they got married."

She squinted at me. "Why?"

"Some bullshit about prejudice. They thought a French name sounded better than an Italian one."

"Better?"

"Well, whiter anyway."

"Worse things than being mistaken for a sexy French doctor, eh?" She fished a jelly donut from the box and took a bite, the powdered sugar spilling down over her chin and onto the checkered tablecloth.

"Jesus Christ," she sighed, wiping at her lips with a finger and then licking it clean. "They're even better than I remember."

"Remember how Fusilli used to sneak them out the back door of the bakery for us?"

"I can't believe he never got caught."

"It was more luck than skill."

Nora took another bite, then set it down on her plate and pulled it close, as though she was afraid I might try to steal her prize. I held up my hands. "It's all yours! I already dropped off a box for Grandpa."

Nora pursed her lips, as if deciding whether to share her thoughts. "He's sicker than he lets on, isn't he?"

I nodded.

"When I hugged him, he was all bones."

"It's cancer," I said, swallowing at the sound of the word. I took a bite of my crumb cake, errant streusel topping falling like pebbles to the table. "Intestinal cancer."

"Fuckin' hell."

"Yeah," I sighed. "Something like that."

"Is there anything to be done?"

"Not much. He's already a couple years past his expiration date."

"It's tragic. Your grandparents are such extraordinary people."

She was right in more ways than she knew. In particular, Grandpa was the one who gave me the grounding I needed when it was time to testify against the priest who had abused my brother. The trial burned our community to the ground; the stress killed my father with a heart attack. His death chastened me at the exact moment I was learning to be my own person, paralyzing me with my own anxieties and making me second-guess myself in emotionally charged situations. I needed Grandpa to pull through, because he offered clarity. He was resolute. He lived his values, without consideration of politics or consequence. There was right, and there was wrong. You did what was right and took your lumps.

Nora used the moment of silence to sip her tea, then change the subject. "So, who's Fusilli's slag, then?"

"I'm not sure what you mean."

"You're so very loyal, Jack," she said, her lips tightening as she swallowed another mouthful of tea. "But you're a terrible liar. She was in your house just the other day."

"How do you know she wasn't there to see yours truly?"

"I'd hang myself if I thought you'd take her to bed over me."

My cheeks reddened. I was a master at talking myself out of the signals a woman might be sending, but there was no subtext for me to mistake. Still, I sat there with my teeth in my mouth. Nora wasn't having my prevarication.

"Oh," she said. "Shall I make myself plainer?"

Too nervous to come up with a witty response, I smiled like an idiot. Nora slunk out from her chair and took a tentative step towards me. I pushed back from the table as she moved my plate aside and rested her bottom against the edge of the table. Parting her skirt, she revealed the length of her leg. I reached for her, sliding my hand along the inside of her knee, then slowly working my hand upwards. She smiled when I reached the place where her thighs touched, then closed her eyes and bit her lower lip, opening her legs fractionally wider. My fingers began to tingle with a mixture of anticipation and anxiety.

"You mustn't tease, Doctor Frére," she breathed. "It's impolite."

She moaned as I slid my fingers into her softness. Rising to my feet, I leaned into her as she laced her hand around my neck and pulled my mouth to hers. Her lips were plush and soft, but her tongue probed with an animal insistence that made me realize we were seconds away from doing something we both might regret. I felt my grandfather's judgment in the back of my head. As Nora leaned back, and I pressed against her, my hard-on flagged as I lost hold of the moment.

"We don't have to make love," she whispered into my mouth, intuiting my embarrassment. "We'll just have a little play."

Nora gave me a gentle push, then slid out to the side, taking my hand from the cleft between her legs and leading me through the hallway and into the living room, where the blinds were still closed. She turned to me and kissed me again, then guided me down onto the couch, pulling my T-shirt over my head as I sat.

Nora fell to her knees before me, unbuttoning my shorts. She ran her hands over me, pulled an elastic from her wrist, and bundled her hair back, then used her tongue to draw a line from my lips to my navel before taking me in her mouth.

"You taste of the sea," she whispered.

When it was over, Nora climbed onto the couch beside me with a smile, then laid me down. She tucked against me, drawing my arms across her breasts. I began sliding a hand under her skirt, but she stopped me.

"If you get me going again, I won't be able to stop myself."

I nodded and pulled her close, kissing her ear. "I just want to make you feel good, too."

"You will," she said. "Soon."

We lay quiet, listening to the hum of the cars on the thoroughfare beyond the fence. Waves of joy and regret washed over me. I'd wanted this but felt bad about it. I didn't *want* to feel bad about it, because I'd desperately wanted it. Nora finally broke the death spiral in my mind by rolling over to face me, taking my hands in hers.

"So," she started. "About Fusilli's trollop."

I laughed.

"Nora . . ." I said, "I don't want to speak out of turn."

"Can we not trust one another now?" Nora asked, eyes wide

as she kissed the tips of my fingers one at a time. I was instantly hard. Holy Christ, what was the matter with me?

"It's just some girl he paid a little too much attention to at a party."

"He paid a little too much attention to her in the Dungeon as well," she said. "You should tell him to mind the windows."

"Are you serious?"

"Sounded like a bleedin' nature program."

"Ugh. I'll talk to him."

"Things will be hairy enough when Katie arrives."

She wasn't wrong. Candy wasn't going to disappear without a fight. Fusilli's latest dalliance needed to be handled quickly and without drama.

"For sure," I said. "I'll lead the mission. We'll take care of it."

"No, better that I go."

"You?"

"I'm no doctor, but I've been Katie's best friend for twenty years," Nora said, leaning back. "I was the first to know she was pregnant."

I started to say something, but my mouth froze mid-syllable as I realized we were having two completely different conversations. Nora's eyes widened in horror.

"What?" I finally asked.

"Oh Lord," Nora said, folding her hands into a tent covering her nose and mouth. "Oh, Christ. I thought he'd told you. From what you said, I mean."

"Holy shit," I breathed, sitting upright. Nora rose to her feet, her hands still over her face as though she'd witnessed an act of gangland violence. Fusilli's reaction to Aldo's abortion story suddenly made a lot more sense. "Nora," I finally asked. "What are you doing here? No bullshit this time."

Nora took a deep breath, then let out a long sigh and sat down on the couch beside me. "I'm the cover story," she said.

"Katie is supposedly joining me for a girls' holiday. She's actually coming to end her pregnancy."

"What? Why?"

"Abortion is illegal in Ireland, Jack. And the UK is too close for comfort. Katie's got doctors in the family."

I liked to think of myself as a modern person, but the idea of unwed pregnancy was still anathema to a mind warped by decades of Italian upbringing and Catholic schooling. Even when married friends told me that they were pregnant, my initial, visceral reaction was invariably *oh shit . . . what do we do?*

"I can imagine Fusilli going for the abortion," I said. "Frankly, I'd be surprised if it was his first. But Katie?"

"To be honest, I don't know that she can go through with it," Nora said. "She genuinely loves your cousin, and I think she'd keep the baby if he'd marry her."

Nora and I stared each other down for another moment before I broke the deadlock. "Excuse me," I said, jumping to my feet and making for the door. "I have to talk to Fusilli. Right now."

"Jack," she called after me. "Go easy!"

My cousin was at the kitchen table, one of our old fishing reels disassembled on a piece of newspaper before him. A rusted can of 3-In-One oil was tipped over, a slow drip from the spout resulting in a darkening circle creeping ever closer to the half-finished donut to his left. I reached over and stood the can upright, then affixed the tiny red cap to the tip. He looked up at me and held out a small gear encrusted in salt. He pinched it between his fingers, and it crumbled, the pieces scattering across the gossip page beneath his arm. How he could dick around with a fishing reel with his baby growing in Katie's belly was beyond me.

"The patient isn't going to make it, Doctor," Fusilli said. "He gave his last full measure."

"We gotta talk," I said.

He made a face at me, then picked up his coffee. "So, talk."

I turned my eyes to where Aldo lay smoking in the bedroom, then to the living room, where our grandparents were thumbing through the morning papers.

"Come with me," I said.

Fusilli followed me out the back door and around the front of the house. We crossed the boulevard towards the bay front on the far side of the park, the sand underfoot warming with the heat of the day. I sat down on the edge of the old blue catamaran and motioned for him to join me.

"What's up, man?" he finally asked. "You okay?"

I didn't waste any time. "Were you going to tell me Katie was pregnant?"

Fusilli looked out over the water. "Nora."

"What the hell, man?"

"I would have told you eventually," he sighed. "I'm as surprised as you."

"Surprised?"

Fusilli's tight lips bent into a half-grin, as though he'd heard a distasteful pun and wasn't sure if he should laugh. This was Fusilli's superpower. There was no situation so grave that he wouldn't try to defuse it with his patented brand of crazy talk or jokes, some shittier than others. "She's not that pregnant," he said.

My cousin was both one of the smartest people I knew and a goddamn idiot.

"Not . . . that . . . pregnant?"

"Barely two months," he said. "If it's even mine."

"Allow me to suggest you don't play the 'is it mine' card."

"I always pulled out. Always."

"Do you know what doctors call people who practice withdrawal?"

"Bareback warriors?"

"*Parents*, you asshole."

Fusilli chuckled for a moment and leaned down, picking up a smooth, flat pebble. He flung it towards the water, watching it skate the golden trail of reflected sunlight. It glanced off the ski ladder of our boat and sank. What were our grandparents going to say? What had they known about Aldo and Wendy? Had they been supportive, their morality becoming more malleable, as often happens when Catholics are confronted with an unwanted pregnancy? I'd seen that scenario play out several times in high school. Or, had Aldo and Wendy been forced to make a terrible choice on their own?

"What are you going to do?" I asked.

"I'm sure she told you the plan," Fusilli said. "I'm not exactly father-of-the-year material."

"Is Katie on board with this?"

"Less sure than me," he said. "But she gets it."

"Well, that's something at least."

"We'll handle Candy tomorrow."

"I gotta go see Mia tomorrow," I said, shaking my head. "Isn't this something you could do by phone?"

"She's got my wallet, dude."

"You got mugged by a fucking Piney?"

"Snagged it off the dresser, I think. Told me I'd have to come to her place if I wanted it back."

"That's a terrible, terrible idea."

"It's terrible now, or it's terrible later. This way, we handle any blowback before Katie gets here."

"You hope," I said.

"I hope," he agreed. "What are you going to tell Nora when you go?"

I wasn't about to bring up Mia to Nora. Not after what we had just done. "That I'm going to see my folks."

"So," Fusilli said, raising an eyebrow. "We aren't as different as you want to believe."

I worried that Fusilli was right, maybe more than he knew. There had to be something as terrible in me as there was in him, some genetic predisposition to infidelity passed down from the old country. Perhaps that was a reason I so tried to emulate my grandfather's character. It was the cornerstone of the wall constraining the base instincts I would otherwise succumb to. Maybe that was why I hadn't slept with Nora. And now I was thinking like Bill Clinton, like the child of an alcoholic who'd taken his first tentative swig of scotch from the liquor cabinet, then tried adding water back to the bottle to cover his transgression.

"That's what I'm afraid of," I finally said.

10

The thing was, Fusilli really loved Katie, or at least he had at one time. I knew this because I got drafted into sending him home to her during the most illegal of our missions. I'd just finished my second year of med school and was back at my grandparents' place for a few weeks. One day in late June, Fusilli's mother showed up in a panic. Fusilli was out of money in Paris. There was also something about immigration giving him a hard time, but she didn't understand the details. She knew he was at a hostel near the Marie Clichy metro stop but not much more. The type who kept all her money in the mattress, she was unwilling to send a wire. Could I bring him the cash for a plane ticket home?

Forty-eight hours later, I was sitting at the top of the staircase that led to the doors of Fusilli's hostel. It reminded me of a Brooklyn brownstone. My head was pounding from a terminal case of jet lag and a bottle of Air France's finest champagne. I couldn't get a bed for a few hours, but the stairs were comfortably shaded and cool. Swiss army knife in hand, I was halfway through a baguette and some strange-smelling cheese wrapped in grape leaves when Fusilli appeared. He looked every bit the quintessential Hemingway expatriate, exiting the metro stop as if ascending from the underworld. He was thinner than I remembered, his face showing a few days' growth of beard. His clothes looked as though he'd slept in them.

"You look just like I feel," I said.

"You deserve it," he said. "What are you doing here?"

"Your mom sent me to collect you."

"That doesn't sound like her." He laid a heavy hand on my shoulder and lowered himself to the ground. We embraced, but he didn't return the back slap I offered.

"She was worried after your last call. What happened?"

Fusilli had outdone himself. He'd been living in Ireland with Katie, working at her family's bed and breakfast after a throwdown with his dad. Though Fusilli ought to have an EU passport through his father, he'd never finished the paperwork. Because of course he hadn't. After a grad school interview in France, the goons from Irish Immigration determined he'd been overstaying his tourist visa and deported him. This would take more than a plane ticket. He needed to go back to Ireland on the down low.

"Do you have a plan?" I asked.

"Who do you think you're talking to?"

Fusilli always had a plan, always some mental Rube Goldberg machine ready to explode in absurd catastrophe. We got to Cherbourg Harbor the following day, hoping to pay someone to take him across on a small boat. We quickly discovered we'd overestimated our foreign language prowess. No one would give us the time of day, figuring we were stupid American tourists, scammers, or both.

Then, we spotted a leggy blonde in a white T-shirt decorated with the Union Jack. She was riding the water taxi from a decent-sized sailboat flying the Irish flag. We watched from a bench as she strolled to a nearby café, stumbling first on the dock and then so frequently on the uneven cobbles that I was sure we'd end up rendering first aid before talking to her.

We crossed the street and had the maître d' seat us near our hopeful benefactor, who was wrapped up in *Zen and the Art of Motorcycle Maintenance*. The tourists around us chatted quietly, having espresso and pastries or the odd glass of rosé and oysters. The tabletops were formed of poorly polished glass pieces that distorted the wrought iron legs beneath, the edges of the metal flecked with rust and peeling black paint. My deranged, cubist reflection asked what series of bad decisions had brought me to this moment.

Fusilli went to work as soon as we put our drink orders in.

"Like I was saying," he said. "The Queen serves at the pleasure of Parliament."

"How can a queen be under the control of a democratic institution?" I asked, unhappy to be playing the idiot in a half-assed Monty Python skit. "It negates the whole idea of a regent."

"I beg your pardon," Fusilli said, offering the blonde a polite wave. "Hi. Are you British?"

She looked up from her book, then down at British Cycling logo on her shirt. Her eyes were the color of the predawn ocean, set above an angular nose that ought to be peeking out from under some kind of fancy hat at a garden party. She could have been an extra from a Sherlock Holmes production.

"What do you think, mate?" she asked, brow furrowed in suspicion.

"I'm just trying to explain the Monarchy to my American cousin here," he said. "I could use a little backup."

"I don't know much about those moldy old farts," she said, diving back into her book. "And care even less."

"So, you're not a Royalist?"

"They'll be first up against the wall when the revolution comes," she said, turning the page with a wry smile.

"A closeted American!" I said.

Her smile grew, allowing me a modicum of hope.

"Would you care to join us?" Fusilli asked.

"Nice try," she said curtly, the smile disappearing. "But I'm here to see my boyfriend."

Fusilli shrugged and continued our conversation unfazed. Even after all the years I'd known him, my cousin could still impress me with his ability to improvise intellectual-sounding bullshit. That was really saying something, given all the maladjusted pricks I went to medical school with. We were soon onto Guy Fawkes's attempt to blow up Parliament, Fusilli perhaps hoping to bring her into the conversation with a more anti-establishment tack. When he finally went to the bathroom, the blonde dog-eared her page.

"Does his rubbish work on Americans?" she asked.

"Not anymore," I said. "But he's mostly harmless."

"Lilly Braddom," she said, taking my hand.

"Jack Frére," I said, extending my hand and leaning towards her. "What brings you to town?"

"My boyfriend is in the big bike race. Tomorrow's stage starts nearby, so I sailed over to surprise him."

"Very cool."

"What do you do, Jack Frére?"

"Medical student," I said.

"Lovely," she said. "What can you tell me about the use of intravenous vancomycin for *Clostridium difficile* colitis?"

"You . . . don't," I said, slightly perplexed. "It doesn't reach the gut lining. You need to give it by mouth."

She studied my face like an Egyptologist decoding a hieroglyph. "You pass," she finally said. "Thought you were bullshitting about being a medic."

"Are you a doctor?"

"The other kind," she said with a wink. "Microbiologist at RCSI Dublin. What brings you to Cherbourg, Doctor Frére?"

"Trying to send knucklehead here back to Ireland," I said, jerking my thumb over my shoulder. "Visa trouble. I saw the flag on your boat and hoped you'd take him off my hands."

She laughed, rising to her feet and leaving a few coins beside her empty glass.

"Would love to help, but I don't fancy a run-in with immigration," she said, screwing up her face. "See you around, Doctor Frére."

Fusilli returned as she slipped out of the patio and onto a side street, tossing her blond mane over her shoulder and giving me a smile that said I might have had a shot with her under different circumstances.

"No luck?" he asked.

"No," I said. "Is it really worth all this? You and Katie have been on and off since we were kids. Meantime, you've fucked half the cast of *Fantasia*."

"Hey! I'm not a shithead teenager anymore!"

"I'm just saying . . ."

"Katie put up with me all these years," he said. "Her folks took me in when my dad threw me out. I owe her."

Fusilli continued his quest after lunch, while I arranged an inexpensive hotel for us. When we reconvened at a bench on the harbor that evening, he was sweating profusely and pushing a supermarket cart carrying a bag large enough to fit a body. Offering him a swig of unpronounceable red, I waited for him to tell me he would hide in the duffel while I carried him onto the passenger ferry like luggage. What he was planning was so much worse.

"Allow me to read you in on Operation Underlord," he said, wiping his mouth on his arm.

Fusilli emptied his duffel onto the pavement, revealing a pair of collapsible oars and a deflated raft of questionable quality.

"Oh my God," I said, allowing my head to fall into my hands.

"Got a great deal at the marine store," he said.

"Where'd you get the money for this?"

"Your bag," he smiled. "Last night, after you passed out."

"That money was for a plane ticket. You think we're rowing there?"

"That was my first thought."

"Fuck you, Fusilli. I'm not drowning in the English Channel."

"Some idiot sailed a bathtub across the channel last year," he said, fishing a foot pump from the bowels of the bag. "Curtain rod and everything. He got an audience with the queen for his trouble. We've been on boats all our lives. If that guy could . . ."

"Fuck. You."

". . . but I knew you wouldn't like that idea," he continued. "So, I came up with a better plan."

"Fly back to the States like an American? Apply for a visa like a law-abiding citizen?"

"Don't be ridiculous," he said, pointing at Lilly's boat. "I'm going to stow away with your new friend."

It took me a moment to realize he was serious.

"We're going to jail," I said. "The frogs are going to sign us up for the goddamn Foreign Legion."

"You say it like it's a bad thing."

I sighed, then drained the remainder of my wine before helping him unroll the gray rubber monstrosity.

"She's off with her boyfriend tonight, right?" he said as he connected the hose and started stomping on the pump. "We paddle out there. We find me a cozy nook to hide in. She sails back tomorrow. After she ties up, I sneak away. I'll even leave some gas money. Problem solved."

It might have been the wine, but the plan didn't seem that unreasonable, as his plans went. When we were nine or ten, he climbed up the widow's peak during a thunderstorm with some hook-up wire and the rabbit ears off the old television. He thought he could gain superhuman powers from a lightning strike. What he got instead was grounded for half the summer.

"She'd better be worth this, Fusilli."

"She is, man."

THE WATER SEEMED cool for July as we launched in the shadow of the breakwater, wading knee deep before jumping into the raft. With Fusilli lying low across the bow and me kneeling in the stern, we made quick progress through the ribbon of darkness cast by the barnacle-encrusted boulders. Making a right at the end of the jetty, we moved into the midst of the boats that hovered beyond the city piers like a wing of plover. Our paddling blended softly with the lapping of the sea against the hulls around us. The cabin was dark as we approached Lilly's boat, but soft jazz was audible over the ripple of the water as we approached. I couldn't tell which boat it might be coming from and hoped to hell it wasn't hers.

The boat was at least thirty feet long, with a tall mast and a low-set cabin. A short gangway led into the cabin. It had a natural wood finish above the deck line. Below, the hull was painted a bright white that was reflected perfectly on the surface of the water.

"Fusilli," I said. "There's no structure on deck. Where are we going to hide you?"

"The hatch up front?" Fusilli groaned. "The bilge, maybe?"

"Dude, you'll drown in there."

"Let's check the cabin," he said. "Maybe there's a closet."

We stood up in the raft, cautiously balancing ourselves against the transom.

"Listen," I said. "Maybe we can sneak you onto the ferry in the ..."

I was cut off by a glass bottle shattering against the gunwale, spraying both of us with shrapnel and opening a gash on my forearm.

"Fuck!" I said.

The deck lights snapped on, offering us a glimpse of Lilly Braddom as she stormed up the gangway from the cabin. She stopped at the steering console, cocking her right arm back and correcting her aim in an effort to brain one or both of us with a (this time, full) bottle of scotch.

"Hello again!" Fusilli started. "Sorry! Wrong boat!"

She eyed us suspiciously, regarding my foot on her stern ladder like I'd been caught with my hand in a cookie jar.

"You're trying to nick my boat," she said, her drunken accent making her sound equal parts absurd and dangerous, a cartoon Ozzy Osbourne. She set her bottle in a drink holder and pulled a small fire axe from the bulkhead.

We were about to die. I was certain of it. I glanced over my shoulder and gauged the distance back to shore, trying to decide if it was closer than the ladder on the side of the breakwater. I wasn't in swimming shape but figured I could still cover a hundred yards in ninety seconds. I wondered how long it would take Lilly to break mooring, start the engine, and run me down like Quint at the helm of the Orca. Maybe she'd just hurl the axe at me and split my skull like a watermelon. It was no less than I deserved for agreeing to this nonsense.

"You're drunk," Fusilli said, putting on his most posh accent.

She lowered the bottle slightly. "Not enough to have imagined you two mongoloid Yanks."

Fusilli looked genuinely offended. "Mongoloid?"

"I already told you two to fuck off," she said. "What's the plan, then? Kidnap me?"

Fusilli and I looked at each other.

"Just tell her the truth, goddamnit," I said, clutching the wound on my arm.

Lilly leaned up against the steering console casually, stretching her long legs out before her. She began shaving the corner of her thumbnail on the edge of the axe blade, like a mobster preparing to dismember a police informant.

"Oh yes," she said brightly. "Do tell."

So, Fusilli told her the ballad of Katie from County Clare. About how they'd met as kids. About how he'd moved across the ocean for her. About how he'd been working as a short-order cook in her family's bed and breakfast and was saving up so they could get their own place. He described the way she tore up the floor of the pub with her traditional Irish dance, how her cheeks got so red that her freckles melted. About how he kept a journal of ridiculous things to say to make her laugh. About how it had gotten harder now that they were out of school, and she needed to think about her future. About how they'd been transatlantic for years, and she just wasn't going to wait for him any longer. He told Lilly he hadn't been hitting on her but was trying to befriend her. When that didn't work, he planned to row across the channel. He closed by throwing me under the bus. It was me, he said, who convinced him to stow away on her boat, since she was headed back to Dublin.

"Guilty as charged," I sighed, raising my hand and taking the hit.

Lilly glowered at me, screwing up her face and shaking the axe accusingly in my direction. She seemed to think it over for a moment, then swung the blade down and buried it in the side of the helm. The polished teak split with a mighty *crack*, scaring the shit out of all three of us. She retrieved her bottle from the drink holder.

"You're a pair of idiots, aren't you?" she said.

"You don't know the half of it," I said.

"Well," she sighed, beckoning me closer. "Let's have a drink, then."

"Yeah?" Fusilli replied, gesturing for me to climb the ladder.

"You're clearly too stupid to be legitimate villains."

"Says the lady who just chopped a thousand bucks of teak for kindling," Fusilli said, following me onto the deck.

"Ha," she said, taking a pull from her bottle and swallowing with a grimace. "That's where you're wrong. It ain't my boat."

"What?" Fusilli and I said in unison.

"Belongs to my bastard ex," she said, passing her bottle to Fusilli.

"I thought you came to see him race?" I asked.

"I went to his hotel after leaving you twats at the café. I caught him shagging the team masseur."

"Oh shit," I said.

"He can fuck right off," she said. "After I empty his bar, I'm going to run this thing aground and forget I ever knew the prick."

"Fuck that guy!" Fusilli cheered, taking a swig from the bottle and passing it to me.

"You'll forgive me," she said. "If I think you're mad for risking prison over some girl."

"Not for some girl," Fusilli said. "For Katie fuckin' Sullivan."

I'd heard my cousin sling every kind of bullshit in at least three languages. This felt like the truth. I believed he was as sincere about this as he'd ever been about anything in his life.

Lilly's eyes filled with the drunken, tearful sympathy of the newly heartbroken.

"That won't be necessary," she finally said, taking the bottle and another swig. "I'll bring you two across in the morning. But you'll have to paddle the last bit on your own. I already told your cousin I'm not fucking about with immigration."

"He'll paddle the last bit," I corrected. "I'll be flying home from Paris, if I survive the night."

We spent that evening drinking ourselves into oblivion with our new friend. Lilly turned out to be a character and seemed like a decent scientist. I might have been interested in her romantically had I not been so concerned that she might decapitate me in my sleep. In the old days, I'd have wagered Fusilli would have tried to bed her. However, he was a perfect gentleman as we helped her to her bunk. We slept in deck chairs under the stars, but not before Fusilli took the precaution of pulling the fire axe from the console and pitching it into the drink.

THEY DROPPED me at the dock the following morning. Fusilli helped me off the boat and took my hand.

"Thanks, man."

I nodded towards his captain, who appeared to be struggling with the GPS unit on the helm.

"You aren't out of the woods yet, my friend."

"What are you going to tell my mother?"

"That I gave you the money and got you passage back to Ireland," I said, handing him the cash. "Which is the truth."

"Part of it," he laughed.

I hopped onto the dock and stood there for a while, watching him recede into the distance, then found my way to the rail station. Lilly Braddom was as good as her word, delivering Fusilli to Rosslare the following night. He paddled ashore under cover of darkness like a commando, then caught the train back to Galway. Katie would inspire him to sort out his immigration issues and help him get into his master's program. Which was how he helped discover those crusty scrolls in Israel, got his face on National Geographic, and netted the fully funded PhD position he always wanted. This allowed him to further develop his relationship with Katie and her family, then subsequently risk both by screwing a leather-clad Piney on a New Jersey beach. A storybook love if I ever heard of one.

11

Fusilli found me in the bedroom as I was preparing to leave for Mia's. He looked approvingly at my neatly pressed khakis and button-down shirt.

"Did you Saran Wrap the car?" I asked.

"It's hermetically sealed," Fusilli said. "Trash bags and duct tape, reinforced with a tarp. I sat in it for fifteen minutes. Nothing leaked through the seat. Just drive with the windows down so you don't smell like Kong when you get there."

"Will do."

"Did you read the stuff I left for you?"

I pointed to his copy of *Sports Illustrated*, which lay atop a pile of newspapers on the bed. Mia's father was a Philadelphia Eagles superfan, and I needed to be able to keep up. Another skit on the *Jack and Mia Show*. I hated sports in general and football in particular. This had always been a challenge, because male culture is so focused on sports-ball. Fortunately, I'd spent years of medical training teaching my brain to regurgitate facts on cue. There wasn't much difference between the names of players on a roster and the list of drugs in the hospital formulary.

"Yeah," I said. "Hit me."

"All right," he started. "Quarterback?"

"Jay Kilderry."

"Tell me something about him."

"He's a good leader but not a great quarterback. He's only thrown more than 4,000 yards in one season."

"Coach?"

"Felix Hackett," I said. "Hired because the Eagles won only four games last season."

"Remember, you don't understand why, since New England fired him a few weeks earlier."

"Right," I said. "But I'm hopeful."

"What do we say?"

"Go Birds!" I shouted, raising a fist in the air in what could have been mistaken for a Black Power salute.

Fusilli nodded in approval. "There's hope for you."

"Christ, I hate football."

"You'll be fine, man. Just act normal."

Things with Mia's folks weren't normal *per se*: it was a . . . performed normalcy, a live-action version of the family news in a Christmas card. This was totally expected. Growing up Italian-American required a focus on appearances, or as my mother liked to say, "don't let anyone see your shit." When someone asked how things were, the answer was *tutto bene,* and woe to those who missed the memo. This was a challenging facade to maintain, given Aldo's drunken vagrancy and my brother's frequent flyer status with the local drug rehab, not to mention Fusilli's exploration of the edges of my sanity. Mia's family had an easier time of it, because they *were* less nuts. Having been raised a Boy Scout in a sea of chaos, the *tutto bene* ethos resulted in a real cognitive dissonance for me. I understood Mia's dance with her parents and accepted it out of loyalty but tried to temper that acceptance with the (possibly mistaken) expectation that we could always be straight with each other.

I got into Pennsylvania ahead of schedule and spent some time driving aimlessly through the development. Navigating Mia's neighborhood outside Philadelphia meant stepping onto a different rung of the social ladder. I was surrounded by sprawling estates with rolling lawns, some gated and guarded by great stone animals, some flanked by gaudy marble fountains. It was as though a caricature artist had been asked to draw a neighborhood for the latter-day Mafia.

The Cerrone home was more modest but still spectacular by any fair measure. It would have fit in well somewhere in Sonoma: two-story, with earth-toned rusticated stonework and an orange tile roof. It was bespectacled with oversized windows and heavy-embroidered drapery. Warm yellow light poured out onto the landscaping and sandstone walkway. Turning into her driveway, I approached a bit faster than I should have and shifted into neutral, killing the engine and coasting in so the exhaust wouldn't draw undue attention. The engine backfired mightily, all but erasing that hope. The neighbors probably thought I was there to rob the family and ransom Mia.

I followed the walkway from the drive to the entrance. Before I could try the knocker, the door snapped open as if spring-loaded. Mia's form exploded from the space, throwing her arms around my neck. "Hi!" she enthused, kissing me with performative *mwahs*. "I missed you!"

"I missed you too."

Her embrace and the toasted vanilla of her perfume were instantly familiar. Mia leaned back but didn't let go, her big eyes taking me in as though I'd been away on a long voyage. She had cut her hair since I'd last seen her, forsaking the wave for a shoulder length, layered look that accentuated her angular features. She'd lightened it, leaving her more legitimately blond and a sharper contrast to her eyebrows. Her work in the gym was paying off, the last remnants of the freshman fifteen she had been carrying since college having melted like spring snow.

She knitted her eyebrows. "You okay? Something on your mind?"

"Ah, you know. Fusilli. Grandpa. Stress."

She stepped back and smoothed her black cocktail dress.

"Oh boy," she said.

"Anyway," I said. "I like your new 'do."

"You think?" she asked, running one of her hands absent-mindedly through the layers in her hair. "It's a big change."

"It suits you."

Mia knitted her fingers around the back of my head and kissed me again, then looked over at the Chevelle. "I can't believe that thing still runs."

"You and me both."

"We'll take my car later."

I followed Mia's bouncing stride across the marble floor of the entrance way, rounding a great staircase and ending up in an open-floor plan kitchen.

Mia's mother, Amelia, had the great chest of an opera singer, with fluffy, curled bangs and shoulder-length hair blown out straight. She wore a red short-sleeve blouse and matching apron. She put her wooden spoon down on its rest and hurried around the island, swinging her ample hips around the edge, narrowly missing a large bowl.

"*Ciao Giacomo!*" she half-sung, sounding like my grandmother with the Italian version of my name. "*Come stai?*"

"*Molto bene!*" I said reflexively, and I meant it. It was impossible to avoid smiling at her enthusiasm. In the moment, it always felt genuine. My misgivings evaporated as she kissed me on both cheeks and gave me a hug, arching her back awkwardly to prevent our torsos from touching.

"Sorry," she said. "I don't want to get you covered in sauce. You look so handsome."

"Thanks."

"There's plenty of food," she said. "So, don't hold back!"

Behind me, Mia's father, Al, meandered in from the living room. He was backlit by ESPN on the projection-screen TV and was slender, balding, and perpetually at ease: shoulders slightly rolled, hips slightly forward. However, his golf shirt and khakis seemed too formal for the Saturday night of a holiday weekend. "*Dottore!*" he said, taking a hand from his pocket and extending it. "How you doin'?"

"Good, thanks," I said. "Can't believe it's summer already. Feels like Christmas was yesterday."

"Ah, it'll be football season before you know it," he said. "What do you think about this Hackett thing?"

I heard Fusilli's voice in the back of my mind: *It's go time.* "You know, I wasn't sure about him taking over, but word from training camp is positive."

"We'll see if they make the playoffs."

"I keep hoping they'll let Kilderry pass more," I said.

"You know, I bet he retires this year. I just don't know who they'll get to replace him."

"It's a crap shoot any way you look at it," I said. "But he barely threw 4,000 yards last season. Maybe it's time for some fresh blood."

"Enough football," Amelia said, rolling her eyes. "You're going to love *Phantom.*"

"I've read positive reviews."

"Another good one is *Cats.* Maybe next time."

"Come on, Amelia," Al said. "That was the worst thing I ever saw."

"The music was beautiful, Al!"

"Bunch-a cats running around for God's sake," he said, dismissing her with a wave.

Mia and I laughed. Her father's curmudgeon act was only half-serious and somehow endearing. He might have been my favorite among her family members.

"Anyway," he said. "Let's sit down."

We ate in the kitchen like family rather than in the formality of the dining room. Mia's parents were warm and kind, genuinely happy to see me and interested in my life. There was no intramural warfare among a half-dozen siblings. No sign of my dad's stuffy, obnoxious parents tearing me down. No drunk uncles making long, politically incorrect diatribes. I felt . . . welcome. Was it worth risking this for an ill-advised tryst with Nora? I was Captain Kirk beaming between different ships. USS Mia: stability and safety; USS Nora: passion and recklessness.

After an antipasto course, a pasta course, a pile of pastries, and an espresso, it was time to leave for the show. Al surprised me by offering up his car. "You want to take the Merc?"

"Wow," I said. "Are you sure?"

"You aren't taking my daughter anywhere in that Chevelle," he laughed. "Maybe you and I can go car shopping in a few weeks."

"I gotta get a few paychecks under my belt first."

"Don't worry about it," he said. "I know a guy."

"I can't let you buy me a car, Mr. Cerrone."

"Sure you can. You're family, *Dottore.*"

Mia winked at me across the table. Al leaned back and reached into his pocket, fishing out his key ring. A Mercedes symbol glittered under the track lighting. "Don't worry about putting gas in it. The company pays."

"Thanks," I said. "This is great."

Mia slipped into the foyer and returned with a gauzy ivory scarf. Amelia helped her put it on, then kissed her. "Have too much fun," she said. "But be careful in the city."

"Who's gonna mess with this guy, ah?" Al said, stepping up

behind me and squeezing my shoulders as he shepherded us towards the garage door.

The black Mercedes coupe looked like some kind of stealth fighter jet under the fluorescent tube lighting. I snaked around the car and got the door for Mia, then waved to Al and climbed into the cockpit. I was careful to avoid dumping the clutch as I pulled onto the uphill and gave it some gas. The engine responded instantly, and I took the corner at the top of the street a little too fast. This was a huge upgrade over Fusilli's car, let alone the junkers I had grown up driving. It didn't have the pull of the Chevelle in her prime, but I should be learning to drive something more civilized anyway.

"How do you like it?" Mia asked.

"It corners like a race car," I said. "The suspension on the Chevelle is shot. It's like steering a litter box."

"You're so funny," she said. "Did Fusilli coach you on the football stats?"

"Gotta bring my A-game for your dad."

She leaned over and kissed my cheek. "You're sweet." She reached into her purse. "I made a mixtape of the music from *Phantom* for you." She pushed it into the player, the speakers swelling with the orchestral score. She reached across and took my hand, squeezing it gently as she sang along with Michael Crawford.

I released Mia's hand to shift into third as we surged up the on-ramp to 476, welcoming the acceleration. The gearshift moved with precision, not at all like the Chevelle's. Wasn't this better? I was Jacques Frére, MD. I was lucky to have the opportunity to marry into a good family and start a different life. Grandpa would not survive the year. Grandma was in her eighties and wouldn't be far behind. I had my siblings, to an extent, but they were young and wouldn't be much of a support structure. Mia was my best option for starting over, for being part of a family that shared my identity and upbringing but lacked the drinking, drugs, and mental illness.

My kids would never be exposed to a backward church or creepy priest. They wouldn't have to be traumatized from birth.

"You're so good with my parents," she said. "They love you."

"They wouldn't if they knew how many nights you stayed at my place."

"Gotta keep up appearances. You know how they are."

"I wish we could get some alone time to talk."

"Don't think you're escaping before you see my new Victoria's Secret number."

"Yeah? What's the plan?"

"The usual. You park up the block. We'll wait for them to go to bed, and then you sneak in through the den."

We'd been running the same scam for years, but it still made me feel uncomfortable. I respected Mia's dad. He was my surrogate father figure: a respected corporate attorney and self-made millionaire. I imagined the disappointment he'd feel if he ever caught me naked with his baby girl.

"Maybe we don't have to keep acting like kids," I said. "You're a lawyer. I'm a doctor, for God's sake."

"Yeah, sure."

"I'm tired of this, Mia," I said, the warm feelings her folks had engendered cooling with each passing minute alone with her, as they sometimes did. "When are we going to drag your parents into the future?"

"My family is a generation behind yours, Jack. My grandparents don't even speak English. We can do whatever we want. We just have to be discreet. What they don't know won't hurt them. Or us."

This was the price of paradise. "Yeah, I know."

She reached across the console and slid a hand slowly up my thigh. "Don't I always make it worth your while?"

"I just . . ." I tried to stop myself, but the words bubbled out like a kettle overflowing. "I love your folks, and I want an honest relationship with them. I don't want to always be sneaking around. And I appreciated your note, but I hate that Ian is still an issue."

"Don't ruin this," Mia said, her eyes hardening as she pulled her hand away. "Tonight has been so nice."

"Mia," I pressed. "We need to talk about it. I need to talk about it."

She left her eyes fixed forward. "So, talk."

"It's just . . . He's just been this weird third wheel in our relationship."

"Jack," she sighed. "I don't know how many different ways I can say it. There's nothing romantic between Ian and me. There never was. I admit it looked bad. So bad."

I loved her, and I wanted to believe her. I always felt like they spent too much time together but told myself I was jealous. Paranoid. Then, one of Fusilli's friends saw her with the Witchdoctor at a school reunion. She'd told me she was going out with the girls. When I confronted her, she said she'd kept quiet because she knew how I'd react. It just felt so underhanded. Now, Fusilli's latest side piece claimed to have seen her around in the off-season, when her house was closed up. Why wouldn't she have told me? Could she have been meeting Ian on the sly?

I shifted again and gave it more gas. The headlights of the oncoming traffic blurred into a stream of starlight. For a moment, I was a child again, imagining launching my spaceship from Bay Shore Park and rocketing away from everyone and everything I knew. Part of me didn't want to find out if she had been up to something.

"Uh-huh," I finally said.

"Things just got . . . complicated."

"What does that mean?"

"I . . ." She paused, taking a deep breath, "I know he's kind of a jerk. He's no good with girls, for obvious reasons. But he's my friend since forever. It's hard to put that aside."

I looked away from the road longer than I should have. Her eyes were welling, begging for my belief. I wanted to believe her, and it made me feel like a fool. Resentment curdled in my stomach like sour milk.

"I know," I said. "We've talked about it before."

"So, why can't we just drop it?" she said, taking my hand. "I know things have been hard between us with distance and everything. That's why I'm leaving DC. I want to do what it takes to make our relationship the priority. You don't need to be insecure because of an asshole like Ian."

"And you aren't going to see him anymore?"

"Jack, I haven't seen him since he was back home for Christmas. I'm not going to see him again unless you're part of the plans. I promise."

I still loved her, and I wanted to believe her, but there was something else. I wanted to *want* her again, the way I used to. I feared that would be the bigger challenge. Maybe that required accepting her explanation, of having a little faith in her. I shut up and didn't ask her about being at the beach in the spring.

12

———

I slept in the following morning but was eventually awakened by Grandma fussing in the kitchen. Barely five-feet tall, she was standing on tiptoes and struggling to reach into the cabinet above the countertop. I reached over her head to get the stack of pasta bowls she wanted. They'd belonged to her mother, workaday china with pink roses and a thin, gold band around the rim. The enamel was crazed in some places and broken in others. Much like my grandfather's blue-plaid mug, at least half of the bowls had dark brown lines marking the places they had been cemented back together over the years.

"I'm shrinking, Giacomo!" She laughed, dropping down to flat feet. "My mother used to say *altezza mezza mellezza!*"

"You've still got a big personality, Grandma," I said.

She shrugged, putting the dishes in the sink. "Eh, I talk too much. Speaking of which, have you talked to your mother?"

She almost certainly knew I hadn't. This was her way of telling me I should make the effort. A terrible distance had fallen between my mother and me after I left for college. That was partly on me. She'd become consumed by religion and I couldn't relate. Our relationship only worsened after my dad passed. She thought that the stress of my testimony during the church scandal was more than his heart could handle. She might have been right. Hearing it recounted for the court record must have been profoundly traumatic, for the both of them.

"Not lately," I said.

"You've got to forgive and forget, Giacomo. Nobody loves you like your mother."

"You always say that."

"It was a terrible thing," she said. "When monsignor came to town, we thought he was God's gift. But he was the devil."

The pedophile priest rode a wave of reform feminism into our parish, seducing women with the idea that they could take their place as men's equals. In reality, he was patronizing them to gain access to their children. Two of the victims would subsequently commit suicide and another pair would die of drug overdoses. My brother Marco and one of his friends were the last men standing.

"You need to care for things," Grandma said, running a finger into the top bowl in the stack before holding it up for my inspection. "They go to pot if you neglect them."

"That's thermodynamics, Grandma," I said. "I took a whole class about it in college."

"So maybe you want to act like it?"

"I don't understand."

She added blue dish soap to the basin. "It's not just this thing with your mother. Where's Mia while you're making time with Nora?"

My stomach sank at an accusatory tone I was probably half-imagining. "Heading back to Washington. The show was good last night."

"I'm glad you had a nice time. I love her, Giacomo. She comes from a family like ours."

"I know, Grandma."

"But it's not enough that *I* love her. *You've* got to love her. And still, that's not enough."

"You lost me again."

"Love is not enough, Giacomo. It never has been. You've got to use your head *and* your heart."

"Yeah," I said. "I get it."

"Yeah, sure. I see the way you look at Nora. It's the way you used to look at Mia. Excitement fades. There has to be something *underneath*. That's where your head comes in. That's how you make decisions."

"How did you decide about Grandpa?"

My grandmother answered as though she'd been waiting her entire life for this exact question. "Your grandfather just fit," she said. "From the moment he walked into the bakery. Sure, he was good-looking, but there were a lot of good-looking guys. And he was a sweet guy, but there were lots of sweet guys. One time, he came to pick me up and take me to the movies, and he saw my niece Claudia in the carriage on the far wall."

"The one who died young?"

"The one who died young. Bad heart. She was colicky. My sister-in-law would just let her scream. Grandpa picked her up out of the carriage and danced her around. The moon was shining through the big window in front. He pointed out the window and sang her nonsense rhymes in Italian."

"He would do that for my sisters."

"He did it for you, too. Where did he get it from? Not from his parents. He came from the orphanage. Not from the nuns. They were hard women. It was just . . . in him."

"My grandfather was a smooth operator."

"No, it's not like that. We all knew Claudia wasn't long for this world. But your grandfather didn't. He couldn't have. He made the decision to love on her. He made himself part of the family that he never had."

"So, you decide to love someone?"

"No, you *fall* in love with someone. You *decide* to stay in love with them."

"I dunno, Grandma."

"Love is an action," she insisted, scrubbing a bowl with her soapy rag and then putting it in the rubberized drainboard. "It's something you do, not just something you feel, you understand what I'm saying? If you stop doing it, you stop feeling it. And then where are you?"

I took a bowl from the rack and started drying. "About where I am now."

"I'm sorry, sweetheart."

The faucet dripped into the basin, keeping time in our silence.

"All I'm saying is," Grandma said, "think about all of it, not just what makes your heart go *boom boom*. Think about what made you love Mia and talk to her about it. It doesn't matter if you hurt each other, as long as you remember that you're supposed to love each other and then forgive."

"Just that easy, huh?

"Sometimes, it's not easy at all. *La vita e fatta cosi.* I'll be pushing up daisies soon, Giacomo. Listen to me while you can!"

"Don't say that."

"It's okay. I got lucky living this long. I was even luckier to live my life with your grandfather. And I worry about you, Giacomo, because I want you to be able to say the same thing when your time comes."

Grandma dried her hands and made her way to the back door, watching Nora hanging laundry beyond the hedge. The southeast breeze carried the curtains around my grandmother, wrapping her in a funerary shroud. Her voice became strangely distant.

"My mother always said I had to marry an Italian boy,"

Grandma said. "You know you don't have to marry an Italian, don't you Giacomo?"

Nora and I walked ankle-deep through the ebbing tide, hand-in-hand. Four years earlier, I would have been running this route in preparation for the annual lifeguard tryouts. I was jealous of my former self. I was soon to start med school, and things were good with Mia. My grandfather's cancer was still an invisible blip in the lining of his guts. Things were their usual mess with my mother, but she had a lot on her plate. My father had been dead for three years, which left her dealing with my brother's drug addiction alone. Still, my day-to-day was as good as I had any right to expect. I always figured I'd feel similarly now, a physician at the end of a long journey.

"How was the trip?" Nora asked. "Your folks well?"

"Sure," I lied, guilt rising in my chest like bile. Nora had been right in her assessment of me. I wasn't a liar. I still had that fourteen-year-old Boy Scout inside of me, and he wasn't going to have this shit.

Nora read me instantly. "What's on your mind?"

"I stopped to see Mia."

"Oh," Nora said, letting go of my hand. "I see."

Her disappointment was palpable. I would have felt better if she'd just called me an asshole. Water streamed faster across the sand bar as the tide fell, drawing shell fragments and pebbles across our feet, towards deeper water.

"Did you break it off with her, then?"

No, I wanted to say, *we had quiet, unsatisfying sex in the den so as not to wake her parents, then I snuck out the back door.*

"We started talking," I said. "I let her shut me down, as usual. I'm ashamed of myself."

"Why do you let her hold you back?"

"Loyalty?"

That was the understatement of the year. Mia's folks had done everything they could to reconstitute my nuclear family, even if they didn't fully understand what had happened to us. They just knew I was more alone than I should have been. I'd abandoned my own immediate family for my mental health. How did I go about abandoning the people who had picked me up and dusted me off?

"You're loyal to a fault," Nora said. "I knew that the moment I met you. But you don't owe anyone anything."

"Look who's talking."

"My Gran likes to say we give the advice we most need to take."

"Wisdom from the old country."

The sand became firmer as we approached the jetty.

"Did you sleep with her last night?" Nora asked. "Maybe that's none of my business."

"Of course not," I said. This was the third time I'd lied to her, and this one felt easier than the others. There was no reason to upset her. Anyway, she had a fiancé. We hadn't made any promises.

"Just askin'," she said, squeezing my shoulder. "I know we're in a kind of limbo, but I'm not keen on sharing you on the day-to-day."

"I feel the same way about you."

A crowd of gulls was gathering over an area of deeper water between sand bars, where a school of baitfish had been stranded. The birds dove on them mercilessly.

"Will you tell her about us?" Nora asked.

My stomach turned. "No, I won't. Will you tell Daniel?"

Nora's head jerked as if I'd struck her. "He would never understand."

"What's there to understand?"

Nora seemed to consider this for a moment, then reached

for my hand. "You were my first love, Jack. I was yours before I was his."

"And I was yours before I was Mia's?"

"Something like that."

It had a strange logic, or maybe I just wanted it to. As a scientist, I understood the value in viewing a situation dispassionately. From an objective distance, the simplest explanation for the twisting of my morals was resentment. I'd let it fester like an abscessed tooth. I needed to address that. Whatever might be with Nora, it couldn't be vengeance for Mia's misdeeds. Nora and I deserved better than that. I needed to make a clearheaded decision so that I wouldn't be wracked by guilt later.

"Which do you think is worse?" I asked. "What we're doing or the cover-up?"

"Neither. It's the lies we'll tell ourselves to make it feel okay."

13

With Katie arriving in forty-eight hours, we needed to deal with Candy. We headed to the far side of the bay, to a small town best known for exporting biting flies and the smell of horse shit when the wind blew the wrong way.

"I want to go on record one last time saying this is a bad idea," I said, turning off the radio.

"We need to take care of business," Fusilli said.

"It's always *we*, never *you*. Why is that?"

"Loyalty until death, cousin."

"Funny how we keep redefining loyalty around here."

"How was Nora this morning? You get your dick wet?"

"Fusilli, I'm not like you," I said, remembering how Nora had gone down on me before I drove off to Mia's for additional, less satisfying sex. But I was different, wasn't I? Nora wasn't some random hookup, and we weren't sleeping together. And I *did* love Mia. I was just figuring some things out. Marriage was forever. I needed to be sure. It was none of Fusilli's goddamn business, anyway.

"Always the Eagle Scout," he sighed. "It's not in your nature, is it?"

"We're just different, is all," I said.

He grasped my shirt. "You cannot sit motionless in the heart of these perils!"

"Hawthorne?"

"Melville."

"Can we get this over with, please?"

We waded across a balding lawn towards a single-floor ranch with apricot paint. The foundation was splattered with sandy mud from the recent rain, and the roof had a few patches devoid of shingles, the exposed-tar paper rippled and torn. A warm breeze stirred the silver maple near the stoop, the white-backed leaves iridescent with moonlight. We exchanged glances as I pointed to Candy's rusting Toyota at the edge of the property, a hand-painted Confederate flag on the trunk.

A dim table lamp shone off-white in the house, affording a view of the living room through the screen door as we approached. There were newspapers everywhere, pockmarked with darkened spots that looked like a liquid spill. The rug immediately beyond the door was heavily tracked with mud. Fusilli pushed the doorbell, but no noise followed. We glanced at each other once more, then I knocked on the aluminum that framed the screen, producing a metallic death rattle.

Suddenly, a pair of glowing eyes appeared in the doorway. Fusilli swore as we leapt back. It took me a moment to realize the eyes were stickers affixed to the top of a black motorcycle helmet, which was then affixed to the head of a small child. He was clad entirely in black leather.

Fusilli tried to say something but was cut short by the child. "Yo, sluts! There are more guys here for you!"

The child disappeared into the shadows as Candy appeared, wearing a sleeveless, banana-yellow tube dress that ran from her armpits to just beneath her crotch. We stepped back from the stoop as she pushed the door wide and saun-tered towards us. She was trailed by another shorter girl with a thick mop of bleached-blond hair and breasts too large for her body. She wore boxers, a tank top, and pink flip-flops.

"This is my sister, Moon," Candy said.

Moon cocked her hips, gave a little wave, and smiled.

"We were in the neighborhood," Fusilli said. "Thought I could grab my wallet."

"Why don't we step inside?" she said. "We'll be more comfortable."

Fusilli and I exchanged glances that said we would not, in fact, be more comfortable. He shrugged and gestured towards the entrance with a flick of his head. Following him through the door, my lungs spasmed at the reek of cat piss. The walls were covered with a variety of Christian iconography. There was a bulletin from someplace called the Church of the Divine Serpentine Canticle on a coffee table. This was going to be worse than I'd thought.

Candy snagged Fusilli's wallet off a shelf and passed it to him. When she turned around, he peeked into the billfold to see if she'd cleaned him out.

We continued into a kitchen at the back of the house. "Hell is empty, and all the devils are here," Fusilli whispered.

The room was lit by dying, frosted fluorescent tubes in the ceiling. The table was strewn with dirty paper dishes, and there were several pots around the countertops and range, caked with burned or dried food. As the four of us sat down at the table, the new and slightly more disgusting fish odor made me imagine us a bunch of kippers crammed into a tin can. Candy threw the soiled plates into the sink and gestured for us to sit.

Fusilli parked directly across from me, his back to a closed door beside the stove. The two girls were on either side of the table. A screen door to the back yard, propped open by a chair, sat behind my left shoulder. A bug zapper illuminated the lawn beyond in an eerie, black-light glow. The leather-suited child was sitting on a large Harley-Davidson, leaning forward and low against a nonexistent headwind, cranking the throttle as he raced down an imaginary highway. He caught me watching him through the door and made his right hand into the shape of a gun. He took aim at me, dropped his thumb, then blew over his index finger as if clearing the smoke from the barrel.

Candy sat expressionless, her arms folded across her chest, while Moon's head twisted and bobbed as if her neck concealed a spring. She twiddled her thumbs and smacked her lips. Drugs? Tourette's? Hard to say. Irrespective of the clinical diagnosis, I sensed danger. We needed to get the hell out of there.

"Nice bike," I said. "You ride?"

She shook her head. "That belongs to the Motorcycle Man. But he takes me to work sometimes."

Fusilli and I exchanged glances.

"Daddy doesn't let anyone else ride his baby," Moon said quietly.

"Don says you don't believe I saw your girl there with some other guy," Candy said, pointing at me like an auctioneer selling the last shreds of my self-confidence.

Fusilli grimaced.

"How would you know her?" I asked.

"I recognized her when she dropped off that letter at your place."

"Maybe someone who looked like her."

"I never forget a face. She sent her eggs back. Twice."

"Listen, Candy," Fusilli said. "We gotta talk. I don't think this is going to work out."

"What happened to your accent?" she said.

"Sorry, it kind of comes and goes."

"Like your feelings for me?"

Fusilli's left eye twitched, "I just mean . . . look. We were really drunk."

"You were sober in the basement," she insisted over the crackle of the bug zapper.

"Candy, you let yourself into my house. That's . . . not cool."

"I saw you through the window and wanted to surprise you."

"You climbed into my bed naked while I was asleep. Isn't that kind of . . . forward?"

Behind Fusilli, a dull thump emanated from the closed door.

Candy rose to her feet, knocking her chair backward. Our quarters were so cramped that the chair didn't even reach the floor but came to rest against the countertop at an angle.

"Are you calling me a slut?" she asked.

Another thump. Another crackle from the bug zapper.

Moon spoke again, her voice pressured now as she rocked back and forth. "Daddy's mad. He's mad."

"Look . . ."

"I said, are you calling me a slut?"

Fusilli met my eyes. He wanted to go for the throat. I gave my head a half shake. *Don't do it. Don't you fucking dare.*

"Candy, no," he said. "I'm really sorry. I thought I could do this, but I've got a girlfriend in Europe. I'm moving overseas and . . ."

"You sonofabitch!"

Candy turned and reached into the drainboard. Before I could see what she grabbed, Fusilli shoved her into the countertop, knocking the wind out of her. She fell into the narrow space between the range and the cabinets. A carving knife clattered to the floor. My heart stopped.

The racket behind the door rose to a crescendo. The door crashed open, and the space behind it filled with an enormous man in denim overalls. He wore no shirt beneath the suspenders, revealing a broad chest and greasy pot belly. His head was like a great stone set above his body, mossy with a two-day-old beard and topped with weedy salt-and-pepper hair. The man was covered from head to foot in smears of what might have been dark-clay earth the consistency of dog shit, or maybe actual dog shit. In his right hand, he wielded a large pipe wrench.

Moon had not moved from her seat. She was shaking her head and repeating, "Daddysmad" over and over, as though it was one word. Fusilli took one look at the wrench and hurdled Candy's chair, scrambling through the back door like he was carrying a football through the defensive line. I dove after him, tripping at the threshold of the door and tumbling down the stoop into the dirt.

Fusilli's footfalls were already retreating around the bend. I took off after him, realizing that I was half a heartbeat and a monkey wrench from having my brains bashed in. As I cleared the front of the house, the Chevelle roared to life. Fusilli peeled out towards the dead end, wheeled around, and started back up the street. He did not stop as I ran aslant towards him, slowing just enough for me to plunge headlong through the passenger window.

He turned another corner with my legs sticking out of the window. There was a loud bang from the undercarriage, and then a second. The rear end slid out from under us, the wheels chattering across the pavement. This forced Fusilli to stop and allow me completely into the vehicle. He dropped the stick into neutral and fell onto the steering wheel. It took a moment for my heart to slow. After catching my breath, I realized that I was seeing Fusilli cry for the first time since our childhood.

"Jesus, Jack."

Perhaps Icarus had flown too close to the sun and finally had his wings singed.

"What the fuck, man?" I said.

He forced a laugh, grabbing the bottom of his T-shirt and dabbing his eyes. "An extraordinary mission."

"It's not funny, man. She was going to kill you."

Fusilli wouldn't meet my eyes. "In the old days, we would have laughed it off and gone for a beer. You'd have evangelized about it like John the Baptist."

"That was a long time ago," was what I said, but it was more than that, even if I couldn't find the words. This wasn't kids' stuff anymore, and on some level, Fusilli knew it. He just couldn't let go of what we'd once been. I felt it too. Seeing Nora again had shaken me awake and sent me in search of the Jersey Shore Time Machine. I wanted to relive skinny dipping under moonlight, making out on the beach, and maybe even Fusilli's goddamn missions. The price of admission was just too high: my self-respect, Candy's dignity, and very nearly Fusilli's life. This shit had to stop.

"Fusilli," I said. "You could be a father."

"Or not."

"Either way, you've got decisions to make beyond which piece of ass you want to risk our lives on."

"My father screwed up with my mom, and then screwed things up with every woman that came after. I'm going to end up the same way, aren't I?"

"You can make better choices than he did."

"I've *been* making better choices," he said, driving his head back against the headrest. "It's not that I didn't want to mess around, of course I did. There was this Israeli girl who'd have fucked me within an inch of my life. But I had my shit together."

I raised an eyebrow. This would take some convincing.

"I'm serious! I can still talk a good game, but that's all. I don't know what made me do this. Maybe the pregnancy freaked me out. Maybe it was a mistake to come back to the shore."

"I'm starting to think it was."

"But what if Katie isn't for me? A kid would seal the deal. You have kids and that's, like . . . it."

"You've been together for years. Shit or get off the pot."

"Look who's talking."

"What's that supposed to mean?"

"Candy saw Mia with another guy. I'll give you three guesses who it was."

I wasn't going to let myself get worked up over a half-assed identification by a homicidal Piney. Mia and Ian meeting halfway between DC and Connecticut to get it on? It didn't make sense. It would be easier for one of them to fly or take the train to see the other. Still, it had a ring of truth I didn't want to admit to.

"She's fucking nuts, man," I said. "She could have made it up."

Fusilli shrugged. "I'm not here to convince you."

We rocked like a playground spring-rider horse as Fusilli put the car back into gear. I reached over and hit the hazard lights as we limped back to Villabaia. I was certain we'd blown the suspension. The instability of the wheels when we cornered might mean we'd taken out the differential as well. It would likely be a death blow to the old girl.

When we got to the house, Fusilli stayed put as I climbed out of the car. I walked around to the driver's side.

"You okay?" I asked.

He nodded, then backed out of the drive and drove north on the boulevard. As the Chevelle rumbled off, the chassis rolling like a boat in the bay, I realized that Icarus hadn't fallen. He couldn't get off the ground for want of wax.

GRANDPA GOT me up the following morning. He sat at the foot of the sofa bed in the living room, silver light streaming through broken clouds beyond the windows, leaving his white T-shirt with an incandescent glow. For a moment, I imagined he'd died, that this was his soul stopping to visit before ascending to whatever reward awaited him.

"I think your cousin could use a hand," he said, gesturing towards the door.

Lacking a jack or ramps, Fusilli had used a pair of boards to drive the Chevelle up onto the curb, which afforded him just enough room to wriggle underneath and inspect whatever damage we'd done. When I looked back over my shoulder, St. Francesco was still there, his glow fading as clouds slowly veiled the sun. He looked down, inspecting the mottled purple tops of his feet.

"Is this a bad sign, Jack? You can be honest."

"It's not good. It suggests poor circulation. Might be worth talking to the cardiologist."

"Francesco," Grandma called. "You need to pick up the cake."

"Maybe better that than the cancer gets me," Grandpa said, rising to his feet and walking slowly towards the sound of my grandmother's voice. He willed his body to do her bidding once more, as he would over and over again until his heart stopped. That's how he showed her he loved her. He paused at the threshold of the kitchen, then looked over his shoulder at me.

"Thanks, Jack," he said. "For everything."

I opened my mouth to say something, then thought better of it. My grandfather was of sound mind, and he understood the practice of medicine better than the average person. If he didn't want to chase another diagnosis, it wasn't up to me to argue with him, or at least that was what the doctor in me said. But the grandson in me was incensed that he was dying before my eyes, and there wasn't a goddamn thing I could do about it. I had studied for years, filling my brain with medical facts and treatment algorithms. They were worthless now that his body was surrendering. There would soon be no more walks for strawberry shortcake. The Yankees game would play to an empty chair. My grandfather disappeared into the kitchen, a fading beam of sunshine following him and inviting him to slip his loosening mortal skin and explode into light.

Blinking back tears, I pulled on my shorts and headed outside to figure out what my cousin was up to. He saw my feet from his position beneath the car.

"Suspension is fucked, Jack," Fusilli said. "We're gonna need the Castellis."

"Oh Christ," I said. "Here we go again."

THE CASTELLI BROTHERS were who you called when all hope was lost. Fiercely loyal, they were latter-day Renaissance men, willing to tow your car, paint your house, or handle the teenage bully who was making your high school existence a living hell. Their ancestors came from the same Southern Italian town as my great-grandmother, which made them family for all practical purposes. Gianni Castelli had been Grandma Elena's contemporary. He founded a wildly successful construction business near my hometown in New York. We grew up with his grandsons, Paolo and Nunzio. Paolo spent nine of the first ten years of his life in Italy after his mother decided she didn't like America. Medium-built and square-jawed, he had a slight southern accent, because he learned English from old spaghetti westerns. He wore a Stetson hat that had seen better days and, during the colder months, a duster coat right out of *High Plains Drifter*. A man out of time and place, he often patrolled the family compound in the country on horseback.

Nunzio was six years younger, which made him our age. He didn't remember much of Italy but looked the part in skinny jeans and a designer T-shirt. Nunzio was the best-looking man I had ever seen. He was shorter than Paolo and shared the familial square jaw but had high cheekbones and wavy, dark hair that fell below his ears. It was the kind of hair women asked to run their hands through when they met him in a bar. He had the thick forearms of a laborer and a pseudo-Latin tattoo on his right bicep: *ILLIGITIMUM NON CARBORUNDUM.*

Paolo still did a little work in the family business but had married an ex-dancer. He spent most of his time managing the deli she'd bought with the proceeds of her first career. Nunzio was a welder by trade and did a lot of auto work but had a side business making medieval weapons for the Renaissance Faire. They loved a good party, and the annual birthday bash they threw for their granddad was legendary. The last one I'd attended featured an illegal fireworks display that nearly burned their house down. Fusilli and I used one of their work trucks to push a flaming tree into a pond. Afterwards, my cousin climbed atop the cab, his arms raised in triumph as the crowd chanted *Fu-si-li* like he was Rocky fucking Balboa.

The Castellis were the people most responsible for Fusilli's acquisition of the Chevelle in the first place. One of their *paisans* owned a small garage, the primary business of which was souping up cars for low-level mobsters. He was known as *Il Dottore Ruggine*: the Rust Doctor. The Chevelle's original owner caught twenty-five to life at Sing Sing, and Il Dottore was left holding the bag. He sold us the car for a song the summer we graduated from high school. Fusilli hoped Il Dottore would be able to resurrect his beloved heap. Given the chaos typically sown by the Castelli family, it was far more likely we were headed for another Faustian circus from which we would barely escape with our lives.

It was after lunch when Paolo stepped out of the weather-beaten crew-cab pickup, the riding spurs on his Frye boots jangling. He adjusted his Stetson and stepped around to join us on the pebbles. He looked over the rusting hulk of the Chevelle with an element of pity.

"The years haven't been kind to our girl," he drawled.

Fusilli shook his hand. "The salt air eats cars like leprosy."

"Doc," Paolo said, his bicep flexing as he tipped his hat. "Been a long time."

"Hey, Paolo."

Nunzio tossed his phone onto the dashboard and got out of the truck, then embraced both Fusilli and me warmly. He gestured at the flatbed trailer hanging off the back of the pickup. "You think we'll need to tow it?"

"Oh yeah," Fusilli said. "See for yourself."

Nunzio took off his shirt, revealing the well-muscled chest and abdomen he'd honed beating metal at his forge. He wriggled under the Chevelle.

"*Madone*," Nunzio said. "Would you look at this?"

"Bad news?" Paolo said.

"He cracked the strut mounts right off," Nunzio said.

"Could you weld new ones, Nunz?" I asked.

"We'll take it back and see what he can do," Nunzio said. "We'd have to heat-treat the whole frame. It's not a small job."

The tinted back window of Paolo's truck opened, revealing Agnese Castelli, their mother. Her hair had gone completely white since I'd last seen her. She'd cut it into a mod bob with an edge so severe that it looked like a wig. Mama Castelli wore dark Jackie O sunglasses and always sounded like she was shouting at you.

"Ciao, Giacomo!" she said. "Ciao, Donatello!"

"Ciao, Agnese," we replied in chorus.

Hearing the commotion, my grandfather leaned out the door and waved.

"Jack," Grandpa called. "Nora stopped in for a cup of tea. Come say hi."

Mama Castelli popped the latch on the door and half-stepped, half-fell to the curbside on tiny barrel-stave legs that supported a much rounder top half. She began waddling towards the house, wielding a pocketbook the size of a bowling-ball bag and swinging her arms back and forth with more effort than should have been required.

"I gotta talk you Nonno before he die," she said.

"Ma!" Paolo said. "Would you watch what you say?"

"He need-a tell my Papa few things when he get to heaven."

"*Madone*," Paolo sighed. "I'm sorry, fellas. You know how she is."

"You think you could refill some of her meds, Jack?" Nunzio called from under the car. "She's impossible to take to the doctor. She put the *malocchio* on the poor guy last time."

"Did it take?" Fusilli said. "Asking for a friend."

Mama Castelli was almost certainly mentally ill, though the language barrier had precluded any definitive diagnosis. They'd tried mood stabilizers and antipsychotics, all to little avail. She spoke to people no one else could see and believed ghosts lived in her house. At the same time, she bore none of the typical stigmata of schizophrenia or frank psychosis. She was not paranoid. She dressed impeccably and kept a house clean enough that you could eat off the bathroom floor. In another time, she might have been viewed as some sort of mystic or visionary.

"I don't think the pills are working," I said.

"She sleeps a little more on the lithium," Paolo said. "Gives us some downtime."

Mama Castelli entered the house with a volley of machine-gun Italian. Grandpa tried to match her energy but couldn't hide the fatigue in his voice.

Nunzio shimmied out from under the Chevelle and rolled down the windows to give us somewhere to push as we rolled it towards the trailer.

"Saw you on cable TV, Fusilli," Paolo grunted as he leaned into the trunk.

"Yeah," Fusilli said, pushing from the driver's side. "That was some shit, huh?"

"You really think Jesus was some kind of revolutionary?"

"It's possible," Fusilli said.

"But it's not in the Bible," Nunzio said, standing at the bottom of the trailer, waving us forward, then signaling Fusilli to adjust the steering wheel. "He was all peace and love."

"Remember when they were about to arrest Jesus," Fusilli said. "When one of the disciples cut the ear off a Roman soldier?"

"Yeah," Nunzio said.

Fusilli stood and mopped his brow. "Where'd he get the sword?"

"Huh?"

"Jerusalem was a Roman outpost. It was demilitarized. If you had a weapon, you were either a Roman soldier, or you were a rebel."

"And since Jesus and his boys weren't Romans . . ." Paolo said.

"Bingo," Fusilli said, pointing finger guns at Paolo.

"Huh," Nunzio said. "I never thought about that."

Nunzio used the winch to pull the Chevelle up onto the flatbed. We cinched down the ties for the trip back to New York, then headed into the house to see what kind of disaster Mama Castelli was fomenting. When we got to the kitchen, my grandmother was pouring coffee. Grandpa was slumped in the chair at the head of the table, looking defeated, his white pompadour splayed across his forehead like he'd been working in the sun. He crossed his eyes at me. Mama Castelli was holding court with Nora, having trapped her on the bench across the table. Nora looked at me wide-eyed, slowly sipping at her tea and probably trying to figure out what the hell she should say.

"Giacomo," Mama Castelli called as her sons greeted my grandparents. "You an educated man. This girl know nothing. Come here."

She slid herself farther along the bench, pinning Nora tight against the wall with her hips, then invited me to join them. I sat down alongside her as she showed me the pictures she'd been discussing with Nora. They were three–by–five snapshots taken with a poorly focused camera and depicted the cream-colored exterior wall of an old building. The windows were shuttered tight, the space above them marked with weathered lettering that was crisscrossed with ivy and almost impossible to read.

"What you think this say?" Mama Castelli asked.

I screwed up my face and drew the photo closer. "Dunno," I said. "It's not Italian?"

"No, it's not Italian," she said. "Look at the letters!"

Fusilli reached across and snatched the photo. "Latin," he said, tossing the picture back like a frisbee. "It's part of a prayer, but the grammar is wrong."

"I don' know from Latin," she said. "But look how high up the wall. No man is that tall."

The first rule of psychiatry is not confronting the patient's delusions directly. I didn't want to suggest the painter might have used a ladder or scaffold. She was clearly trying to get at something.

"What do *you* think it is, Agnese?" I asked.

"I think it the language of the vampires," she said with a frown. "That's why the shutters all close. To keep the light out. I think they write a curse."

"Good thing we cook with all this garlic," Fusilli said.

"He know the garlic keep them away, see," Mama Castelli said, elbowing Nora and pointing at him.

"Christ on a bike," Nora said.

"Well, you no see any, do you?"

"Ma, would you stop with this?" Nunzio pleaded. "There's no such thing as vampires."

Mama Castelli leaned in to Nora. "My boys no believe me," she said. "But I know things." She gestured around the room with a finger. "I talk to the spirits."

Nora's voice caught in her throat, producing the strange vocal fry of a woman who couldn't imagine what the fuck she'd done to get involved in this and had no idea how to extricate herself.

"If you talk to the spirits," Paolo asked. "Why did you come bother Uncle Francesco? Call Nonno direct."

Mama Castelli shook a crooked finger at him. "You Nonno too far gone now. They gotta move on. But Francesco find him when he go."

My grandmother was a devout Catholic but still retained many of the superstitions of the old country. There was a part of her that believed Mama Castelli was legit.

"Right," Grandma said. "Of course he will."

"Francesco, you no forgetta what I say, right?" Mama Castelli said.

"No," he said quickly, trying and failing to smooth back his hair, the natural wave spilling forward like geriatric Elvis Presley. "I've got my marching orders."

"And you no forget," she said, poking Nora in the ribs with fingers in the shape of devil's horns. "You too beautiful. You hold your fingers like this so no one put *il malocchio* on you."

"Thanks very much," Nora said.

"And you, Giacomo," Mama Castelli said. "You put a baby in her, quick."

Nora flushed a shade of red I'd never seen in nature. Fusilli burst into laughter. My grandmother launched a salvo of *Napoletano* expletives at Mama Castelli.

"What?" Mama Castelli said, her eyes wide with feigned innocence. Then, she reached across her body and squeezed

Nora's left breast as she might a ripe eggplant. *"Guarda queste tette!"*

Nora yelped, bouncing from her seat in surprise and slapping Mama Castelli's hand away. Her knees caught the underside of the table and spilled the drinks everywhere.

"You see?" Mama Castelli cackled. "She ready for you, Giacamo!"

14

———

I met Nora at the beach the following night, my barefoot passage marked by the gurgle and belch of the sump pumps emptying at the curb. Earlier showers had left a starry sky behind broken-gray cloud cover and a stiff wind from the west. Nora was in the gazebo at the top of the street, wrapped in a beach blanket the size of a parachute. It streamed down her legs and gathered around her feet like a royal-blue cape. I saw her before she saw me, my mind twisting as I wondered what the hell I was doing. Nora and I hadn't slept together yet. Avoiding that ultimate betrayal was the right thing to do. But there was also a decent chance Mia had been up to no good, and now she was saying she wanted to come home to be together. Was the move really about being closer to Ian? Was Ian banging someone else as well, making me the better bet again? What was "right," anyway?

Fusilli's moral relativism was filling my brain like quicksand. Maybe living with him again was warping my mind. My nihilistic turn was aborted by Nora raising a hand in greeting. Down the boardwalk, Mia's house was dark. No sign of her folks, and no cars in the lot behind. No witnesses. My heart drummed against my chest with a combination of anxiety and desire. I wanted Nora. I also wanted to be loyal to Mia. Even if she was running around on me, I should be a better person than her.

"How you keeping, Jack?"

I found my way to her bench. "Been a rough few days."

"Any old bats grab you by the tits?"

"Sorry about that," I grimaced. "She's got a screw loose."

"Screws, I reckon."

Nora produced a flask from beneath her blanket and raised it in offering. I placed a hand over my guts. "I'm not sure I've recovered from the last round you poured."

"Hair of the dog, love."

I chuckled and sat upright again, taking the flask and a swallow. We sat in silence for some time, passing it between us, a swig at a time.

"How was the slag, then?"

"She tried to stab him," I said. "Her father nearly brained me with a monkey wrench. Then we wrecked the car."

She giggled. "You're having quite a holiday!"

Nora offered me the corner of the blanket, and I snuggled in beside her, my head swimming with whiskey and the freesia vapor of her skin. We entwined our fingers and sat for a time, the southeast breeze rustling the dune grass and goldenrod behind us.

"You're not your usual chatty self," I said.

"Ireland on the brain."

"Tell me."

"*You're not getting any younger, Nora!*" she sang in a soft falsetto. "*Wouldn't little Fusilli love a playmate?*"

"You're afraid they'll keep the baby, and it'll increase the pressure on you."

"If'm tryin' to put off the wedding, this ain't gonna help."

I put my arm around her, and she tucked in tight, her head resting in the crook of my neck. What did she need to go back to Ireland for, anyway? I liked the way she felt. I liked how whiskey took the edge off my anxiety. I liked the hint of possibility, of freedom from the constant self-doubt I felt with Mia, of never knowing what was real and what was being kept from my view.

I took her hands and pulled her upright. We crossed the dune bridge and began walking north, her arm around my waist and mine around her shoulders. We stopped several streets down in the shadows of the dunes, out of the glow cast by the boardwalk lights.

We folded the blanket in half like a giant sleeping bag, then crawled inside and lay in each other's arms as the crescent moon rose and the tide slid in. The world began to feel unstable under my elbow.

"Jack," she said, "I'm so fuckin' lonely."

"Me too."

"Can you keep a secret?"

"It's what I do best."

I shuddered as her lips drew close to my ear. "I don't love Daniel. Not really."

"I'm so sorry, Nora."

"Do you love Mia?"

"Not the way I should. Not anymore."

"You're such a good lad. You're so earnest and kind."

"You can see it has done a lot for me."

"You deserve so much better than you've gotten."

Our hands began to drift over each other's bodies: first the shoulders, then the small of the back, then under the shirt. I took her face in my hands and kissed her. She tasted of whiskey and salt, of every fantasy I had imposed on her memory for more than a decade. I unhooked her bra, and she lifted her shirt and mine, her nipples like Jordan almonds against my chest, her gooseflesh on mine like rare sea creatures entwined. Our drunk, fumbling fingers struggled with the remainder of our clothing. The ocean lapping at the high tide line beyond our feet, I imagined the mysterious Daniel somewhere east of us as dawn broke over Ireland. Would he swim that day? Could I take him in a fight?

Naked, our skin pressed together, I had a detached thought of Mia. I imagined her coming out of the water to me, even though she hated swimming. She was folding her arms across her chest, her expression more of curiosity than judgment. Nora dragged me back into the moment, rolling me over with surprising strength and climbing astride my hips. Taking hold of me and guiding me inside her, she yelped as it began, then smashed her mouth against mine and sucked the breath from my lungs. Our bodies began to rock gently with the rhythm of the surf but grew more frantic with each passing moment, as if we each felt the ticking of some invisible clock.

"Is it like this with Mia?" Nora gasped as she reared back and pulled my hands to her breasts, burying me inside her. "Does it feel this good?"

"I'm not going to last like this, Nora."

"Go on, Jack," she said. "Make me yours."

WHEN I AWOKE, I was clothed again, lying prone in the sand, the tide in retreat at my feet. The climbing sun was working me over like a mafia enforcer with a blowtorch. Nora was already awake beside me, bundled in the blanket. I moved to her and put an arm around her shoulders, but she pulled away.

"Christ, Jack," she whispered, resting her chin on her knees. "Jesus Christ, what have we done?"

I didn't know what to say. We'd wanted this. Well, *I* had. I thought she did, too. Had I misinterpreted something in my excitement?

When Nora finally looked up, her eyes were hollow, like an abandoned car with the windshield taken out.

"I ruined everything," she whispered, her voice breaking.

I tried to put my arm around her again, and she did not resist this time. "I'm sorry, Nora. I didn't mean to . . ."

"No, I wanted it. More than you." She shook her head, weeping openly now. "I still do. And that's the problem."

Buyer's remorse? Was she feeling guilty over Daniel? Panicky over a desire to remain in the States and pursue whatever this was? She stared out to sea, unwilling to meet my eyes. Maybe she was imagining Daniel across the water or looking for a reason to return to him.

"You don't have to do anything you don't want to, Nora. You don't have to marry him."

"Oh, I'll just have you instead then?" she snapped, squinting at me. "You with the girlfriend you can't seem to shake? I don't need rescuing, Jack."

"I just . . ."

"Just what?"

"I just want to understand. If I'm just a diversion, okay. But I think there's the possibility of something more. Shouldn't we talk about that?"

"What are you in such a rush about? We're only twenty-six. We haven't seen each other in twelve years, and we only just got around to sleeping together. Why does everyone push?"

"I'm sorry," I said. "I'm sorry for last night. I'm sorry for making you angry. I'm not good at this."

"No, I'm sorry," she said, losing the edge in her voice. "I need to sober up. Maybe we can talk more once I have my head together. Right now, we gotta think about Katie and what she's gonna need. There will be time for us later."

"Okay," I said.

"I don't regret it, Jack," she said, reaching over to squeeze my hand. "I don't. You're grand. When I was a girl, I wanted you to be my first."

Nora rose to her feet and rolled up the blanket. She paused for a moment to kiss me on the top of the head, then began a slow walk south. I waited for her to look back, but she never did. I followed her trail of wet footprints with my eyes as she approached a crowd of gulls near the jetty, the birds scattering as they leapt into the sky. It took me a moment to realize I was watching her disappear in time, fading into a Kodachrome memory just as she had more than a decade earlier.

I lay down again as she receded from sight, listening to the chatter of the seagulls and the beat of the waves against the sandbar. I felt dirty and wondered if this was how Fusilli felt after his antics. I thought of the things I had whispered to Mia between damp sheets only weeks earlier. Rekindle an eighth-grade transatlantic romance, that was the fucking plan? Nora drank her face off, wanted to fuck, and then got upset about it. She was an unbroken horse. We barely knew each other anymore, and still I wanted her. In spite of my better judgment, against my natural risk aversion, and contrary to every promise I'd made to Mia, I wanted her. I wanted her and was disgusted with myself for it.

When I got back to Villabaia, Aldo was passed out on the couch, an empty bottle of tequila beside him. A note from my grandparents said they'd gone up north for the day. There was no sign of Fusilli.

I showered and shaved, but the water made me feel no cleaner, no matter how hot I cranked it. I'd become my cousin, accepting a family pattern I'd long derided. This was who I was. There was no denying it anymore. I spent the rest of the day hiding in the Dungeon, sleeping off my hangover in broken jags. When I finally went back upstairs to find some food, Aldo was gone, but his bottle sat on the coffee table as some grim reminder of what I had done. The Cross of Death had been planted in the mouth of the bottle. The attached Post-it read "R.I.P. Jack."

15

The dash of Grandpa's Plymouth was chalkboard green, cracked, and uneven, as if it had been upholstered with badly tanned ogre hide. "This is a travesty," Fusilli said from the passenger seat. "I can't believe we've been downgraded to this . . . thing."

"It's only got sixty-seven thousand miles on it," I said, signaling to change lanes. "It's thirty-years old! Talk about reliability!"

"It's a scow," he said. "The Chevelle had class."

"The Chevelle smelled like you were making moss bunker gravlax in the back seat."

"It was our chariot," he moped, leaning forward and trying to tune in the Yankees game. "The Phantom of the Parkway. State troopers talked about it the way airline pilots discuss UFOs."

"What did *Il Dottore* have to say?"

"Doesn't sound like it's worth fixing," he said. "I guess it doesn't really matter anyway, since I'm headed back to Europe. May she rust in peace."

Nora leaned in from the back seat. "We'll find you a proper car when you get back to Ireland."

"I don't want to endanger anyone by driving on the wrong side of the road."

"Like you haven't been wreaking havoc on the right?"

I laughed and reached a hand back to receive Nora's high-five. She seemed like herself again. I wanted to believe that, after some sober thought, she was realizing there were possibilities between us.

The ride to Newark International was uneventful, since Katie was landing in the middle of the day. We left Nora sweet-talking the cop at the curb while Fusilli and I dashed through the cloud of jet and car exhaust that hung over the terminal like a plague, finding our way to International Arrivals.

We arrived just as Katie darted through the customs exit, her round cheeks flushed with excitement as she dodged slower travelers struggling with jet lag. She dropped her duffel and tucked her blond bob behind her ears when she picked us out of the crowd, then opened her arms wide and cockeyed. Fusilli trotted towards her, gathering her up and lifting her off her feet. She giggled as he spun her around. As they turned, I saw something in my cousin's squinted eyes and toothy grin, something more genuine than sardonic, open rather than strategic. I knew when he was putting on a show. This was for real. Fusilli was a fuck up. He made terrible decisions. But he still loved her, just as he had when we were trying to sneak him out of France.

"I missed you, Donnie!" she squealed.

"Hello, love!"

"Donnie?" I called from twenty feet off. "What's this bullshit?"

"It sounds more Irish than *Donatello* or *Fusilli*," she said as they strode towards me, an unfamiliar bounce in my cousin's step. "Don't you think?"

I laughed as she got on tiptoes to hug me and kiss my cheek.

"You're the expert," I said.

"So good to see you, Jack."

"You too," I said. "How long has it been?"

"Had to be Christmas? Three . . . four years ago? I think I was still at uni. So were you. You were waiting to hear about medical school."

"Feels like a lifetime."

We started walking towards the exit. "I'm looking forward to a few weeks at the beach," she said. "It'll be like the old days."

Her breezy attitude made me uncomfortable. Did *she* know that I knew what she was doing here? That was the problem with other people's secrets. You never knew who exactly you're supposed to be keeping them from.

"It'll be a little cooler than you remember. Though warmer than Ireland, I'm sure."

Katie rolled her eyes, tugging at the cream-colored cable-knit sweater that struggled to contain her breasts. Probably the first physical manifestation of her pregnancy.

"I was hoping to put this jumper away for a few weeks at least," she said.

"Soon."

"I guess Fusilli told you the news?"

Fusilli's eyes widened. He shook his head infinitesimally and flashed two-two with his left hand. A baseball sign from our youth: Let the first pitch go.

I raised an eyebrow. "About you coming?"

"His opportunity in Italy!"

"Yeah, he was saying."

"Italy is so romantic. I'm hoping we'll get to do some traveling together."

"With a little luck, you'll live long enough to regret that."

"Hey!" Fusilli protested, re-balancing her bag on his shoulder.

She laughed and gave me a backhand to the chest. "Stop that! Who would have thought our lad would become an archeological phenom?"

"Certainly not me."

"You thought he would just talk bollocks all his life," she said. "But I had faith."

"Two things can be true at once, right?"

She laughed and backhanded me again, then reached into her handbag and pulled out a purple paisley hair band, pushing her bob back from her face. Our pace slower than the crowd, the sea of chattering bodies began to part and flow around us like a stream.

"Where's Nora?" she asked.

"Watching the car," Fusilli said.

Katie's eyes turned towards the sliding glass doors, where Nora was standing beside the Plymouth, waving her arms as though she were directing runway traffic. She winked and pointed at the cop she was chatting up, then gave the OK sign. I felt a pang of jealousy. Perhaps it shouldn't have been surprising since we'd slept together, but what right did I have to be jealous when I still had a girlfriend? My feelings for Nora were progressing faster than they probably should have. Nora wasn't as invested as I was based on our conversation on the beach. I was no longer thinking clearly, and that was dangerous.

Katie stuffed her handbag into my arms and ran towards Nora.

"I missed you, chicken!" Katie called as the doors slid open. The cop turned and smiled at the second beautiful Irish woman he was about to meet in ten minutes.

"Did you guys think I would miss her getting a goddamn abortion?" I muttered.

"How would you know she was pregnant?" Fusilli asked.

"Her rack, for starters."

"Magnificent, isn't it? Maybe fatherhood *is* for me after all."

"I hate you, Fusilli."

CAPTAIN KIDD'S began its history as a whorehouse in the 1800s, but gradually became more civilized with the waning of the fishing industry. It evolved into a bar and restaurant before I was born. Three stories tall, the original stucco had been sheathed with some kind of vinyl faux-shingle siding, as if Disney had tried to graft a background check from Martha's Vineyard onto the Dirty Jerz. Still, they'd kept the original black shutters, and the same hardwood sign had been hanging crooked above the door on wrought iron stanchions since my mother's childhood. Its success was entirely predicated on its bayfront locale: smack between the fishing piers, with a direct view of the sunset.

The ceilings were low enough that I had to duck beneath the hand-hewn beams to avoid braining myself. The original dark hardwood floors remained uneven and authentic, contrasting with plaster and lathe walls that had been ruined with a mixture of classic and cheesy nautical decor. A phony, old-time street sign accenting a vintage brass sextant hung next to a crucified, dry-rotting rubber crab, which hung alongside couch art that belonged in a derelict nursing home. You could not have imagined a better metaphor for the Jersey Shore.

We made our way through the late-afternoon crowd to the center of the room. Nora stepped behind the well-worn bar and put her hip into one of her coworkers with a soft *sorry love*, making room in front of the Guinness tap. She began pulling a pint as the rest of us grabbed stools at the long mahogany counter. Katie was shorter than I remembered, her legs barely reaching the brass rail at our feet. She looked down the bar at the bed of ice pockmarked with littleneck clams and oysters, the barman shucking them as fast as he could. Katie blew up her cheeks and stuck her tongue out. Her reaction wasn't wrong. You didn't eat at Kidd's if you could help it.

"What are you havin', Katie?" Nora asked.

"Just a lemonade for me," Katie said.

Nora rolled her eyes, put the first pint aside to allow the head to form properly, and poured the second, then brought the first back to the tap and finished it off before passing it to me. I smiled at the heart shape she'd fashioned in the head of my beer. Katie's eyes flashed to the heart, then to my face. A knowing grin began to form in the corner of her mouth. She waited for Nora to step away before she struck.

"Do you know the kind of trouble you're in for, Jack?" Katie asked.

Fusilli leaned forward, flashing two-two with the hand that wasn't clutching his pint.

"I don't know what you're talking about," I said.

I didn't. Not really. But it was time to get off the fence. I was falling for Nora. I deserved to start over in something better and healthier, rather than constantly wonder whether it was the Witchdoctor or I who was the side-sausage. But Katie didn't need to know that and neither did Fusilli. I had the feeling Nora was going to take some convincing. She had a lot more to lose than I did. She was formally engaged, and it sounded like there were several connections between the families. Maybe we could stay in Jersey and make a place for ourselves or move back up into the mountains near where I'd gone to college. It could be a good life and one worth living.

Katie glanced over at Fusilli. He offered a shrug before taking a sip of Guinness, the head forming a milk mustache above his lip.

"I don't know nothin'," he said.

"I'm sure you don't," she said, shaking her head.

"Getting soft in your old age?" I said, gesturing at her fizzy drink and hoping to change the subject.

"I need to watch my figure."

"Guinness has fewer calories," I said, raising my glass.

"Sure," Katie said, "but the trouble is, I'm pregnant."

Fusilli coughed up whatever beer remained in his mouth, while Nora put down the rum and Coke she'd made for herself, then crossed her arms and leaned back against the shelves of hard liquor, offering a half-surprised laugh.

"What?" Katie asked. "He wasn't going to figure it out?"

"I mean . . ." Fusilli said, his eyes begging me to play along. "We could have eased him into it."

"We'll need his advice sooner rather than later, right?"

"It's not really my line of work," I said, relieved that I didn't need to play stupid anymore.

"For fuck's sake, Jack," Katie said, "Are ye a doctor, or aren't ye?"

"I mean, yes."

"All right, then. Because we find ourselves in a bit of a pickle."

We were quickly earning side-eyes from nearby patrons, and gossip had a way of finding its way back to my grandparents. My mother said it was the main reason Uncle Aldo had never gotten away with anything in his youth.

"How about we take over that table in the corner," Nora said, draining her rum and Coke, then fixing herself another. "Fewer ears."

We gathered around the corner table, the lack of A/C vents leaving the air still and smelling of seafood on the verge of expiration. Katie leaned towards me expectantly, Fusilli sitting alongside her with his hand over hers. Her cheeks were flushed, blurring the space between her freckles. I was anxious. I'd only done two rotations in obstetrics and gynecology, and both had been in a Catholic hospital with strict rules about abortion. One of my earliest clinical experiences was with an undocumented Palestinian woman having a miscarriage. We weren't permitted to intervene. After a short labor, I delivered a fetus small enough to fit in the palm of my hand, his slick, translucent skin yellowed and crisscrossed by veins. His head gave the slightest twitch as I moved him to the gurney beside the bed, perhaps struggling to breathe through the lungs he didn't yet possess before dying. Later, we used an ink pad to make tiny footprints on a card for his mother. She was inconsolable, wringing her hands and crying to me in Arabic. I couldn't understand the words, but the meaning was clear: *Why didn't you save my baby?* I felt sad and useless and realized I would never be an obstetrician.

"I don't want to talk out of turn," I said as Nora snuck in beside me. "I don't have a lot of experience in women's health."

Katie sipped her drink cautiously, her lips tight and feline. Bubbles percolated around her nose.

"Just do your best, man," Fusilli said.

"Let's say I decide to get rid of it," Katie said, her glass loud against the tabletop. "What does that entail?" She was trying to appear tough about it, but the royal sapphire of her eyes was wet with tears, looking for a reason to burst.

"They'll give you some anesthesia, at least enough so you don't remember and probably enough that you're completely unconscious. They'll dilate the cervix and then use some combination of vacuum and curettage..."

"Curettage?" She asked

"Sorry. Instruments that will scrape the lining of the uterus and remove the products of conception."

"The baby, you mean."

I took a moment to breathe before responding. "The baby."

"Fuck's sake," Katie said, bowing her head and covering her mouth to stifle a small cry. Nora pulled her chair around to the opposite side of the table, pressing a napkin into her hand and throwing an arm around her shoulders.

"Katie," Fusilli said gently. "We can figure something else out."

"It's what we decided," she said. "It's better this way."

"It's a difficult situation," he said. "I'm not sure there is any *better*."

On one hand, I was happy my cousin wasn't trying to pressure her. On the other, I was frustrated that he wasn't more responsible to begin with. Katie was becoming yet another casualty of Fusilli's long line of bad decisions.

"She wouldn't be in this situation if you'd been careful," I said.

"Spare me the sanctimony," Fusilli said.

"It took two of us," Katie said. "No one twisted my arm."

Fire flashed behind Nora's eyes. "You didn't exactly beg me for a rubber the other night, did you, Jack?"

A stunned silence fell on us like an avalanche. I couldn't believe she'd just come out with it. From the looks of it, neither could anyone else.

"Jesus, Mary, and the fucking donkey," Katie said, her mouth falling open. "Have you learned nothing?"

Nora rolled her eyes. "Calm yourself. I've been on the pill for years."

"Unprecedented!" Fusilli said, taking my hand in congratulations.

"Fuck off, Fusilli," Nora said.

I'd spent so long trying to be respectable and then trying to seem so even when I wasn't. That possibility was now gone. I felt a strange liberation as the shackles of my self-image loosened. It was simultaneously disorienting and thrilling, perhaps like an astronaut experiencing weightlessness for the first time. The thing about weightlessness, though, is that you weren't *actually* weightless. You were in free fall but moving fast enough that you never hit the Earth. I suspected my impact was coming sooner rather than later.

"So, what's the plan, then?" Katie asked. "You're going to stay here with Jack and tell Daniel to fuck off?"

"Maybe," Nora offered, taking a pull of her drink. "Or maybe Jack will . . ."

"We don't have a plan yet," I said.

"Make one fast, love," Katie said. "Her Da's gonna have your balls in a sling after what he paid for the reception."

I looked at Nora, who grimaced and nodded gravely. "The Da will skin you alive, if Daniel doesn't first."

"They'll need to get in line behind Mia," Fusilli said, his smile widening.

"Who's Mia?" Katie asked.

"Jack's girlfriend of six years!" Fusilli said, tenting his fingers and drumming them together like a cartoon villain. "Isn't it exquisite?"

"The same one from back when?"

"The same!" Fusilli cheered, raising his fists in the air, thrilled at our apparent role-reversal. "My cousin is a man, where there was once only a boy!"

"You mad cow!" Katie said, giving Nora a shove before turning her attention to me. "And you! What's your excuse?"

"I think Mia's been fucking the Witchdoctor," I said. "I doubt she'll be too broken up about it."

Katie's mouth hung in wonderment. "A witch . . ."

"Wiccan," Fusilli corrected.

"Fuck off, Fusilli," I said.

We sat looking at each other for a few moments, Jimmy Buffett's inane lyrics dribbling through the overhead speakers as the dinner crowd began to filter in. Nora waved at one of the barmaids and signaled for another around. We were going to need it.

GRANDPA WAS SCHEDULED for chemotherapy the following day at noon. He seemed unusually chipper that morning, whistling Benny Goodman as he flitted about his morning chores. Grandma was working at the stove, frying the eggplant rounds she'd make *parmigiana* for supper. The air was heavy with aerosolized olive oil and toasted breadcrumbs as she stacked the eggplant between layers of paper towels. Closing my eyes, the smell instantly transported me to some August Saturday of my youth, coming home from the beach to stacks of crusty Italian bread, fried cutlets, and bubbling tomato sauce. Hunks of fresh Romano and mozzarella cheese. My grandmother would lean up against the sink and smile to herself as my siblings and I dove in, eating like we'd been marooned on a desert island.

"Francesco," Grandma called, "you've got to get a move on, or you'll miss your treatment."

"Breathe through your mouth, Elena," he called from the basement. He appeared short of breath as he crested the stairs, like a free diver who'd chased a lobster too far into the reef and had to turn back. He put the gallon can of olive oil he'd been looking for on the countertop, then kissed my grandmother on the cheek.

"You smell good," she said.

"Want to be at my best for Dr. Landry," he said. "She's nice looking."

"You're a regular comedian," Grandma said. "She's welcome to you!"

"You hear that, Jack?" he said, winking at me. "Now that I'm *futtut*, she's willing to let me off the hook."

"I had too many headaches when the kids were young," Grandma said. "We should have made more whoopee when we had the chance."

"Grandma!" I said.

My grandparents giggled like a pair of teenagers.

"It's fun to scandalize you once in a while, Giacomo," Grandma said.

"You want me to drive you, Grandpa?" I asked.

"No, no," he said. "I'll be fine."

My grandmother looked up from her pan. "Yeah, Francesco," she said. "Why don't you let Jack take you for a change. He might like to see Sloan Kettering."

"I think he'd rather see the Irish chippies next door," Grandpa said with a wink. He went into the bedroom laughing over his shoulder, then returned in a clean linen shirt.

"Well, you can call your brother-in-law if you have any problems," Grandma said.

"*You* can call Vinny. Tell him I said to go shit in a hat."

Grandma and I laughed. "You're terrible!" she said.

"All right, Elena," he said, kissing my grandmother again. "I'm off. Love you."

"Love you, sweetheart," she said. "Drive safe."

Grandpa waved as he headed out the door. It all seemed so breezy and carefree, like it wasn't the last time any of us were going to see him alive.

16

———

More than anything, I wanted out of Mrs. Costa's apartment. I was numbed by the loss of my grandfather and bewildered by his decades-long betrayal. I needed time to process what had just happened but was offered only the hot, stale air of the bedroom, cut with the smell of the festering trash and car exhaust blowing in off Metropolitan Avenue. There would be time for reckoning later. We needed a plan—and quickly. Our grandmother thought we'd gone to the city to help Grandpa with some car trouble. Every minute would both increase our exposure and invite her suspicion.

"How are we going to get him out of here, Fusilli?" I said, looking down at Grandpa's body. "We can't just carry him down the goddamn stairs."

"The fire escape out back?" Fusilli said, his chest still heaving after running to give Aldo the news, then back.

"Past all those windows?"

"The freight elevator," Mrs. Costa piped up. "You could go right out the back door. The super's office is there, but I can distract him."

"Do you really want to be involved in this?"

"Like I'm not up to my wrinkled tits in it already?" she said. "I was in the war, boy. I can handle myself."

Fusilli offered a short, surprised laugh, like a burst of sidearm fire. Then, we got to work. We dressed Grandpa, gently pulling his clothes over limbs limp with the departure of his spirit, then used the top sheet to roll him up like a burrito. Before we closed the flap over his face, Mrs. Costa bent down to smooth his hair, then gently kissed his lips.

"I hope you found Ellsworth and the lads waiting for you," she said softly. "I hope you'll introduce me when I get there."

She patted his shoulder and nodded, then stepped back as we closed the shroud. My eyes filled with tears. I had questions, too many questions, but this wasn't the time. Focus on the task at hand. This was what my medical training had been about. How does the patient survive the next twenty seconds? The next twenty minutes? The next two hours? Manage one disaster at a time. Don't let it get ahead of you.

We used some of Mrs. Costa's stockings as ties around Grandpa's chest and legs to be sure the sheet wouldn't unroll in transit. Mrs. Costa sat in a small navy-blue armchair in the corner of the room, silently working her way through a decade of the rosary in her hand as we did our work. Wartime visages of her and my grandfather stood sentry over her shoulder, guardians of a past rendered in black and white. What were they like then? Had their love been carefree under the constant specter of death? Could they have imagined what life had in store for them in the coming decades?

Mrs. Costa dabbed at her nose with a balled-up Kleenex and found my eyes, as though she was reading my thoughts. "We weren't always these dried-up old husks, Jack. We once shone as bright as you do right now in your prime."

I cinched her stockings tight around my grandfather's chest. I didn't know how to respond. My entire world felt upended.

"I think we're good to go," Fusilli said, checking my knots one final time.

Mrs. Costa placed her Kleenex and rosary on the end table beside her chair, then rose to her feet. She lifted a finger in pause, then stepped into the walk-in closet. When she reappeared a few moments later, she wore a tan, pleated skirt, white blouse, and matte-black flats. She looked almost elegant as she adjusted her hair in the mirror on the door, then turned to face us, bringing her heels together and squaring off her shoulders.

"Ready for duty," she said.

"I need to borrow your phone first," Fusilli said.

Mrs. Costa nodded and led us back to the kitchen. Fusilli dialed an international number. When Katie picked up, the volume was loud enough that she sounded like a cawing raven. Mrs. Costa must have been hard of hearing.

"Donnie?" she said. "Are you *mad*? Do you know what an international call to a mobile costs?"

"Listen to me carefully," he said. "In two hours, you and Nora need to take my grandmother shopping."

"What? Why?"

"Tell her to take you to Portofino's to buy the makings for pasta carbonara. You want her to teach you, because it's my favorite dish."

"It is?" she asked. "What the hell is it?"

"Like macaroni and cheese with bacon," he sighed. "Look, it doesn't matter. We just need her out of the house in two hours. Keep her away for an hour or so. We'll be fishing across the street when you get back."

"You're going to explain this to me later, right?"

"No," Fusilli said, his eyes locked with mine. "We're never going to talk about this again."

∼

I NEVER UNDERSTOOD the term "dead weight" until we lifted my grandfather, my hands under his armpits, Fusilli's under his legs. Grandpa couldn't have been more than 150 pounds, but he might as well have been a ton of cement. Mrs. Costa cracked the door, checking for anyone in the hall, and then motioned for us to follow her. We shuffled down the corridor and around a corner to a door half the height of a typical elevator. When she pushed the button on the wall, a low groan began to radiate from somewhere deep in the building.

"Give me time to get to the ground floor," Mrs. Costa said. "When you get out of the elevator, the service door will be down the hall on the right-hand side. Walk right out, don't look back. Understood?"

"Understood," Fusilli said.

Mrs. Costa hurried to the steps and started down, the report of her leather soles fading slowly into the lower floors. When the doors finally opened, Fusilli and I stooped to muscle our grandfather into the cramped space. We had to bend him at the waist to fit. The floor creaked under our weight, rocking gently on a cable that probably wasn't far from its limit.

There were no controls inside the car. Fusilli reached outside and pushed the button labelled B. The doors rattled closed, enveloping us in a suffocating darkness. The car lurched as we started our descent. I imagined the doors opening to Dante's hellscape at the bottom, Satan eagerly waiting to deliver the prescribed punishments for our misdeeds.

"Be a real kick in the balls if we plunged to our deaths now," Fusilli said from the void to my right.

"Fusilli," I said, the atmosphere souring with the heat and our sweat. "I can't wait to die."

"That's my boy."

We reached the bottom of the shaft with a muted crunch, as if we'd landed on a pile of empty beer cans. The doors opened to a dank basement. The only light was provided by a pair of bare bulbs dangling from wires overhead, each protected by a small metal cage. I lifted a finger to my ear to signal Fusilli to listen. Indistinct voices were coming from around the corner, one of them female. Ten yards away, a seam of light between a pair of doors marked the way to the alley.

Fusilli and I nodded to each other, took hold of our grandfather's body, then shuffled into the passageway. We were able to move more quickly once we were upright. As we reached the corner, Mrs. Costa's voice became clearer. I took a quick glance to see her blocking a doorway at the far end of the hall. Backlit by the office light, her long shadow stretched towards us like an apparition. I pushed through the doors and into the asphalt cauldron of the Brooklyn afternoon.

Aldo spotted us as we hurried towards the back of the El Camino. Squeezing out of his door, he stepped around, opening the tailgate and cover glass. He stood silent watch against the wall as Fusilli and I slid our grandfather along the filthy corrugated metal floor of the bed. Mrs. Costa's footsteps clipped up behind us, arriving in time to witness us up close.

Mrs. Costa and Aldo nodded at each other, then Aldo ducked into the cab and started the engine. Fusilli hugged Mrs. Costa as Aldo drove off, then followed behind to collect Grandpa's Plymouth. As they disappeared around the corner, Mrs. Costa and I looked at each other for a long moment.

"What were you to him?" I asked.

"I was his angel," she said. "He was my deliverance."

Mrs. Costa fell into my arms and kissed my cheek. Before I could ask her what the fuck any of that meant, she turned and hurried back towards the loading dock. She paused at the corner. Her shoulders slouched, she brought her hands to her mouth and sobbed to the brickwork. Then she glanced back at me, wiped her eyes, and straightened her skirt as she might her old army uniform. She disappeared around the corner with the formal gait of a soldier, leaving me standing alone in the alley and wondering what was going to happen next.

New Jersey was one of the few places in the world where it was possible to get stuck in a traffic jam doing seventy miles per hour. Fusilli was holding position too close to Aldo's bumper as we merged onto the Garden State Parkway.

"Back off a little, would you?" I said.

"I don't want someone pulling in between us and seeing Grandpa laid out in there."

"I can't believe he's in the back of the El Camino," I said, pulling the visor down to shield my eyes. "It's so undignified."

"Maybe we should have taken the bread truck?" Fusilli asked.

"From the bakery? Are you fucking high?"

"Like this is more normal?"

We followed Aldo over the Raritan Bridge, the coastal wetlands spread out before us as we approached Amboy. This was my favorite view as a kid on my way to the shore for the summer. It was my first sight of harbors clogged with boats, of rafts of cattails sheltering the crabs and weakfish my grandfather and I would hunt for supper. It was where I might catch the first whiff of salt air or boat exhaust, depending on the wind. The first evidence of communion with a family legacy that stretched back close to seventy-five years. I'd hoped to bring my own brood here someday. To initiate my own children and grandchildren into the sacraments of August. To feel them blessed with steaming plates of pasta and shellfish, the recipe passed down through the family for generations, a lineage unbroken from Southern Italy a hundred years ago. Now, all of it seemed like some kind of mirage.

"So, do you think he died while they were, you know . . ." Fusilli made a fist and pantomimed a punching motion.

"Jesus fucking Christ," I said. "Can you just . . ."

"What do you want to talk about, then?" he said. "This is so fucked up. I feel like I'm watching myself."

I shrugged. The AM radio crackled, losing the Yankees game as we passed into the marshlands.

"Everything we grew up with," I finally said. "Family. Loyalty. Honor. It was all bullshit."

"I think . . ." Fusilli said, "I think we aspire to a kind of order that doesn't exist in nature."

"What does that mean?"

"You studied physics," he said. "Even I understand Newton. Simple equations. Cause and effect. Then Einstein came along and told us space is bent and we can't trust our perception of time. Then Heisenberg invented quantum mechanics. Told us two things can be equally true, until an observation forces a choice. So, whose observation is reality? It's all dependent on your point of view."

"So, what?" I said, "he's both a philanderer and a saint? Schrödinger's Grandpa?"

"No," Fusilli said. "Schrödinger was German."

"You're such a dick."

"Look, man. I'm saying we all live in realities of our own construction. Until today, Grandpa was the most upstanding guy we knew. A hero. And everything he did to earn that was real. All of what we knew of him is still true. We lived it."

"But?"

"But . . ." Fusilli sighed, flexing and extending his fingers around the steering wheel. "There was shit we couldn't see. Another reality, one that was for him and Mrs. Costa alone. Who knows what they went through in the war? Can anyone who wasn't there understand it? Our grandmother? Us?"

"Fusilli," I said. "There's one reality. We're all playing in the same sandbox."

"I think we just learned that reality is highly subjective," Fusilli shrugged. "You and I are proving it this very minute by creating the history this family will accept for decades. Grandpa came back from chemo and died peacefully at home, a loving husband and father. Idolized by his grandchildren. Sainted by his parish. No one will question it."

"And we ignore this . . . other reality?'

"We don't concern ourselves with it. It's not our business. Our grandfather was a good man, and he had his reasons for keeping things from us. We should trust his judgment."

This felt like a bridge too far for me. Fusilli was accustomed to living different lives, to showing different parts of himself to different people. It wasn't my experience at all, at least not until Nora turned up. My grandfather was all-American: Army, truth, work, family, honesty. Did he really believe in those things? Or was it a front to keep up appearances and hide his dirty secrets? I couldn't square this circle.

"This is breaking your brain," Fusilli said. "I can feel it."

"This isn't how it should be."

"Jesus Christ," he said. "Stop with the *should*. There's only what *is*. People get desperate, and they do the best they can. Are you a horrible person because you fucked Nora?"

"That's different."

"Is it?"

"I'm not having a sixty-year affair while extolling the virtues of monogamy!"

"No, you aren't," he agreed. "But you ritually give me shit when I fuck up, and I'm not even married. And you're quick to pass a harsh judgment on our most important role model, without knowing any of the circumstances. And you're doing all these things after screwing Nora behind Mia's back, I'm guessing more than once."

"So, you're saying I've given up any claim on a moral compass?"

"No, Jack," he sighed. "I'm saying you should quit taking your self-loathing out on the rest of us."

GETTING Grandpa into the house was much easier than getting him out of the apartment in Brooklyn. Katie had done her part: There was no one at Villabaia to witness our labor. Aldo got the back door while Fusilli and I carried Grandpa in. Gently lowering him to the floor in the kitchen, we unwrapped his shroud and bagged it up, then moved him to the couch, placing a pillow under his head and folding his hands across his chest, as he typically would have for an afternoon nap. I started the fan in the window. It was the first thing Grandpa would have done before lying down.

Fusilli grabbed our fishing poles from the rack in the mud room beyond the kitchen, while Aldo retrieved a half-empty bottle of Drambuie from the pantry. It was my grandfather's favorite after-dinner drink. We headed across the street to the park, where Aldo disposed of the shroud and stockings in the trash. We found our way past the merry-go-round Grandpa used to push us on, then past the swing set he and my grandmother often sat on together this time of day, watching their gaggle of grandchildren swarm the playground equipment.

"When I was a child," Fusilli said, "I spoke as a child, I understood as a child, I thought as a child. But when I became a man, I put away childish things."

"Shakespeare?"

"1 Corinthians 13:11," he said.

We reached the edge of the bay as the tide was coming in, the bottle-green water warm as it lapped at our feet. Aldo uncorked the Drambuie with his teeth and spit it to the sand, then took a long swallow.

"To my old man," he said. "May he find the peace in death that I never gave him in life."

"Amen," I grunted, taking the bottle and a swig as my throat tightened with emotion. "So long, Grandpa. You had a good run."

I passed the bottle to Fusilli, who polished off what was left.

"Best of British, old man," Fusilli said. "May flights of angels sing thee to thy rest." We stood there in silence for a moment, then Fusilli dropped the bottle at his feet and cast his metal lure in a high arc towards the westing sun. "*That* was Shakespeare," he clarified, beginning a slow retrieve.

"If you're done talking shit," Aldo said. "We need a plan."

"We're going to stand here and cast until Grandma and the girls get back to the house and find your father," Fusilli said. "When they start yelling, we're going to act surprised."

"Surprised?" Aldo said.

"He wasn't feeling great after chemo and wanted to take a nap while we fished."

"I'm going to run back to the house like it's still possible to save him," I said. "When I get there, I'm going to pronounce him dead. I know his internist. I'll call and tell him it was natural causes resulting from his cancer diagnosis. No autopsy needed."

"Aldo," Fusilli said. "You'll call D'Acquisto's and make arrangements for them to send a hearse."

"Glad to be of service," Aldo said. "Happy to send my father to his great reward, his sins unpunished."

Fusilli squeezed his eyes shut in frustration. "What's with you judgmental fucks? There's no punishing the dead. Whatever was between you two is *done*. Get over it. The only person we need to be concerned with is Grandma."

"Yeah," Aldo said. "Except, you didn't have to live with his secrets all these years. I did. You think that was fuckin' easy?"

"What are you talking about?" I asked.

"I used to see the bread truck in her alley when I would cut school," he said. "I'm not an idiot."

"If you've kept quiet this long, you can keep quiet a little longer," Fusilli said. "We all can."

"Yeah," Aldo said. "Sure. Except I caught beatings for whatever I did wrong, while he gets off for fucking Isobel Costa for sixty years. Maybe it's time he got taken down a peg."

Aldo threw his rod down and lit a smoke, then walked over to the faded blue catamaran Nora and I had once made out beneath. He plopped down on the end of a pontoon, elbows on his thighs, eyes studying the pebbles at his feet. Fusilli and I held our ground, soldiers defending Villabaia against the sunset, casting and retrieving as though we hadn't a care in the world.

My mind was in knots. If learning about my grandfather was scrambling my brain in my twenties, what had it done to Aldo as a kid? What was it like to know your father was running around on your mother with a family friend? Did my grandfather know Aldo knew? What did an argument look like at the dinner table when a volatile child had a family-ending bullet locked and loaded? As a parent, how did you discipline a child when you knew they might open fire at any time? What was it like to resist the urge to press that attack on a parent for decades?

The tension was finally broken by the inevitable shouting behind us, closing quickly. We turned in unison to see Nora and Katie running across the park, tiny rooster tails of sand kicking up into the air behind them. Nora's longer stride length delivered her first into our midst.

"Jack," Nora gasped. "It's your granddad. Something's happened."

"Come on," I said. "Let's go."

I dropped my pole and started running towards the house. The surprising part was that it didn't feel contrived. I moved with purpose, as I would have rounding the bases as a Little Leaguer, Grandpa shouting encouragement from the dugout. I was doing this for my grandmother, for her peace of mind. I was doing this for my family, so that Grandpa would remain forever golden in their memories. As we climbed the front steps to the porch two at a time, I looked back to see Katie and Fusilli trotting together, with Aldo bringing up the rear with cement legs and a tuberculoid cough. Our family suddenly looked very different. I wondered who would join and who might depart.

The living room was filled with the thick orange light of the evening sun when we entered, the linear shadows of the jalousie windows and power lines beyond dividing the far wall into orderly segments above my grandfather. A sea bird's silhouette crossed the demarcations towards the ceiling, like a soul climbing a ladder to heaven.

Grandma had brought a chair to the head of the couch and was bent forward, smoothing my grandfather's hair with one hand, squeezing his arm with the other.

"I think he's gone, Jack," she said. "I think he's dead."

I knelt beside her and pressed my ear to his chest, then felt for the pulse in his neck that hadn't been there for hours. I met my grandmother's eyes and shook my head sadly. She nodded.

"He would have wanted you to pronounce him, Jack," she said. "He was so proud of you."

I nodded, then looked at my watch. "Time of death, 17:12." I imagined the coroner checking my grandfather's body temperature and disagreeing with my assessment, then trying to convince him of the pressing need to cosign on my deception.

I leaned over and hugged my grandmother as Fusilli and Katie spilled into the room. Fusilli raised his eyebrows expectantly.

"He's gone," I said.

"What happened?" Nora asked.

"He was feeling pretty run down when we got back from the city," I said. "He wanted to take a nap when we went fishing."

Katie's eyes narrowed. She didn't believe a word I was saying. I kept my expression impassive. Clinical. I needed to sell it, to Grandma at the very least.

Aldo was the last to arrive, wheezing as he supported himself against the door frame. My grandmother led him by the hand to the couch. I was surprised when his tears began to fall, which in some way gave the rest of us permission to join. My grandmother reached for Nora's hand, who then reached for mine. Katie and Fusilli completed the human chain on my left side.

"He was a good, good man," Nora said quietly, her eyes focused on Grandpa's face. "I was lucky to know him."

Grandma looked down the line of us. "We're going to pray now." She began reciting the Our Father, the rest of us falling into the familiar cadence. My grandmother spoke with the conviction of faith, safe in the knowledge that her husband had given everything to and for his family, for as long as he was able. I looked to Fusilli and then to my uncle. Our motley crew was now the guardians of my grandfather's legacy. It was up to us to keep the faith, whatever that meant anymore.

17

The funeral home was a converted Victorian mansion in Central Jersey, reminding me of Herman Munster's house in the eponymous television series. My mother was out front, wearing the kind of black dress Johnny Cash might sing about, bare arms and a long skirt that had too many pleats and folds to count. Mom had started dying her hair dark brown at the first sign of gray, then cut it to shoulder length when I was in college. The rest of her look went from reformed hippy to middle management around the time she'd finished her doctorate in psychology. She used some of the insurance settlement from my father's death to start a career in counseling. It was a reasonable idea, given what my brother's stints in rehab cost. She might even have been good at it. Perhaps our family tragedy had given her a perspective that seemed lacking during my childhood.

"That's your mum, right?" Nora said, squeezing the words out of the side of her mouth.

"Yup," I said, looking over my shoulder for some moral support from Fusilli. He and Katie were a few steps behind, but they'd been collared by some other relatives. We were flying solo.

My mother sidestepped to get out of the traffic on the walkway as we crossed the last few yards of wet asphalt. The tall, white hydrangea gathered around her bowed with the weight of the rain caught in the flowers.

Mom opened her arms first. We exchanged a hug that was both familiar and lacking in warmth.

"Hiya, Ma," I said.

"Hi, sweetheart."

"You remember Nora, don't you?"

"I couldn't believe it when I heard you were back!" Mom said, a genuine light in her eyes.

Nora took Mom's hands in hers. "I'm so sorry, Mrs. Frére. Your father was a wonderful man."

Mom pulled Nora close and wrapped her up in a hug. "It's nice to see you again, Nora. It was good of you to come."

"Oh," a voice interrupted us from behind. "The Jack-Meister General!"

An open hand fell hard between my shoulder blades as I turned. My brother was four years younger and a head shorter than me but had put on considerable weight in rehab. The added bulk seemed to somehow equalize our relative sizes. He'd straightened his blond surfer curls since we'd last gotten together, transforming him into a latter-day Tony Hawk. He offered a hug, and I accepted. His big pupils, sky-blue iris, and animated face were a relief. He wasn't high, or, at least, not on opiates.

"Marco Polo!" Nora said.

"Hi, Nora," he said, cocking his head bashfully and putting his hands in his pockets. That look had been slaughtering girls since his adolescence. "Long time no see."

"You're all grown up!"

Marco slapped the beginnings of the pot belly that was

forming above the beltline of his jeans, then loosened his tie. "I'm grown, all right."

He laughed, but I knew it bothered him. The cocktail of medication he took to try to control his bipolar disorder and addictions left him unmotivated to exercise and constantly hungry. As a kid, he'd been on the cover of the town newspaper a half-dozen times, owing to his combination of good looks and sports prowess. He'd walked onto the team at a local community college, but both school and his game had been derailed by rehab. It had been a long fall for him.

"Come down to the beach and do some swimming," she said. "Be good for you. Your brother could use the company."

Marco squeezed between Nora and me, hugging Mom. "Hi, Ma," he said, kissing her on the cheek. "You doing okay?"

"As well as can be expected," she said. "Where are your sisters?"

"I missed them at the house, so I got on the train. They're probably stuck in traffic."

Mom's eyes narrowed fractionally as she studied his face. "You didn't stop in the Bronx did you?"

"Want me to piss in a cup?"

"I'm not accusing you of anything," she said. "I just know this has to be stressful, and relapse is part of recovery."

"I go to my program every day. I get tested every other week. What more do you want from me?"

My stomach soured as the parking lot bustle was replaced by gangrenous silence, our family and friends tuning into whatever embarrassment was about to unfold. My mother's concern wasn't misplaced. Marco didn't do well with family drama. At least two of his overdoses had come on the heels of major family upheavals. It was among his top triggers to abuse the substance *du jour*. Marco wasn't wrong, either. No one gave him the benefit of the doubt anymore, not after what he'd put the family through. It had to be hard living under perpetual suspicion.

"The same as I want for all my children," Mom said. "Happiness."

"So how about…"

I reached for Marco's sleeve. "Hey," I said, tipping my head towards the gathering crowd. "Let's not do this here."

Marco yanked his arm away. "I don't give a fuck about them!"

My brother was spiraling. I didn't want this for him again, but anything I said was going to make matters worse. I spun my head to look for Fusilli, but he and Katie had their backs to me. Nora caught my eye, then leaned in close to my brother's ear.

"They're fuckin' tossers, Marco," Nora said. "The lot of them. Don't give them the satisfaction. Let's you and me go have a drink."

Marco's posture softened. He took a deep breath. "Maybe it'll straighten my head out."

"No shame in it," Nora said. "No one in my family has been sober since the famine."

Marco laughed, lowering the tension a bit more. Nora hooked her arm through his, then turned and guided him across the asphalt lot. "We'll have a pint, your brother and I," she said over her shoulder. "Join us after you pay your respects, all right?"

"Sure thing."

Marco had been back from rehab for maybe two months, but I wasn't going to fight about it. I gave her a pleading look. She offered a wink and mouthed, "I've got him." I hoped she did. Every time my brother relapsed, there was a greater chance of something terrible happening. The guy may have had nine lives, but he'd been through at least seven already.

Mom crossed her arms as they strode off. "Typical Irish. Drown your problems in booze."

"Cultural differences, Ma. She's just trying to help."

"You two been spending a lot of time together?"

"It's been nice catching up with her."

Mom cocked her head, offering her patented *don't give me that shit* look.

"What?" I said. "This is why I don't tell you anything."

"I remember you *running* to the mailbox to check for her letters. Where's Mia?"

"Hung up with work. She'll be here tomorrow."

"You've got a lot invested with her. Be careful."

"Ma, you don't even like Mia."

"Well, she wouldn't have taken your brother to the bar, right?"

"Ma!"

"I'm sorry," she said, raising a hand. "I'm upset. We'll love and support whoever you end up with. I'm just saying things can get fraught and complicated in a family crisis."

"That's for damned sure."

"Think things through. Make good decisions."

"Sure, Ma."

I would have liked my mother to be supportive rather than political. Mom thought Mia was too eager to please. She also knew Mia represented my escape hatch from the family. Still, she'd always refused to come out strongly *against* Mia, lest we end up together. She'd said as much to me in the past, which defeated the purpose of her faux neutrality. At the same time, she didn't want to come out strongly *for* Mia, lest that be perceived as encouraging it. Mom thought she could play both sides of the fence in everything. It wasn't worth getting into with her. We just needed to survive the next couple of days together, and then I could return to my self-imposed exile. I gestured towards the entrance of the funeral home, and we headed inside to face whatever fresh hell lay in wait.

MOM and I joined a platoon of oldsters from Brooklyn. Close to a foot taller than most of them, I scanned across the patio of liver-spotted bald spots to where Grandpa Francesco was lying in repose. He didn't look like himself, and it wasn't just the heavy-handed makeup of the funeral director. Grandpa's jowls hung low and inanimate, his cheeks filled with cotton or gauze as if he were a chipmunk suffering overzealous taxidermy. I had to remind myself that this was just a shell, the husk that was left behind when the soul fled the body after a lifetime of insult. It didn't look like my grandfather because it wasn't. Not anymore.

"Where's Aldo?" Mom asked.

"Dunno, but I'll give you three guesses," I said.

"Typical."

Grandma Elena stood at the foot of the coffin, backed by sprays of greenery taller than she was. She was surrounded by parade-float floral arrangements that would have fit right into a grotesque Rose Bowl carnival. She looked strong and in control but had tired eyes for the first time in my memory. We hugged and kissed. Before I could offer a suggestion for rest she would not heed, we were distracted by the arrival of Fusilli. He was glad-handing with some of our younger cousins by the door, Katie on his arm. They jumped the line to greet Grandma and my mother before I pulled them aside.

"You seen Aldo?" I asked.

"At the bar," Fusilli said. "He zipped over while you were negotiating the peace treaty. Well done, by the way."

"Temporary ceasefire at best. Any sign of your mom?"

"Behind schedule, as usual. She'd be late to her own wake."

"Olivia was a week late to her own birth," Grandma piped up. "Dr. Fallocaro was talking about a cesarean, until my contractions started!"

My aunt Olivia was Grandma's youngest child. She'd met

Fusilli's dad in the early '70s, when he was a soldier attached to the British Consulate in New York. According to my mother, he'd always been kind of an asshole, but Olivia fell in love with the accent. So did a lot of other women, apparently, which was how Fusilli's parents ended up divorced by 1987.

I was about to say something when Fusilli bugged his eyes at me, reached up to scratch his ear, then flashed three fingers as he put his hand back in his pocket: check the runner.

I turned to see Mrs. Costa approaching in a black-pant suit, the bun in her hair perfectly spun, her stride elegant and smooth. She walked right up to us without a hint of hesitation.

"Jack and Don," she said warmly. "I haven't seen you since you were boys!"

Fusilli was quicker on the draw. "Mrs. Costa? Is that you?"

"It's sweet that you remember," she said. "I'm so sorry about your grandfather."

So, this was how we were going to play it. Barely remembered, let alone acquainted. Definitely not partners in the family caper of the century. Not at all like she'd been my grandfather's *cumare*. Certainly, not like we'd found him dead in her geriatric love nest. Absolutely not like we'd illegally smuggled him across the state line like prohibition moonshine. And positively not like we'd left him on the couch for my grandmother to find, who, holy fucking shit, was standing right behind me and watching this farce play out before her eyes.

Fusilli introduced Mrs. Costa to Katie. Hearing her accent, Mrs. Costa offered a wry smile.

"Irish?" Mrs. Costa asked, winking at Fusilli. "Making time with an American?"

"Yeah," Katie said. "There's no accounting for taste, you see."

"I was married to one for fifteen years, child. Go home while you still can!" She turned to me as they laughed along with her. "And you, Jack. You don't remember me at all, do you?"

"A little," I said. "We used to eat chocolate in your living room. Your daughter Carolyn babysat us once in a while."

Mrs. Costa hugged me, then moved on to my mom. When she got to my grandmother, the two of them broke down in tears. It was the first time I'd seen my grandmother cry since Grandpa passed.

"I'm so sorry, Elena," Mrs. Costa said. "I owe my life to Francesco. And my husband. My children. Everything. We loved him so."

"I know, sweetheart. I know," Grandma said, hugging her close and rocking her side to side. "And he loved you all, too."

Fusilli and I exchanged an incredulous look. Katie recognized the telepathy between us. As we stepped away from the group, she grabbed me by the shoulder and whispered forcefully in my ear.

"When this is over, don't think for a second you two aren't going to explain this whole bleedin' thing to me."

I looked over my shoulder one last time as we headed for the door. As my grandmother turned her attention back to the greeting line, Mrs. Costa genuflected at the kneeler before my grandfather's body, then reached into the casket and grasped his hands. Her fingers wrapped around them, depositing something. It happened so quickly that I wasn't sure exactly what I'd seen. Our eyes met as she stood up, and she drew a finger to her lips as if to shush me.

More fucking secrets. We were going to have a serious conversation before the night was over.

18

Set across the street from the funeral home, Serotta's Tavern was a corner building that easily could have been mistaken for a residential structure. That was probably the idea; it was almost certainly a mob front. There was no sign advertising the joint. The first floor was brick, with dark-tinted windows dressed in green-canvas awnings. The entrance was similarly protected by an overhang, this one slightly torn, the frame canted to one side. The second floor was a complete mismatch, the once white-washed shingles now coated in the depressing gray of automotive exhaust. The top layer of paint was peeling like week-old sunburn.

The front door was windowless and constructed of some kind of heavy wood, painted a dark green that didn't quite match the awnings. I pushed and pulled at the knob, but it seemed to be locked, despite the audible crowd inside. Fusilli gave me a quizzical look and then tried himself. Shrugging at me, he pounded on the door and tried to look through the peephole.

The knob turned from the other side, then opened about six inches, the space between the door and jamb filled with a short, squat man in his sixties with a sour face. What little remained of his hair was dark gray and slicked back from a forehead the size of a truck mirror. His black sport coat fell open, revealing a shoulder-holstered pistol. I felt Katie stiffen beside me, then take a step back.

"We're closed for a private function," the man said through thick lips.

Behind him, the crowd parted to reveal Nora, Aldo, and Marco holding court at the corner of the bar, which was little more than a hollow rectangle of Formica with an island of ancient looking liquor bottles in the center. I couldn't imagine a worse place to mourn my grandfather.

"Aldo!" I shouted.

"Let them in, Lumber Head," Aldo shouted, raising a bottle of Peroni. "They're with the family."

Lumber Head looked over his shoulder, nodded, then offered a half-bow and stepped aside.

"We're limiting it to Francesco's family and friends today," he said. "Very sorry for your loss."

"Thanks," Fusilli said as we stepped past him.

The room was filled with every character and crone I'd ever seen in the old neighborhood. My grandparents' generation was dressed in black, the women in hats and veils that looked older than they were. A decrepit disco ball missing half of its mirrored squares turned lazily in the center of the room, casting irregular shooting stars across the scene. Fragments of *Napoletano* flew like bullets between the '70s wood-paneled walls, the hard-leading consonants and dropped final syllables making the words sound more violent than they were. They were intermittently drowned out by peals of my brother's laughter.

"Wait," Marco said. "What do you call 'washing the dishes'?"

"Pot walloping," Nora insisted, pushing her empty glass towards the bartender for a refill. "What do you call it?"

"Washing the dishes!" he said, laughing harder and pointing at the ketchup bottle on the bar. "And what's this?"

"Tomato sauce."

"You come from a magical land."

"It's a mad place, Marco. Truly."

Marco's eyes lit up when he spotted Fusilli alongside me. "The Dungeon Maestro himself!"

Marco stumbled as he hopped off his barstool but recovered quickly. He was already shitfaced and no longer practiced at hiding it after a few months sober.

"How you doing, cuz?" Fusilli said.

They embraced warmly. It took Marco a moment longer to place Katie. Fusilli tried to facilitate by introducing her, but Marco hip-checked him aside and hugged her.

"Of course, I remember Katie," Marco said. "I just can't believe she's still slumming it with you."

"It's a probationary thing, you see," Katie laughed. "If he doesn't settle down, your brother has offered to neuter him."

"He's a medic, after all," Nora said.

I took Marco's seat as he, Fusilli, and Katie got into it. Nora leaned into me, running a hand up and down my thigh. She'd reversed her Claddagh ring, the point now facing outwards. I wondered if it was purely symbolic or if she had actually spoken to Daniel and derailed the impending nuptials. If I wasn't in the middle of hiding the circumstances of my grandfather's death or wondering what the hell Mrs. Costa was up to in his casket or worried about my brother falling off the wagon, this would have been an exciting development. The barman put another drink in front of her.

"How much has my brother had?" I asked.

"Enough to improve his mood."

"I was hoping you might be a . . . moderating influence."

"Have you met your brother?"

"I know. He's a lot. But you said you had him."

"To get him away from those arseholes," she said. "I wasn't volunteering to become his sponsor."

"Twelve-step is for pussies!" Marco said, raising his beer. "To Grandpa!"

About half the bar raised their glasses.

"Quit being a wet blanket, Jack," Aldo said. "Have a drink. This is a celebration of my father's life! Got any good stories you wanna share?"

"Aldo," I said. "Come on."

"How about some of his adventures in Brooklyn?" Aldo pressed. "You've spent time there."

Fusilli and I locked eyes. We needed to end this immediately. I lifted my right hand to my chest and flashed two-three-two: steal second. Fusilli opened his mouth to derail the conversation but was interrupted by a voice at the door.

"I have a few tales I could tell."

Fusilli and I turned to see a thin woman in a short-sleeved blouse and long, gray skirt stepping past Lumber Head. Her neck was as pink as her cheeks, although she didn't appear to be wearing makeup. A small cross hung around her neck on the thinnest of gold chains. Her eyes were green and kind, aged by the crow's feet at the corners and protected by small, oval wire-frame glasses. She floated across the floor towards the bar, but she was looking past Fusilli and Katie, past Nora and me.

Aldo's mouth hung slightly open, as though he'd been struck dumb. He finally swallowed, the motion of his Adam's apple reassuring me that he hadn't stroked out.

"Who's this joker?" Marco asked.

The woman looked over her shoulder, smiling gently.

"Sister Marie Claire," she said. "But I went by Wendy when Aldo and I were together."

Fusilli's eyes widened, his beer bottle frozen to his lips. I was equally amazed, feeling like we were witnessing a scene out of a bizzarro-world *Casablanca*: Aldo's long-lost love reappears after escaping to the convent decades earlier.

"Aldo got down with a nun?" Marco said.

"Jesus Christ, Marco," I said.

Marie Claire glanced at me, then tipped her head infinitesimally.

"Sorry," I said.

"You're one of Francesca's, aren't you?" she asked.

"I'm Jack. The oldest."

"You look just like her."

"*Jolie Marie*," Aldo croaked, then cleared his throat. "They let you pick your name in the end?"

"*C'est gentil de t'en souvenir,*" Marie Claire said.

Nora stood without a word and offered her stool. Marie Claire nodded and sat down. Aldo had not blinked since she entered the room, sitting with his hands folded like a chastened schoolboy. I flicked my head towards Fusilli and the others and Nora took the hint. We hurried across the floor, simultaneously fascinated and realizing that whatever was about to happen was not for us or anyone else in the bar. Aldo and Marie Claire fell into each other, the disco ball painting them in tiny points of silver light. Aldo's eyes were squeezed tight, his ruddy cheeks stretched in a pained grimace. His tanned, sinewy arms were wrapped around her back, his chin resting heavy on her shoulder, and he was crying.

I wasn't sure exactly when Mrs. Costa arrived. When Fusilli pointed her out, she was seated alone in the back corner of the bar, slowly stirring the ice in a half-empty rocks glass. I made my way through the throng and took the chair across from her.

"I was wondering when you would turn up," she said,

draining the remainder of her glass. She signaled to the bartender for another.

"I have a lot of questions," I said.

"Understandably so."

"I want to know what you were to each other."

"You can't possibly be that thick."

"I took the risk of sneaking him out of your place and ..."

"Lower your voice, Doctor," she said. "Loose lips sink ships."

I leaned in, forcing a whisper across the table like a gangster out of film noir. ". . . and I think I'm owed a better explanation."

"And *I* think I'm owed the last shreds of my dignity," she said, taking a deep breath. "Leave an old woman her few remaining secrets, eh?"

"I know you were in the war. I know about China."

Mrs. Costa smiled sadly, nodding her thanks to the bartender as he delivered a fresh cocktail. "Rubbish bourbon," she said, taking a sip and grimacing. "You don't know the first thing about China, Jack."

"I know a lot of his men were killed."

"Killed isn't the word for what happened to those lads," she said. "For what happened to my parents and the nuns. For what happened to the children who were in my charge to protect."

"Parents and nuns?"

Mrs. Costa knit her eyebrows in thought, then took a long pull on her drink. "Perhaps I can offer you something more precious than dirty laundry."

"Like?"

"Context."

Mrs. Costa was born Isobel Warner. She'd trained as a nurse in London and was barely twenty-years old when she shipped off to China. Her parents were Catholic missionaries who ran an orphanage with the Sisters of Saint Joseph, the same order that had raised Grandpa in North Philadelphia. She'd had the bad luck to arrive a few weeks before Japan invaded in 1937. That's what brought Grandpa to her door in the first place. He was with the Twenty-Second Reconnaissance unit, a small band of soldiers tasked with covertly monitoring the Japanese occupation and fostering a guerrilla resistance.

His Chinese limited to what he was taught in training, Grandpa recognized the uniforms of the sisters while on patrol and made fast friends with Isobel and her parents. The Americans established a base camp in the hills a few miles from the orphanage, near a mountain reservoir. Grandpa only visited Isobel and her family at night to avoid being noticed by the children. The orphanage became their most important source of intelligence about local happenings, troop movements, and rumors of the resistance. They used what they learned to network across the countryside.

"Is that how you fell in love?"

"Don't know how it happened, really. In fact, I was considering taking my vows. We would meet after midnight near a creek behind the orphanage. I'd give him what news I could and help him with his Chinese. He taught me to whistle like the silver orioles that roosted in the forest."

"Was there something about him?"

"He made me laugh. He understood British understatement. He wasn't an insufferable American."

"That's all it took?"

"We were young, and it was war," she shrugged. "We did what came naturally."

The orphanage was both small and remote enough to avoid scrutiny, until it wasn't. When the Japanese finally came, Isobel was out gathering firewood. She stayed hidden in the trees as they dragged her parents and the nuns out into the grass. Knowing the horror stories of Nanking, she tried to run west to the American encampment but caught up to a small Japanese patrol that was already on the way there. The Americans had been betrayed. She was forced to turn back.

"Where did you go?"

"I hid in the hollow of a fallen tree near the creek. I reckoned Francesco would look for me there if he survived. If the Japs didn't find me first."

"How long were you there?"

"Long enough to hear the first and last screams of my parents and the children," she said. taking a long swig from her glass. "Long enough to hear the beginning and end of the gunfire in the direction of the American camp. Long enough to hear what the Japs called the orphans as they bantered on the march out: *Niku.* Meat."

Grandpa came in the middle of the night, whistling a bird-song to signal her. He had been on patrol when he saw the smoke but was too late getting back to do anything. He told Isobel what she already knew: Her parents, the nuns, and the children were dead, their bodies burned in the orphanage or left to rot in the sun. The soldiers were long gone. Grandpa and Isobel were faced with two choices: March a hundred kilometers to the coast or conduct a suicide mission against the Japanese lying in wait for them at the American campsite. They agreed on the latter.

"Why not get out of Dodge?" I asked.

"We wanted vengeance more than we wanted to live."

They created a plan and moved out before dawn, infiltrating the ridge above the north corner of the American encampment. The Japanese soldiers were helping themselves to the supplies. There was a clear line of sight through the trees to the campfire. Grandpa set himself up beneath a blowdown with his rifle, perhaps a hundred yards from the tents, while Isobel hid in a rocky outcropping on the opposite side of the clearing with Grandpa's pistol.

When their captain moved into his line of sight, Grandpa

shot him through the hip. He fell screaming to the ground. His men took cover and fired wildly into the forest, unsure of where the first shot had come. Mrs. Costa fired twice to attract their attention. When they shot back, she stayed behind the rocks and screamed as though she'd been hit, then went quiet. After a few minutes, the men broke cover to help their commanding officer. Grandpa shot all three of them in quick succession. Only the captain was left alive, moaning in the firelight at the bottom of the hill.

"Did Grandpa finish him off?"

"No," she said, draining her bourbon. "I did."

"You?"

"I ran down the hill and beat your grandfather into camp. The officer had propped himself up against a stump. He was trying to draw his ceremonial dagger, presumably for *seppuku*. I stepped on his arm, put the pistol to his forehead, and pulled the trigger. I didn't even think about it. It was a reflex. When I close my eyes at night, I still see the way his head exploded. The way his brain scattered like pumpkin innards. Some of it hit Francesco's boots and trousers."

"Is that why he never talked about China?"

"No, it's because of what they'd done to his mates. They'd been tied to trees at the far side of the clearing and disemboweled. The one called Ellsworth was partially skinned alive. He was still breathing when we got to him."

"What did you do?"

"There were medical supplies in the camp, but no way to help except the obvious. I administered a lethal dose of morphine as your grandfather gave Last Rites."

"Jesus Christ."

"Our Lord was AWOL in China," she said, reaching for my glass and finishing what was left. "Dereliction of duty. We'll have words when my time comes."

A man fifteen or twenty years older than me appeared at

the door and waved to her. It took a moment to recognize him as her youngest child, Matteo. She raised a finger to indicate she wouldn't be long.

Grandpa was able to make contact with some of the guerrillas his squad had been fostering, who helped smuggle them out of the country. Isobel and Grandpa ended up joining a medical unit together in the Philippines, where his brother was stationed. Grandpa became a surgical technician, Isobel an OR nurse. Grandpa was able to function in the operating room, because surgery focused his attention. Nighttime was another matter.

"He was haunted when he slept and would wake up screaming," Isobel said. "I wasn't much better off. The nurse's quarters were separated from the men. There was no fraternization. But your grandfather had an idea. He'd kept Ellsworth's fishing pole. He ran fifty yards of line through the jungle between us, a small bell on each end. If one of us were struggling at night, we could signal the other and meet in the mess tent."

"It's good that you had each other."

"It's the only reason we survived. So, when I told you I was his angel, that is quite literally true. I watched over him while he caught some shuteye in the mess."

"And he delivered you from China."

"From hell to purgatory. We told ourselves the good we did in the hospital was penance for the sins we'd committed."

"There was no sin in what you did."

"I expect I'll learn soon enough," she said with a shrug. "We killed so many on our way to the coast. You know the rest of the story. I was an only child, and my parents were dead. After the war, I followed Francesco to New York but quickly realized he wasn't going to jilt Elena. In that way, I suspect the two of you are quite alike."

"What's that supposed to mean?"

"He frequently conflated morality, duty, and loyalty," she said, rising unsteadily to her feet. "As you do when you weigh your girlfriend against that redhead over there."

"What do you know about it?"

"Your grandfather worried about you."

"He could have told me himself."

"He would have, had he lived longer. People die slowly, then all at once. You should know that by this stage of your training."

"Mrs. Costa . . ."

"Isobel," she said. "We're conspirators now."

"Isobel, then. What did you put in his casket?"

"That's not for you," she said, her eyes hardening.

"I need to know."

She stirred the ice in her drink. "A patient will give you the diagnosis, if you ask the right questions."

I looked over her shoulder to where Matteo Costa was navigating the crowd towards us. Then, something struck me. My grandparents had helped raise her entire brood after Mr. Costa's death. They'd grown up around the bakery. Her daughter babysat Fusilli and me for a time. Most of them still lived in the old neighborhood.

"Where are the rest of your children?"

"Very clever, Doctor," she said with a sad smile, taking her son's arm. "Very clever, indeed."

"Do you feel better?" Fusilli asked. "Now that you know?"

"I think I'm still trying to process it."

"They had a connection that just couldn't be undone."

"But he still married Grandma."

"How much did they understand? They were even younger than us."

"And then I start thinking about shit I've done and . . ."

"Dude, Grandpa and that lady fucking *killed* people. They euthanized one of his friends."

He was right, of course. I'd been so wrapped up in our drama and my own self-flagellation that I'd missed what was staring me in the face. My problems were stressful, sure. Fusilli and Katie got bonus points for wrestling with ending her pregnancy. It all seemed weak in comparison to the stakes Grandpa and Isobel had faced. I suddenly felt very young and foolish. Whatever Grandpa and Isobel did to live with what they had faced all those years ago, it wasn't up to me to pass judgment. They were entitled to their secret. It would die with us.

Before I could reflect on any of that to my cousin, we were interrupted by my mother working her way through the crowd. Her face was shiny with perspiration. She pulled the neck of her dress away from her chest.

"Grandma wants to know what you might like of Grandpa's," she said.

"How do you mean?" Fusilli asked.

"His ring? His watch?" she said.

My grandfather wore a gold ring set with a square onyx that had rounded edges. There was a small diamond in the corner of the onyx. It was from the original engagement ring he'd bought my grandmother. He'd gotten her a nicer diamond for their twenty-fifth wedding anniversary, when they had some savings. He'd never removed his ring in all the years I'd known him. It was still on his hand in the casket, the same hand that was now holding whatever it was Isobel had put in it.

"You're just going to take them off him?" I asked.

"Tomorrow morning," she said. "After the family viewing. There's no reason for them to be buried. He'd be happier if you had them."

"The ring wouldn't fit me," Fusilli said. "But I'd like his watch. What about Marco?"

"You're the eldest grandchildren," she said. "And valuables have a way of … disappearing … when Marco's around."

Fusilli nodded in sad understanding. Marco had stolen from all of us at one time or another. Drugs were expensive, and he'd never held a steady job. Mom melted back into the crowd, but my wheels were turning. Depending upon what Isobel had put in his hand, the whole thing could blow up in our faces.

"Fusilli, we've got problems."

"Now what?"

"Mrs. Costa put something in Grandpa's hand when she was standing at the coffin."

"What do you think it was? Something sentimental?"

"She wouldn't tell me, so it can't be good."

"Fuck," Fusilli groaned.

"We can't let Grandma find it."

"What do you want to do?"

"We need to get in there."

"I'm not burgling a funeral parlor," Fusilli said. "Are you insane?"

"I think that's my line, stranger."

Across the room, the Castellis were waving us over to their table.

"Let me think about this a minute," he said. "Come on, we need to get back in the game here."

We picked up Nora and Katie as we passed the corner of the bar. Mama Castelli patted the seat beside her as we approached. Nora reflexively reached for Katie's arm.

"Oh no," Nora said.

"Calm down," Katie said.

"Easy for you to say. You weren't felt up by the daft bint!"

"Oh, she doesn't mean any harm."

"You sit next to her, then! When she grabs you by the tits and divines you're eatin' for two, don't cry to me!"

Paolo and Nunzio were on one side of the table, with Mama Castelli and Paolo's wife Brandi seated across from them. Brandi was formerly an adult dancer who'd bought the most popular deli in our hometown. Her sleeve-tattooed arms flailed like a technicolor octopus as she tried to contain their kids, hyperactive three-year-old twins named Gianni and Emma. Gianni's small dark eyes widened at the sight of new people to interact with, while Emma was immediately spooked, tucking her chin into her polka-dotted dress and sticking her thumb in her mouth.

Fusilli solved Nora's problem by sidling up next to Mama Castelli, who kissed him on both cheeks and told him she was sorry about Grandpa. Beside them, Gianni pulled back from his mother, then fussed with his pants.

"Mama," he said, furrowing his brow and pawing at her arm. "My *pishadeel* is hard."

"A challenge in every young man's life," Fusilli laughed. Brandi leaned back, her well-muscled arm rippling as she reached behind Mama Castelli to sock him in the shoulder.

"He takes after his father," Nunzio said.

"That's called an erection, sweetie," Brandi said, glaring at Nunzio.

"What do I do?" Gianni asked.

"We'll talk when you're in high school," Fusilli said, earning another jab from Brandi, this one aggressive enough that he winced.

"It's okay, sweetie," Brandi said. "You just tell mommy."

"He's gonna spend a lot of money repeating that to his shrink someday," Paolo muttered.

Brandi let go of Gianni and raised a fist, her painted eyes widening. "There's a fresh one for you too if you keep it up!"

The children giggled in delight. Gianni took the opportunity to clamber across Mama Castelli and into Fusilli's lap. He settled into the crook of Fusilli's right arm. My cousin looked as though someone had handed him a live grenade.

"*Puoi salutare Fusilli?*" Mama Castelli said.

"Ciao, 'Seely!" Gianni said, planting a slobbery kiss on Fusilli's cheek and hugging him like a starfish.

Perhaps jealous of the attention her brother was getting, Emma let go of Brandi, crawling across Mama Castelli's lap and squeezing herself under Fusilli's left arm.

"Foo-see-lee," Emma enunciated, slapping at his chest and giggling with each syllable.

"I think I just found my new babysitter," Brandi said.

Fusilli's eyes widened in terror. Before he could say something horrible, the radio station changed from whatever Sinatra-centric nonsense was playing to a New York commercial station. The room was suddenly pitched into the early 1990s as the opening beats of Sir Mix-A-Lot's most famous song poured through the speakers.

"Big butt song!" the twins cheered. "Big butt song!"

"Dance, Seely, dance!" Gianni said, sliding off his lap and pulling him towards an empty spot in front of the bar.

Emma joined her brother, jumping up in the air and stomping down with both feet.

"Big butt dance party!" She insisted.

"I was dancing to this the night I met Paolo," Brandi explained. "It's kind of our song. And theirs now."

Fusilli rolled his eyes and got up. The twins began slapping their diaper-armored bottoms and hopping from foot to foot, throwing their matching blonde curls around in time. To his credit, Fusilli joined and did his best to match their frenetic energy. Noticing the chaotic scene, the older Brooklyn crowd began elbowing each other and pointing, then clapping in time with the music and cheering them on. Sister Marie Claire was unable to resist the preschool mayhem, her eyes lighting up as she hopped off her stool to join.

When the twins started bumping their hips into each other, Marie Claire and Fusilli did likewise, eliciting whoops from Nora and Katie. Marco grabbed Nora by the arm and dragged her onto the makeshift dance floor. He lifted her hand and spun her around, her skirt twirling like something in a 1950s prom scene. Brandi came next, her moves serpentine and professional as she twisted around and between her children.

At the edge of the melee, Katie stood clapping, her big blue eyes full of tears waiting to spill. Across the bar, Aldo sat frozen, a paw wrapped tightly around his beer like a modern-day Ghost of Christmas Past. One of them was imagining what might have been, the other what might yet be.

"Look at him," Katie said as Fusilli threw Emma up in the air. "He could be a father. A good one."

"So," I said, putting an arm around her shoulders. "Ask him to be."

As the song trailed off into a commercial break and the group headed back to the table, I leaned down to stick my head between the Castelli brothers.

"Fellas," I said. "Can I get a word outside?"

Nunzio leapt to his feet like a superhero, head on a swivel.

"Trouble, Doc?"

"No," I said, catching Fusilli's eye and flicking my head towards the door. "A mission."

19

———

We gathered by the lamp post on the corner, the air thick with humidity and the stench of Elizabeth's petroleum cracking plants. Union County was called "Cancer Alley" for a reason. How much of my grandfather's disease ought to be attributed to Exxon or Shell? Was I signing myself up for the same by continuing to work at a local hospital? Maybe Nora would place something in my casket someday, or maybe Mia. Maybe I'd die alone, some descendant of the D'Acquisto family rifling through my coffin to find nothing at all.

We talked in hushed voices as we planned my first mission.

"Wait," Nunzio said, running a hand through hair thick with product. "She stuck something in his hands?"

"Yeah," I said. "And I don't want any drama when Grandma takes his jewelry off."

"What are you thinking?"

"Who knows what was going on back in the day?" I said. "Maybe she had a thing for him."

"She was around a lot," Paolo said ominously.

"Exactly," I said. "Grandma doesn't need any surprises. You gotta get me in there to check it out."

"All right," Nunzio said, as casually as if I'd asked to borrow a couple bucks. "Is the place alarmed?"

"Just like that, we're breaking and entering?" Fusilli asked.

"First floor might be wired. Not the second," Paolo said, looking over his shoulder at the funeral home. It was an old Victorian with minimal updates. The rear of the building was three-stories tall, shingle-sided with a gabled roof. There wasn't a porch or first-story roof for us to work from. Well-groomed hedges grew eight feet tall and about as wide against the building.

"They never bother with the second floor," Nunzio said. "We've worked on a lot of houses like this."

"Yeah," Fusilli said. "What kind of asshole breaks into a funeral home, anyway?"

"Original windows," Paulo said. "Piece of cake."

"We could hit Home Depot real quick for a ladder," Nunzio offered.

"The light is still on upstairs!" Fusilli said, "Best case, we get arrested. Worst case, Lumber Head sees us and blows our fuckin' brains out!"

"So, we come back after they split," Paulo said. "I wasn't saying it was go time."

"What about Mama?" I asked.

"We'll give her an extra lithium. She'll sleep like a baby."

"Lithium might not do it," I said. "You got any Xanax? Benzos are amnestic as well."

"I'm down," Nunzio said.

"She could use the rest," Paolo said. "So could we."

"We aren't drugging Mama Castelli!" Fusilli said through clenched teeth. "Jesus fucking Christ, how did *I* become the voice of reason here? Just leave her with Brandi and the kids."

Paolo and Nunzio exchanged a look.

"Brandi will have our testicles, bro," Paolo said.

"How do we know they didn't lock Grandpa in the icebox for the night?" Fusilli said.

"Fuck," I said. The Castellis unleashed a chorus of Italian swearing. None of us had considered this possibility.

"Hear me out," Fusilli continued, raising a hand. "How about we just go knock on the front door?"

Nunzio and Paolo looked at each other, then back at Fusilli.

"Yeah," Paolo said. "Maybe that's a better idea."

"Pretty lame, as missions go," Nunzio said. "I'm just sayin'."

Fusilli rolled his eyes and started across the street. I followed him to the entrance. After a few knocks, the door was opened by Mr. D'Acquisto himself. People in the parish called him Tank because he'd driven one in the Second World War and because of his size. His clean-shaven head accentuated his eggplant shape. He resembled an olive-skinned Grimace of McDonald's fame.

"You okay, fellas?" he asked. "What can I do for you?"

"Mr. D'Acquisto," Fusilli started. "My cousin got here late with the traffic. Would it be cool if he had a couple minutes alone with Grandpa?"

"Of course," he said, stepping aside and pointing us to the parlor on the left. "Of course."

"Thanks," I said. "It means a lot."

"Francesco was a good man, fellas. We're all gonna miss him," Tank said. "I'll be upstairs a while yet. The door is locked. You can just pull it shut when you go."

"Yeah?"

"Sure," he said. "Whatcha gonna do, steal the body?"

∾

FUSILLI WATCHED the door as I entered the parlor where our grandfather lay. The room devoid of friends and family, this was the first time I'd been alone with him. I tried to imagine him napping at Villabaia, the curtains adrift in the bay breeze, the westing afternoon sun warm on his skin. However, the funerary stench of the chrysanthemums stuck to my tongue like rancid peanut butter. The wallpaper was a gray-patterned blur around me, like being surrounded by a fog bank, God-knows-what lurking just out of sight. There was no redirecting my mind; I was there to do something impossibly grim.

"I'm sorry," I said to the shadows gathering around my grandfather. "I'm sorry we didn't get there quicker. Maybe I could have done something."

When your number's up, your number's up, Grandpa would have said. *You know that better than anyone.*

"Is it hard being here alone?"

Being dead is easy, he'd say. *It's the dying that's hard.*

"Yeah."

You sure you want to do this?

"I have to know."

I know. After I bought you that telescope, you could never stop looking.

I rested my hand on his for a moment, then slid my fingers into his palm, finding something metallic. Oblong. I retrieved a locket on a thin gold chain. I looked it over in the soft light of the floor lamps. It wasn't fancy jewelry, heart-shaped with a fine patina sorely in need of cleaning. Someone had worn it for many years against their skin.

"What's this?"

You promise to keep the secret?

"I promise. It's what I do best."

My neanderthal fingers struggled with the edge, then it popped open, the space within filled with a tiny black and white photo. I moved to the lamp in the corner to get a better look, adjusting the angle to minimize the glare of the bulb beneath the muslin shade. The room grew darker in my peripheral vision as my eyes adjusted. A younger Mrs. Costa stared back at me, though she was older than she appeared in war photos. A small child was seated on her lap, my grandfather's face positioned behind her and resting on her shoulder. The child's features were inscrutable.

"Who is this?"

My grandfather's memory offered no response. No defense.

"Who is this?" I demanded, looking back at him in the casket. "Who?"

His lips remained still. Something stroked the back of my neck as the central air kicked on, making me swear and jump towards the seats. It was one of the palm fronds in the flower arrangement. Fusilli's face appeared in the doorway, looking at me across a sea of empty chairs. His features were ghostly, alternately hollowed or accentuated by the meager throw of the lamp.

"You okay?" he asked.

I raised the locket. He hurried across the carpet towards me, his footfalls silent on the thick shag.

"What's that?" Fusilli asked, taking it from my hand carefully.

"Have a look," I said.

Fusilli squinted in the gloom, his eyes widening in recognition. He plucked at the photo, perhaps hoping to find an inscription on the back, but it remained stubbornly in place.

"What the fuck?" he whispered.

"This is nuts."

Now you know. The whole damn mess.

"You think..." Fusilli stammered.

"You got a better explanation?"

We were careful. She was a nurse, for God's sake.

I took the locket from my cousin, wrapping the chain

around it. I walked back to the coffin and slid my hand behind
my grandfather's lapel, finding the inner pocket of his suit coat.
I tucked the locket inside and cinched it with the button.

"Who do you think that is?" Fusilli asked.

I thought for a long moment and remembered my promise.
"No one."

20

———

Our Lady of Perpetual Help was a tall, gothic structure that was poorly matched with the surrounding low-slung neighborhood shops and three-flats. Its twin spires flanked a smaller central basilica, the granite walls streaked with green after decades of runoff from leaky copper drainpipes. The features of the saints on the facade were soft from weathering, the steps below worn beneath the feet of generations of the immigrant faithful. As a child, I'd drawn comic strips with Grandpa that began with Batman lurking in the shadows of the gargoyles perched at the roof line. The Gotham aesthetic was spoiled only by the flower boxes around the entryways, which had been freshly replanted by the Altar Rosary Society. The granite containers were over-flowing with petunias, marigolds, and geraniums. Their prox-imity to the polished oaken doors left the church resembling a deep-sea anglerfish trying to lure unsuspecting prey into its maw.

Neither Marco nor I had been inside a church since our father's funeral, and we weren't keen to break our streak now. We stood on the sidewalk, my brother working his way through his third cigarette in ten minutes. We'd walked over ahead of the hearse and family because he didn't want to see Grandpa in the coffin. I understood why he never made it into the funeral home, but I didn't think this would be any better for his mental state.

"What's going on with you and Nora?" Marco asked.

"What do you mean?"

"Don't bullshit me."

"Let's just say you aren't the only one who has made some bad choices."

"Like what?"

"You want to hear my confession, Father?"

"I hear it's good for the soul."

I looked at my watch, the sun gleaming off the polished titanium. Mia would be proud to see me wearing it. 9:45 a.m. I traced the slide rule around the bezel with my eyes. There was no calculation that could unfuck this situation in the fifteen minutes before game time.

"Okay," I sighed. "Any minute, Mia is going to roll up. A few minutes before or after, Nora will get here. Neither of them knows I'm sleeping with the other."

Marco's eyes widened, his mouth open and breathless, a curl of smoke wrapping around his face. For a moment, we were teenagers again, awaiting the inevitable consequences of something horrible one of us had done.

"Get the fuck outta here."

"Scout's dishonor," I said, holding up a three-fingered salute.

"You're knee deep in the shit now, Action Jackson!"

"Oh, yeah."

"I don't know whether to high-five you or call you a dirty bastard."

"How many Hail Marys do I have to say?"

"Nah, fuck that. Which one of them gets the boot?"

"I'm not sure it's a choice."

"The hell it isn't," Marco said, flicking his cigarette to the ground and stamping it out with a Vans-clad foot. "You're no Fusilli. This has to be killing you."

"*Fusilli* isn't even Fusilli anymore."

"I know, right? I'm in the 'hab for a few months, and now it's mayhem around here."

Mia arrived first at the field of battle. She made a turn through the traffic island and parked her black Acura sedan at the end of the block. She hopped from the door and waved, offering a sad smile that included her mouth but not her eyes. She wore a black single-piece dress that clung to her hips and fell to her knees. Her smile widened at the sight of my brother.

"You're the doctor, Jack," Marco said. "I shouldn't have to tell you to close one surgery before starting the next."

Mia was upon us before I could respond. She greeted Marco first, getting on tiptoes to hug him and kiss his cheek.

"Hey, Marco," she said. "I'm so sorry about Grandpa."

"Hey, Mia," Marco said, making eyes at me. "Thanks."

She kissed me and offered a longer hug. Mia and Marco continued making small talk while I tried to nod and smile at the proper times. My guts were twisting like an alien parasite. Mercifully, I didn't have long to suffer. Fusilli pulled up in Grandpa's old Plymouth, Katie riding shotgun and Nora in the backseat. The alien transformed into an expanding balloon of panic.

"I'm making my choice, Jack," Marco said, throwing an elbow to my ribs as he went for the car.

"What was that about?" Mia asked.

"I think Marco has a thing for the redhead," was the best I could come up with.

My brother stepped to the curb and helped Nora from the car, then offered his arm and steered her away from the widening group of mourners and towards the church. I appreciated his effort, but it was for naught. Nora saw me and course corrected, pushing Marco through the throng and aiming right for Mia and me. This was the worst of all possible worlds. Fusilli caught sight of the unfolding debacle too late to intervene.

Nora leaned in and kissed my cheek.

"Is this your girlfriend, Marco?" Mia asked with a wink.

"She should be so lucky," Marco said, laughing in my direction.

"Indeed," Nora laughed, meeting my gaze with wide eyes as she stuck out her hand at Mia. "I'm Nora. My family used to stay next door to Villabaia. Lovely to meet you."

"Oh, you too," Mia said. "I'm surprised we never ran into each other."

"I'm from before your time, love."

The women stared each other down in the way women do, leaving me to guess who would throw the first punch. They were of similar height and build. Nora knew how to fight but Mia carried pepper spray in her purse. A cold hand reached up through my guts and encircled my heart. This was the natural outcome of my treachery, so twisted that Fusilli could not have imagined the like: My long-term, probably unfaithful girlfriend facing off against my betrothed side-chick, at the funeral of the grandfather who'd died in his mistress's bed.

"We grew up together," I said quickly, hoping to force a blink out of one of them.

"Those were good days, Jack," Nora said, reaching for my forearm and offering a squeeze. "Come on, Marco. It's gonna be standing room only today."

"You used to talk about an Irish girl you had a crush on when you were a kid," Mia said, her eyes following Nora like a raptor guarding a nest.

"That's her," I admitted.

"You've been seeing a lot of each other?"

"She's a barmaid at Kidd's. You know how Fusilli and Aldo drink."

"Yeah," she said, her gaze still locked on Nora.

I was rescued by the arrival of the hearse. It was followed by my mother piloting the old family van, a dark blue Chevy. It was a shell of its former self, the wheel-wells bubbling with corrosion, a hubcap missing from the rear. My father never would have tolerated it. The side door spilled my three sisters onto the pavement, but it was Gabriella who made a beeline for me. Eight years my junior, Gabriella was the youngest of my siblings. She would be going to Northwestern in the fall and had recently scored an internship with one of the big accounting firms. She acted the part. Her black dress and heels were impeccable, as were her makeup and jewelry. Her confident stride didn't seek attention but commanded it. Gabriella could easily be mistaken for someone in her early twenties. The chaos of her shoulder-length curls belied the sharpness of her mind and tongue. Despite her abrasive streak, Gabriella and I thought most alike of my siblings. At opposite ends of the family, we each saw the bullshit for what it was. She gave the rest of the mourners a wide berth as they coalesced around the arriving priest, who was offering some kind of instructions.

"Nice to never call me, jerk," Gabriella said.

"Sorry," I said. "It's been a lot."

"We'll talk later," she said, poking me in the chest with her index finger even as she turned to Mia. "How are you?"

"Hiya Gab," she said. "You look great."

"Someone's gotta keep it classy, right?"

"Ouch," I said.

"That suit is so '90s, Jack," Gabriella said, winking at Mia. "I'll take you shopping if Mia won't."

"I'm still paying off the *last* time you took me shopping."

Gabriella rolled her eyes at me, but her response was short-circuited by little Gianni, his voice amplified by his position atop Paolo's shoulders.

"I have a 'rection in my diaper!"

The pastor burst into laughter, his oversized eyeglasses bouncing on rosacea-festooned cheeks.

"Wrong person to tell, little guy," Gabriella said. "Ask us how we know."

"I'll take things you can say in nursery school or nursing home for 400, Alex," I said.

Gabriella and I giggled like children. Mia turned and slapped me in the chops. She might have meant it playfully under different circumstances, but there was something more behind it. Or perhaps it was my guilty conscience investing every gesture with imagined meaning.

Nunzio and Paolo began handing the kids over to Brandi and Mama Castelli, waving at me to join the pallbearers for our entrance. Marco hurried down the stairs from the church with Fusilli and Aldo in tow, leaving Nora, Katie, and Marie Claire waiting at the top. Katie and Marie Claire turned to enter, but Nora waited a moment longer. Her stare split me like firewood beneath an axe. There would be no mistaken interpretations. Whatever had just happened between us, I was going to pay for it. That was fine. I deserved it. But I was ready now. I was ready to give anything, suffer anything, deal with anything for a chance at happiness in an authentic relationship. I just didn't want Nora to give up on me.

THE FUNERAL CEREMONY itself was unremarkable, save for the feeling of Nora's eyes boring through the back of my skull from three rows behind. How had my grandfather lived this way for decades? The anxiety was crippling. My discomfort grew stronger each time Mia reached for my arm to offer support, which she did more often than I might have expected.

At the end of the service, Fusilli and I led the coffin, draped in the American flag. We were followed by Nunzio and Paolo, with Marco and Aldo at the rear. When we reached the pool of daylight spilling through the great oaken doors, we each grabbed a handhold and lifted the coffin off the trolley, then carried him down the steps and guided him into the back of the hearse. Despite the casket's weight, he felt lighter with six men carrying him than when it was just Fusilli and me in Brooklyn. The twenty-yard walk was costly in the heat, and the effort left me sweating through my clothes. The graveside service was going to be brutal when the sun reached its zenith.

Marco and I rode with Mia to the cemetery, a small field that lay atop a hill several miles to the west. The military honor guard was waiting for us when we arrived, a full-bird colonel and two other men whose stripes I had trouble deciphering. Beads of sweat popped at the edges of their crew-cut hair, but there was no hint of discomfort in the efficiency of their movement or speech. They conferred with my grandmother and the pastor as our family gathered around the grave atop the hill. When the time came, Fusilli and I corralled the Castellis, Aldo, and my brother. We collected Grandpa from the hearse and carried him to the winch straps that lay atop the grave.

The pastor bid us closer to start the service. He had traded his gilded vestments for priestly blacks, complimenting the murder of crows roosting in the trees at the edge of the cemetery. We formed a semicircle at the foot of the grave, while the honor guard stood at attention behind the headstone. Grandma, my mother, and Fusilli's mother formed the center of the throng, while the pallbearers and I stood at the far right. My sisters lined up behind Grandma, joined by Mia. It took me a moment to spot the Irish, who had taken up position at the back of the crowd. The priest opened his mouth to speak, but Grandma held up a finger, silencing him, then reached back into the crowd to pull Isobel and Matteo Costa into line beside her. Grandma squeezed Isobel's hand tightly and didn't let go as she nodded her assent to the priest.

As the priest began, Marie Claire moved from the back of the crowd, coming up behind Aldo and putting her arms around him. His face softened from an expression of impatience to something calmer, the skin relaxing beneath his eyes. His right hand clutched the place where her wrists crossed in front of his heart. You could have mistaken them for a married couple in late middle age. I didn't know what to make of this strange duo, of their familiarity after not having seen each other in decades. Had the years between frozen them in a kind of amber, leaving each to feel the other as they had been so long ago? The tenderness she offered, and the comfort he willingly accepted, seemed such a contrast to what I knew of him. What might have become of them had this life not been so cruel? What was going through their minds as we buried the man they might feel was partly responsible for Marie's maiming by the abortionist?

"Look at Matteo Costa's ass," Fusilli whispered, nodding across the crowd to where he stood beside his mother. "That's an Iannucci ass. If he was a teenage girl, he'd be dating a rapper."

"Seriously," I whispered. "What the fuck is wrong with you?"

"I'm just saying."

"That could be our uncle," I said, studying Matteo's graying hairline and strong jaw. Once you knew to look, it was impossible to ignore the family resemblances. Was *he* aware of his parentage? Were the rest of his siblings? Was that why the rest of them hadn't shown up for the services?

Mia knitted her eyebrows and leaned forward, shushing us.

Beyond her, my sisters each offered some variation of a scowl. I lifted a hand in acknowledgement and leaned back.

"Considerable improvement over Aldo," Fusilli continued. "Don't you think?"

"Fusilli. Enough."

The priest began the prayers of intercession, the crowd murmuring *Lord, hear our prayer* at the end of each stanza. His cheeks grew redder with each utterance, the heat seeping into his flesh. The crowd didn't seem to be in much better shape, save for Isobel and Grandma, who stood resolute against the day, their hands clasped. Their eyes remained sharp and dry until the priest's final line.

"For the men of the Army's Twenty-Second Reconnaissance unit, who deserved better than this world offered them, whose service in Asia remains untold, and who even now stand guard with us and await the arrival of their brother Francesco, we pray ..."

Isobel's British reserve finally broke at the mention of China. Silent tears spilled from her eyes, slipping into the tightening corners of her mouth. Some part of her was still secreted in that forest, in the hollow of the tree where she waited for my grandfather. Some part of her was frozen in time, pushing morphine into whatever vein she could find in poor Ellsworth. Some part of her was forever pulling that trigger, forsaking the most beautiful, human part of herself for a moment of primal vengeance. I ached for her, for what she suffered, for her decades as the other woman, for all the happy years she and my grandfather were owed and were denied. I hurt for my grandmother, who'd sent the love of her life off to war and gotten back a different man, a different relationship than she had signed up for. They deserved so much better than they'd gotten. All of them.

I was relieved when the honor guard began playing "Taps." When they were finished, they folded the flag and offered it to my grandmother, who accepted it, and then pulled Isobel's hand on top of hers. They thanked the colonel, who rejoined his men. At the conclusion of the service, they marched off in formation.

As the crowd began saying their goodbyes, Gabriella found her way over to me, with Mia on her heels.

"Are you coming to Grandma's with us after lunch?" Gabriella asked.

"Most likely," I said.

"So, you aren't coming back to the beach?" Mia asked, reaching for my hand.

"No, why?" I asked.

Gabriella raised a perfectly tailored eyebrow, her barracuda eyes darting to mine.

"I just wanted to know your plans," Mia said quickly. "I'm headed back to my folks."

"You're welcome to join us at lunch, Mia," Gabriella said. "You're family."

"Honestly, I've been working on a case for thirty-six hours straight and I'm shot. I just need some sleep."

"No worries," I said. "I get it."

"Anyway, if you're not coming back, I won't wait up," she said. "But come for dinner tomorrow. My mother wants to do something for you."

Gabriella pursed her lips in thought and looked like she might say something but let it go.

Mia hugged me and said goodbye, joining the scattershot of mourners headed for their cars. I moved to join Fusilli and the Irish beneath the twisted boughs of an old magnolia tree that stood nearby.

"Are you okay?" I said as I approached Nora.

"What do you think, Jack?" Nora said, her syllables clipped. "You've had Mia hanging on your arm all day. Meantime, I'm a body hidden in the boot."

"I'm sorry," I said. "I know it's uncomfortable. I was just trying to avoid a scene."

"That's the trouble, isn't it? There's never a good time to end a love affair."

"I'm just saying . . ."

"I understand, Jack. I'm not daft. I'm just saying sort yourself out." Nora turned on her heel and stormed towards the car.

Katie grimaced at me and mouthed the word "sorry" as she chased off after Nora.

"She's wrong, Jack," Fusilli said.

"Is she?"

"You did the right thing by keeping the peace here."

"I did what I had to do in the moment. So, why do I feel like dog shit now?"

"There's no good time," he said, unbuttoning his suit coat and digging the keys from his pocket. "But there are bad times, and this would have been the worst."

21

____

After the repast, Fusilli's mom took mine for a drink, leaving my sisters and I to take Grandma Elena home. Grandma's neighborhood was a mishmash of Victorian and Colonial designs. Originally a farmhouse, my grandparents' place lay at the end of a long block that dead-ended against a forest preserve. The clapboard siding had recently been painted a brilliant white, while the shutters stretched wide like dark angel wings. Once hemmed in by tall hedges, the old growth had been trimmed back to waist height since my last visit. The old wicker porch furniture had been renovated, the seats of the armchairs and rocker re-strung with freshly varnished material. Alongside the house, the garden hose had been screwed onto the tap in the side yard, the hose unfurled and stretched into the plot behind the house, a relic of my grandfather's garden. One of his neighbors must have been tending to what remained of his tomatoes and peppers.

We followed the hose around the back, the reptilian green eventually connecting to a length of black tubing that snaked back and forth between the young plants in the yard like the coils of a toaster. The tubing was riven with perforations that leaked thin streams of water into the darkening soil. The contraption didn't appear store-bought. Whereas my father had kept tool chests akin to the best-equipped auto mechanics, my grandfather's had been a study in improvisation; a meager collection of second-hand hardware and hand-me-down gadgets. The results of his labor were always creative, if not perfectly functional. He'd probably spent a day or more puncturing the tubing with an awl or icepick.

We entered through the back door, which opened directly into the kitchen, reflexively kicking our shoes off into a pile on the back porch. The room had been renovated years before, but the changes still surprised me. The rear wall of the house was home to a long countertop with a white and blue patterned backsplash done in subway tile. The wall on the right was home to a pair of large ovens and a variety of cabinets. The center of the room was occupied by an island with a stove top and room to seat about a half-dozen people around it. A few pots and pans hung above it that were purely for show; my grandmother was less than five feet tall and could never have reached them. The workaday pots she'd cooked in since the '50s lay in the cabinets beneath the range.

Grandma was ready for bed and asked me to help her upstairs, which was surprising, given all of the women present.

"Thank you for all you did for your grandfather," she said, stepping into a walk-in closet that had formerly been one of the bedrooms.

"It was the least I could do," I said.

"I think you've gone above and beyond, don't you?"

I didn't know what to say. Did she know about Isobel Costa? If so, what? I decided to play it cool and see if she pursued what could be a ruinous conversation.

"What's the matter, Jack?" she said, sticking her head out from behind the door. "Cat got your tongue?"

"I'm not sure what you mean, Grandma."

"I saw you with Isobel last night. I know how she looks when she talks about the war."

Grandma stepped from behind her door in her nightgown and took my arm. I guided her towards her bedroom. The center was occupied by a queen-sized, mahogany four-post bed, the surrounding walls by old dressers and shadows. The dressers were topped with a variety of religious icons. Her mother's rosary hung around the neck and arms of St. Anthony, patron saint of lost things.

"It sounds like she and Grandpa saw some . . ."

"I don't want to know," she said, sitting heavily on the bed and swinging her legs up. "It haunted your grandfather. He refused to talk about what he'd seen and done. I only knew it was terrible."

"How do you mean?"

She sighed as she lay back on her pillow, folding her hands across her chest. "Your grandfather was a different person when he came back from the war. A car might backfire, and he would duck. Sometimes, he would check corners on the street or in the bakery before walking around them. Some nights, he woke up screaming."

"I . . . I can understand why."

"At first, I thought it would get better," she said. "Shell shock, they called it. I tried to talk to him, but he would just get . . . quiet. Like he was ashamed."

"There was nothing for him to be ashamed of," I said. "It's called post-traumatic stress disorder nowadays."

She nodded. "One night, Isobel and John were over. They were still newlyweds. Your grandfather fell asleep on the couch and woke up screaming about the Japs. It was like . . . it was like he was dreaming, but awake. He asked where his rifle was. He tried to get Isobel to hide in the closet, and when John tried to stop him, Grandpa knocked him on his ass."

"Jesus."

"I was scared," she said, reaching for her rosary on the nightstand and wrapping it around her right hand. "We'd only been married a year or two. I thought they might take him to a mental hospital."

"Did you call someone?"

"No," she said. "Isobel grabbed onto him and hugged him tight. She said something about the mess. I said, there's nothing messy here! I keep a clean house!"

"The mess tent," I said. "It's where they would sit together."

"Anyway, they went downstairs to the bakery, to the room in the back where we stored the flour and my brothers played cards. When we peeked into the room later, your grandfather was asleep in a chair at the table, and Isobel was next to him. She sat with him like that. John slept on the couch, but I kept going back. Isobel never moved. She never slept, not that I could tell. She just stared down the night. Watched over him, like a guardian angel."

"That's what she did for him in the jungle," I said. "That was their secret."

"I know your grandfather loved me," she said. "I know he loved her, too. And I'm smart enough to know she made it so he could live with whatever they saw and did. I don't understand what they were to each other, but I know she was able to find some piece of the person I loved and bring him back to me."

"I understand," I said.

"So," she said, closing her eyes. "I don't know what she told you, or what you and Aldo and that cousin of yours did in New York. I don't need to know. I'm just thanking you for whatever you had to do to get him home for the last time. Now he can rest."

~

MY SISTERS WERE SEATED around the living room like melting popsicles, waiting for the central air to take the edge off. They'd assumed positions as far as possible from each other. The furniture was typical Art Nouveau, armchairs and a couch flanked by end-tables with intricate carvings and topped with painted porcelain lamps. Aurora occupied one of the armchairs in the bay window. She was the eldest of my sisters, two years younger than me and two years older than Marco and Lidia. Aurora had recently landed her first good job after completing her graduate work as a pediatric nurse practitioner. Her blond hair was darkening with age, which she tried to rescue with highlights and a bob she was too young to pull off. She'd recently had her heart broken by her douchebag college boyfriend, but I knew she could do better.

"No sign of Marco?" I asked as I descended the stairs.

"No," Aurora said. "He was with Aldo and Sister what's-her-face. They took off in the Camino. How does Aldo know her?"

"She was his girlfriend before she went to the nunnery," I said.

"Wow," Aurora said.

Lidia had taken up the couch on the wall opposite the stairs. She was Marco's twin and the most intellectual of the family. Fluent in both Greek and Latin, she'd studied classics abroad and was applying for a PhD in philosophy. She'd worn the same straight-cut bangs since high school, the rest of her hair pulled back into a tight brunette ponytail. Her small round spectacles were perched at the end of her nose, leaving her resembling a youthful Benjamin Franklin.

"You never imagine clergy having a former life," Lidia said. "It's silly, really."

I fell into the armchair at the bottom of the stairs, physically and mentally exhausted. "Honestly," I sighed, "the priesthood sounds ideal right about now."

Gabriella was banging around in the kitchen behind us, the

cacophony of ice cubes, glasses, and liquor bottles testifying to her inexperienced bartending.

"Let me fix that for you," Gabriella said, turning down Sinatra on the oldies station.

"I'm afraid to ask," Aurora said.

"Uncle Chris taught me how to make these at the family reunion. He used to bartend someplace Tony Bennett owned, you know."

"Jack Benny," I said.

"Whatever," she said.

"Your girlfriend was on her best behavior today," Aurora said. "Are things getting better?"

"She can play the part when she needs to, I guess."

Lidia leaned forward and adjusted her glasses. "You think she's insincere?"

"She's a lawyer," Gabriella called. "It's a professional requirement."

"She's nice enough," Lidia said.

"She's a phony," Gabriella said, stepping into the kitchen doorway as she muddled mint leaves in the crystal pitcher Grandma reserved for holidays. "I've had enough of her reindeer games."

"Careful with the pitcher," Aurora said. "It was Great-Grandma's."

"I prefer gin and tonic," Lidia said. "Bombay Sapphire, if you have it."

"We don't," Gabriella said. "What are you, ninety?"

"I run with a . . . different crowd."

"British cat ladies?"

The three of us laughed, but Lidia offered a thoughtful expression. "A few, if we're being honest." It only made us laugh harder. Lidia finally joined.

The phone rang in the kitchen. Gabriella snatched it up to avoid waking Grandma.

"Jack," she called, waving the receiver overhead. "Fusilli."

I took the phone from her. Fusilli started talking before I even had it fully pressed to my ear.

"You need to get back here," he said. "Right now."

"Why? What's going on?"

Gabriella raised an eyebrow at my response, crossing her arms and leaning back against the sink.

"We're convening the Inquisition. Time to burn the witch."

"Burn the witch?"

Gabriella closed her eyes and bowed her head, shaking it gently. She had no patience for Fusilli's hijinks. She'd have thrown something at him if he were within range.

"Wiccan," Fusilli said. "Whatever."

"Fusilli," I said. "For God's sake. It's been a long day. Can we not . . ."

"It's about to get a lot longer. Ian's car is parked up the block."

The world slowed on its axis for a moment. We'd just finished burying our grandfather. Could Mia possibly be this underhanded? What the fuck was he doing there?

I agreed to get on the road, then carefully replaced the phone on the cradle. A haphazard array of pictures hung on the corkboard beside it. My eyes settled on the one of Mia and me standing behind Grandma and Grandpa at the party celebrating their fiftieth wedding anniversary. Just out of frame would have been Mrs. Costa, her kids, and their spouses at one of the tables reserved for the Brooklyn crowd. So much in the picture, and so much unseen by the lens.

Gabriella's charcoal eyes telegraphed suspicion. "What did your degenerate cousin want?"

I didn't want to get into it with her. "You know, the usual."

"You are the worst fucking liar," she said.

"Pour me a tall one of those," I said, pointing at her pitcher. "Please and thank you."

"If you don't want to tell me, just say so."

"The Witchdoctor is at Mia's house," I said, my shoulders slumping incrementally with each word. I opened a cabinet to find the first vessel that would hold a mojito. I took a coffee cup and filled it to the brim, then reached into the pitcher barehanded and grabbed some mint to garnish with. My other sisters leapt to their feet and crowded into the doorway.

"I fucking knew it," Gabriella said, her finger in my face. "The way she was trying to pin down your plans tonight!"

"I can't believe it. I can't believe we're going to do this."

"Tell me you aren't going down there."

"You're goddamn right I'm going down there," I said, taking a slurp from my mug. "I need to catch her in the act and tell her to fuck off."

Gabriella raised her hand like a crossing guard, then grabbed the drink from my hand and took a big swallow. "What you *need* is a tall glass of shut the fuck up."

"This is why I don't tell you guys anything."

"No," Gabriella said. "You don't tell us anything because you're ashamed to admit you're as fucked up as we are. Mia is your disguise."

"He's a child of chaos," Lidia said, peeling off her glasses and cleaning them on a dishtowel. "We all are. Playing house with Mia doesn't change that."

There was probably more truth to that than I wanted to admit. There was something old-fashioned about Mia, something that made me feel like I was both accepting my grandparents' example and modeling it for my siblings. Only, things were a lot more complicated than I had ever imagined. Every generation had its own trials to survive, its sins to atone. Any reassuring image of simplicity was just that. This was a terrible shaking of my foundation. My sisters had no idea how lucky they were not to know what I knew.

"Don't get philosophical," Gabriella said. "The point is, he's too nice. If he gets into it with her again, she'll lead him around in circles."

"Can you stop talking about me like I'm not here?" I said. "I'm a scientist. I want the truth."

"You know the truth already," Gabriella said.

"I feel like I'm losing my mind."

"Because this is crazy behavior," she said. "This isn't some laboratory experiment. You don't need to collect evidence, Sherlock. You need a girlfriend who isn't a fake."

"It doesn't make any sense," Aurora said. "Why move back to Jersey if she was screwing someone else?"

"Men in Mediterranean cultures frequently take lovers outside the primary relationship," Lidia said. "Grandpa was likely an exception among his peers. Why should it be different for women? Mia's a generation closer to Italy than we are."

An exception to his peers? A part of me wanted to let loose. Let me tell you a little story about Grandpa and Isobel Costa. I was suddenly a lot less willing to pass judgment on Mediterranean men. Who knew what stories were behind those relationships?

"Mia's been part of this family for years," Aurora said. "It's hard to believe."

"Aristotle would say a statement is true if it accurately reflects reality," Lidia said. "We don't need to understand Mia's motives, only observe her actions. Gabriella is right. You're most likely being cuckolded."

"I don't like the word 'cuckold'." Aurora said.

"It's nothing obscene. It comes from Middle English and refers to the..."

"Enough out of you," Gabriella said, before turning to me. "Never forget what she did to you. Never let her know you remember. Just dump her already."

22

I had to borrow Aurora's car to get to the beach because Fusilli had Grandpa's. When I arrived, the atmosphere in the kitchen was that of a different kind of funeral. Katie was sitting against the wall on the bench, head in hands as if nursing a hangover. Nora sipped her cup of tea expectantly, both hands wrapped around it, steam rising around her cheeks. Her eyes narrowed as she studied my face, perhaps curious as to how I would respond to Mia's deception.

Fusilli was sitting at the head of the table, humming and stringing a garlic bulb onto a loop of fishing line. Before him lay a roofing hammer and a section of tree branch, slightly crooked, one end whittled to a fine point. The wood shavings were scattered about like confetti.

"What the fuck is all this?" I asked.

Fusilli knotted the fishing line and stood up, hanging the garlic bulb around my neck like an Olympic medal. He gestured towards the table.

"I'll place the stake over his heart," Fusilli said. "You'll raise the hammer and strike in the name of the risen Christ."

I yanked the garlic from my neck, the monofilament digging into my skin before snapping. I hurled it in the direction of the trash. "You're a real asshole, you know that?"

"Take care," he shouted, channeling Abraham Van Helsing. "For the sake of others if not your own!"

"How do you live with this shite?" Nora asked, leaning into Katie.

Katie shook her head without looking up. "It's a wonder, isn't it?"

"I'm sorry, man," Fusilli said. "I'm just trying to lighten the mood. Everything is fucking terrible."

I leaned against the wall and took a deep breath. "I know."

"What are you going to do?"

"I'm going up there to dump her," I said. "I ought to kick his ass on top of it."

"You haven't thrown a punch since we were fourteen."

"It's not on him anyway," Katie said. "He's not the one claiming to love you."

"She's not wrong," Nora said, dropping her eyes. Had I not been so angry, I might have considered what she was feeling. She was probably seeing in me everything Daniel would feel if he learned what she'd been up to on her "girls' holiday."

I'd spent a lot of time hating Ian, and for what? He hadn't given a shit. Mia obviously hadn't given a shit. All I'd done was give myself *agita* and waste time I could have put into a more productive relationship. There was no point worrying about it now. Mia had finally forced the moment to its crisis. I threw my keys on the table and made for the back door. As I sprung the latch, I looked back at my cousin.

"You joining the mission, or do I have to do everything myself?"

~

FUSILLI and I entered the beach from a couple of blocks north of our street. The sand was cool underfoot, like sugar after being taken from a dark cupboard. Walking in the shadows of the dunes, we came up on an overturned lifeguard gig that still bore the branding of a long-defunct restaurant, the aqua paint bright under the half-moon. The splintering keel was rough beneath my palm, triggering memories of the times I'd pushed it into the surf over the years. I was tougher then, a waterman hardened by years of training and hurricane surf. I needed to find that fortitude again. Then, I thought of how many times Mia and I had made love beneath that same hull, and my insides turned to jelly.

We stopped behind the dune in front of Mia's house. I hopped the fence, then scrambled up and peered over the top. The salt breeze from the southeast swirled against the thick humidity from the bay, the contradiction in flow unsettling. A single Tiffany lamp burned in the middle pane of the three great-picture windows on Mia's second floor. The stained-glass shade cast a supernatural kaleidoscope on the walls. The telescope Grandpa had bought me stood alongside the lamp. Mia's dad liked using it to look for whales. What would she see if she trained it on me? Anger? Pain? Determination?

The backs of three heads were visible in silhouette before the big-screen television in the rightmost window, while Mia stood at the far left, her features lit by the refrigerator as she put something away.

"Gabriella called ahead of you," Fusilli said from behind me. "Asked me to keep you from doing anything stupid."

"It's time we hashed this out. Mia needs to choose."

"She's made her choice, man."

"No, she needs to tell me to my fucking face. I'm so angry."

"At Mia? The Wizard of Yale?"

"For starters."

"Bullshit," he spat. "You're angry at yourself."

"Fuck off."

"You let it come to this. No one else. Your relationship was a grenade. This shit just pulled the pin."

"I'm better than that motherfucker in every way."

"Your pride won't allow losing to him," he said. "I get it. But she's never going to come clean and admit being the bad guy. So, just dump her in the morning. Make it easy."

I hung my head. "She deserves that?"

"No," he said. "*You* do."

"I'm not sure I understand the logic here."

"Look, man. Life is crazy. People fall in and out of love. People fuck people they shouldn't. We're all gonna die someday."

"Story of your life."

"Yours now, too."

"Thanks."

He commando-crawled up the dune and lay beside me. "Jack, we've been partners from birth. We pissed our diapers together in the crib. You go, I go. You lie, I'll swear to it. But you gotta be honest with yourself."

"I know."

"All right. So, what now?"

"We're going to observe the specimen in her natural habitat."

"This is a bad idea," he said, propping his chin his hands. "But I'm all in, man."

We watched as her parents slipped off to bed. Ian eventually rose, his lanky silhouette moving slowly across the room, then descending the staircase that led to the first-floor guest room. Mia pulled the blinds and switched off the lights.

"So much for a peep show," Fusilli said.

"We'll give her a few minutes," I said. "If I know Mia, she'll sneak down to the guest room once she thinks her parents are asleep."

"We can't see anything."

"I'll check her bedroom in a few minutes."

"Dude."

"I deserve to know."

"There's a special place in hell for the man who does the wrong thing for the right reason."

"Augustine?"

He smiled crookedly. "Actually, I think I just made it up."

After about twenty minutes, I darted over the dune and down to the boardwalk, then through the tall grass planted alongside her house. I circled behind and up the back stairs to the deck. I'd done this a hundred times before, under very different circumstances. When Mia came home on summer break, her parents enforced a 10 p.m. curfew, but that never stopped us. Her bedroom window opened onto the deck. Once her parents went to bed, I'd meet her at the window and help her out, filling the space under her sheets with a pile of laundry that vaguely resembled a body. We would creep down the stairs and around the side to the boardwalk. From there, we found our way to the beach and crawled under my lifeguard boat.

I was awash in a different kind of anxiety as I prepared to find an empty bed and confirm my worst fears about Mia. The swirling atmosphere shifted in favor of the bay, the iodine crisp of the sea lost in the sulfur of the drying weed beds. I got to Mia's bedroom window and crouched down to peer inside, a nervous sweat pouring from my brow and stinging my eyes. What was the point of any of this?

As expected, Mia wasn't in bed. In her stead lay Daisy the Springer Spaniel, who regarded me with a cocked head and questioning eyes. The edges of the ceiling fan gleamed in the moonlight, turning like switchblades in a Springsteen song.

I moved to the kitchen window, Daisy whining nervously as

I disappeared. Both the kitchen and living room were mausoleum silent and empty, the door to the bathroom open and dark. The stairs that led down to the guest room and entrance to the downstairs apartment were bathed in shadow. She couldn't be in the apartment, since it was under construction. That left the guest room. His room. His room which used to be mine when I would stay there.

I floated down the steps to the rear lot. The lights flicked on in the guest room as I circled to the side of the house. Mercifully, the blinds were shut tight. Still, I'd been behind them enough times to know what was going on, the movie playing relentlessly in my head as I tried to divert my mind's eye. They were under a thin cotton sheet. Mia's pajamas were in a ball between the pillows. She was on top to ensure the rhythm was restrained, to avoid suspicious noises that might reach her parents' room. The bile rising in my throat tasted like defeat.

Fusilli was still watching from the top of the dune, ready to spring into action. I'd give Mia and Ian a minute, then bang on the window and scare the hell out of them, probably waking her parents and causing a scene. That was fine. She should have to live with it. I'd fooled around with Nora, sure, but that paled in comparison to years of infidelity. What the fuck was she thinking? Was she really planning to keep stringing me along? Why not just leave me for him? Of course, I knew the answer. He was wealthy and had a good job, but he was a WASP. He didn't understand the immigrant way. He couldn't speak Italian to her grandparents. It would never fly in Mia's house. In the same way, his old-money Mayflower family would never accept her. She lacked the pedigree.

I waved at Fusilli and pantomimed a knocking motion. He shook his head and trotted down the dune, hurdling the low fence at the bottom. We met on the boardwalk.

"Jack," he said. "Don't do this."

"The only thing worse than knowing is not knowing."

"Or vice versa."

I took a deep breath, pressing my feet against the splintered wood to center myself. My head spinning, I didn't notice my own tears until I tasted them. He set a hand on my shoulder.

"You know what you need to know, man," he said. "Let's go home."

23

W e turned the corner at the bay to see a figure tucked into the shadows of our porch. It took me a moment to realize it was my brother and not Aldo. He sat on the porch swing, the end of his cigarette glowing sunset orange. His tie, dress shirt, and Vans were missing in action.

Marco rose to his feet. "Where the fuck have you two been?"

"Secret mission," Fusilli said.

The door opened as we mounted the brick staircase. Nora and Katie spilled into the fray, their faces grave.

"We've got problems. Aldo's been arrested."

"That's the best news I've heard in days," I said.

Katie gave me a stern backhand to the chest.

"What happened?" Fusilli asked.

"We were on a bar crawl," Marco said. "Aldo got snagged for DWI. They impounded his car."

"Did they arrest Marie Claire, too?"

"No, she asked us to drop her off after the second bar. Smart lady."

"What will it cost to get him out?" I asked.

"He was arraigned a couple hours ago. Bail is $1,500."

"I don't have that kind of money, and we're not going to Grandma, not after all she's been through."

"She's going to find out sooner or later," Marco said. "He was talking about moving in with her since Grandpa is dead."

"Fuck that."

Grandma didn't need her prodigal son complicating her life, never mind that they couldn't stand one another. My grandmother felt Aldo was her great failure in life. She sincerely believed she could have prevented his alcoholism and anomie had she loved or disciplined him harder. She shouldn't spend what little time she had left in a quixotic effort to straighten him out.

"First things first," Katie said, turning to Fusilli. "Can you call your mother?"

"Don't bother," Marco said. "Aldo said there's money in his room."

We found our way to Aldo's flea-market dresser. I tugged on the bottom drawer, which opened only halfway but was clearly empty. I then began rifling through the three upper drawers, which contained a variety of clothes emblazoned with the logos of booze or cigarette companies. I stood up and shrugged.

Nora pursed her lips and bent down to pull on the bottom drawer again, a puzzled look on her face as it bounced at the end of its abbreviated travel. "I think there's . . ." She reached under the dresser, her eyes widening as she grasped something. There was a tearing sound, and then she produced a gallon Ziplock bag covered in an inordinate amount of duct tape. She stood up and peeled it open, her eyes widening in either surprise or disgust. She passed it to me. I fished out a roll of $50 bills and another Ziplock containing more OxyContin tablets than I could count.

"What are those?" Nora asked.

Fusilli took the bag from me, his eyes about to explode from his head. "Holy shit, Jack."

The sympathy I'd begun feeling for Aldo at the wake was quickly evaporating. "Now we're living with Pablo fucking Escobar?" I clamped my eyes shut. "Fuck!"

"This is, like, intent to distribute," Marco said. "I can't get caught with that."

"What does that mean?" Nora asked.

Fusilli held up the bag and shook it. "You go to jail for this."

"For a long time," Marco said.

"And now our fingerprints are all over it," I spat, kicking the drawer shut, my anger feeding on itself. "Fuck this shit. Fuck that drunk asshole. Let him rot."

"Aldo's a dick," Fusilli said, "but he's blood."

"Bullshit. No one has seen him in years."

Fusilli looked at Marco, who shook his head. "I'm with Action Jackson. I spent a couple days in Rikers last year. I'm not going back."

"We spent today burying Grandpa and supporting each other. Are we just going to forget about all that?" Fusilli said.

"Let's just take a breath and think this through," Katie said.

I dropped the wad of bills on the bed and snatched the drugs from Fusilli, then made a beeline for the bay. Fusilli, Nora, and my brother gave chase. Katie stopped on the porch, hands on hips, shaking her head like an exasperated schoolmarm.

The trio pulled up alongside me as I barreled across the street, through the dune grass and into the sandy park beyond.

"What are you on about?" Nora said. "Slow down."

"You remember when we were kids, Fusilli?" I said. "When we hung out in this park?"

"Yeah, sure."

"We played ball. Went to the beach. Met girls." I pointed to Nora. "Nice girls. Not crackheads with homicidal fathers and a murder basement! No drunk uncles knocking me off ladders while selling drugs on the side. No grandparents with secret lives. This place was heaven."

"What are you babbling about?" Marco asked.

"Yeah," Fusilli said. "I feel you."

"Good," I said, holding up the bag. "Do you know what this is?"

Nora started to say something, but I cut her off. "This is the end of everything. If the cops found this, we would lose the house. Marco would probably do real time. The girls would get deported. That's what nonstop crazy gets us."

Marco reached for my arm. "Quit overreacting. Let's call Mia and ask..."

Nora recoiled at the sound of Mia's name.

"Mia works for the federales, Marco!" I pulled away from him and began marching into the water. "And she's up the block screwing the Witchdoctor! Everything is fucked!"

"Witchdoctor?" Marco said, looking at Fusilli. "Someone slip him some acid?"

"He's lost the plot," Nora said.

"Maybe," I said. "But I'm sure as hell not losing my medical license on a drug charge."

Fusilli pointed to the bag. "Do you have any idea what that's worth?"

"Not my future," I said, my progress slowing as the water came up past my knees and approached my hips, soaking my khakis as though I was about to be baptized by immersion. "Not Marco's. Not yours. And not your kids."

"Kids?" Marco erupted. "You? How many ways did you guys shit the bed while I was away?"

I took a handful of the tablets and threw them as far out into the bay as I could. I repeated this until the bag was empty. Then I rinsed the bag the way someone with OCD might wash their hands after visiting a public bathroom.

When I looked up, the group was staring back at me, their mouths slack.

"Aldo is going to freak the fuck out," Fusilli said.

"Fuck. Him."

"What now, Jack?" Nora asked.

"We police the house for any remaining evidence. And then we collect our drunk, vagrant uncle before he calls Grandma and gives her a heart attack. You know . . . because he's family."

THE POLICE STATION WAS A SLENDER, deep building constructed of unassuming red brick and fronted with Georgian columns that held up a white facade, like a country church without a steeple. Two of the town's three police cars were parked out front on the southbound side of the road, while the side lot was almost entirely empty. I pushed through the double-glass doors. The desk sergeant was sitting behind a long counter. Aldo was handcuffed to a tall-backed wooden bench.

Marco took in his surroundings, pushing his blond hair back over his ears. "I've never seen the inside of this place before."

"That makes one of us," Fusilli said.

I recognized the sergeant from our childhood; his name was Dean or Deke or something. He was maybe five years older than us. His ballcap was too tight for his great round head, the band forming an uncomfortable-looking indent in the sunburned skin underlying his blond buzz cut. His great-grandfather was one of the first members of the police department in the early 1900s, the family name now immortalized on both a bayside bandshell and a local liquor store chain. Dean/Deke had started his career as a rent-a-cop, busting teenagers for drinking his grandfather's products on the beach.

Aldo looked like an old Mylar balloon stuck on a power

line. His neck deflated and hanging, he was snoring with his chin lolling against his chest, his small round sunglasses balanced on the end of his nose. A rivulet of drool hung from his lower lip, dripping onto one of my old volleyball tank tops.

Fusilli shook his head and pointed at Aldo. "How much for the drunk guy?"

"You know him?" Dean/Deke asked.

Fusilli nodded. "Our uncle."

They stepped into an office and did whatever business needed doing. Fusilli came out a few moments later carrying a sheaf of papers.

"Is there anything else we need to know?" Fusilli asked.

"He's all yours," Dean/Deke said, adjusting his belt. His navy-polo shirt pulled free, riding up over his ample paunch and exposing his navel. He tried to tuck it back in. "Just remember, you forfeit the money if he doesn't show up in court."

"What makes you think he won't?"

"He said he's from here but has an Alaska license and plates," he said. "I've never seen him before."

"He's been away a few years. Your folks probably grew up with him."

"Aldo, love," Nora said, leaning over him and gently shaking his shoulder. "Time to go home."

Aldo snorted and looked up at her, then tugged at his handcuffs before Dean/Deke bent down to unlock them. Aldo rubbed the raw spot on his wrist, then pushed the sunglasses up on his nose as he found his feet. He walked past me without comment and elbowed his way through the doors, then veered west towards the bay. A pair of giggling teenage girls turned the corner in front of us, then redirected across the street to give Aldo a wide berth.

"You're welcome!" I called after him.

Aldo didn't break stride. "Cops are pussies now. In the '70s they just took your keys and made you walk."

"So, it's their fault?" I asked.

Nora touched the upper part of my arm, shaking her head.

"I wasn't going to die three blocks from home," Aldo said.

"It's not about you," I said. "The drunk doesn't usually die in the wreck."

"I forget how wise you are, Jack."

"Kiss my ass."

"Let's talk when he sobers up," Marco said.

We turned the corner at the bay. Captain Kidd's lay just beyond the next intersection. Windows propped open, the sounds of a terrible band aping Jimmy Buffett streamed out at us. Aldo began to walk with purpose. He might make last call.

"Are you fucking kidding?" Fusilli said.

"Let him go," I said. "There's not enough money to bail him out again."

"Aldo, man," Marco said. "What are you doing?"

"Make sure you put my stash back," Aldo said.

"I got rid of it," I blurted.

Aldo stopped at the curb. "What?"

"We didn't know what you got pinched for," Nora said. "We were afraid they'd search the house."

"It's a family home, not a drug den," I said.

Aldo stormed towards me. Fusilli jumped between us. "You think you're so fuckin' smart. You don't know shit."

"Educate me."

"What do you think I was doing in Alaska, Jack? I was back from 'Nam and I got in trouble protesting. I went to fucking prison."

"What does that have to do with anything?"

"You try getting a decent job when you've done time," he said. "You think commercial fishing was my dream? It destroyed my body. I'm in constant pain. I'm not selling drugs. I'm buying them. I do what I have to do to survive."

I should have shown more empathy. I was just so angry and

Aldo was in the line of fire. "One bad decision can't fix another."

"I hope you never make a stupid mistake," he said, his eyes narrowing. "One that haunts you for the rest of your life."

"The difference is that your mistakes could cost your mother her house and me my medical license."

"Now who's making it all about them?"

"So, what's the plan, Aldo? Keep digging the same hole?"

"To die before I'm fifty, you arrogant prick."

He crossed the intersection towards the bar, narrowly missing being struck by an old convertible Blazer driven by the police chief. I started after him, but Fusilli stopped me. We waited for Aldo to go inside, then continued towards home, Nora and I trailing Fusilli and Marco. She hooked her arm through mine as we walked the boulevard along the bay.

"You might go a little easier on him," she said.

"Fuck that guy."

"What are you so angry about, Jack?"

"The constant insanity," I said. "The excuses. The idea that we were all raised with a set of values, but no one actually lives them."

"Not even you. Or me, for that matter."

We looked at each other for a moment. Nora wasn't wrong, and I didn't like the way that felt. "And we'll probably pay for it. We need to do better."

"Aldo has had his fair share of punishment, don't you think?"

"I just . . ." I felt my throat tightening. Aldo had not had an easy life. Still, he didn't have the right to take that out on the rest of us.

"Families change, Jack. They're dysfunctional. They're universally mad. You can't control them or fix them. The normal one you're looking for doesn't exist."

"You think?"

"You're imagining this romantic life for us. I have too. But it won't be that way. My brothers will get drunk and fight. Da will struggle to make payroll and argue with Mum about the money she gives to the church. Life is hard."

"So what? We don't aspire to do better?"

"I think everyone is trying their best. Even the people who hurt us."

"That's one way of looking at it."

"What you're really angry about is Mia, isn't it? What happened up there?"

"They were fooling around."

"You saw them? On the beach? Holy Christ."

"No," I said. "In the guest room."

"Now you're a peeping tom? Can you not see what this is doing to you?"

"It's not like that," I said. "I didn't actually *see* them. I used to sneak her out the window after . ... whatever, it doesn't matter."

"So, you didn't confront her? You're making a lot of assumptions here."

"Fusilli stopped me banging on the window like a psycho. It'll have to wait until tomorrow."

The others turned into our driveway, while Nora and I went the long way around the corner to her place. Her flowers were thriving in their window boxes, the stems firmer, the bright orange petals turning upwards, waiting for the sun. In my heart, I believed there was a possibility between us that could take root in the same way. I was done with Mia. I'd been totally betrayed. Did I need to look at Nora more closely, given how willing she was to mess around behind her fiancé's back? She said she didn't love him, but more importantly, that she'd felt bad about it. That meant she had a conscience. Mia had never shown any misgivings over the time she spent with the High Priest of Wicca.

When we got to her door, Nora was pensive, like a cat testing a puddle of sunlight with a single paw.

"You all right?" she asked.

"Can we be honest with each other?"

"About?"

"Us."

She sighed and sat down on the stoop, pulling me down by the hand. "You want to do this now?"

"It's time to make some changes in my life."

"Maybe best to let bygones be bygones, eh?"

"How do you mean?"

"We wouldn't be the first to have a bit of fun before a wedding," she said. "Who knows what Daniel might get up to at his stag do."

"I mean, if that's all this was to you . . ."

"No," she back-pedaled, eyes widening. "I don't mean it like that."

"Nora, what if it wasn't just a bit of fun?"

"This again?" she asked, leaning back on her hands. "Jack, you should get some sleep. You've had a hell of a week. We all have."

"Maybe we could be something to each other. More than just a regret."

"Are you serious?"

"Why not?"

Her mouth twisted into a frown. "Because after all this, you're still hung up on Mia. Or the idea of her. Or the future you thought you could have with her. I see that clear as day now. *That's* what has you so angry. And I'm still engaged. I can't be your rebound."

"You told me you didn't really love him."

"I was drunk."

"*In vino, veritas.*"

"Don't give me that shite. The Irish invented the drunk confession."

"If you have doubts, you should sort them out now," I said. "Marriage is supposed to be forever."

"You really are this earnest, aren't you? It's not a put-on at all."

"I want to believe in something. I wondered about you for a long time when we were kids. Didn't you wonder about me?"

"Of course." She squeezed my hand, her mouth relaxing. "And you're exactly who I remember, Jack."

"So, what's the worst that could happen?"

"We fall in love. Then what?"

"How about we jump off that bridge when we get to it?"

"Jack, I come from a tiny place. Do you have any idea what this would look like?"

"I come from a town of five thousand, Nora. It's not exactly a metropolis."

"And I come from a village of five hundred," she said. "Three generations of Daniel's family sit behind me at mass. They live two houses over. My parents would never live it down."

"They don't need to know yet. We can spend the summer together and figure out our feelings. It's only an hour commute from here to my hospital. We could have a normal relationship."

"We spend the summer together here . . . and just lie about it? That's the plan?"

"We don't lie," I said, surprising myself with Fusilli's words. "We keep it to ourselves."

She seemed to think it over for a minute. "I take it back," she said. "Maybe you aren't who I remember at all."

"It's not ideal. I'm just saying I don't expect you to blow up your life for me. At least not before we're sure."

Nora started to open her mouth and then stopped, her

tongue resting on the back of her upper teeth. The back door of Villabaia opened behind me, but I didn't hear anyone come down the steps. I felt their eyes on us.

"I can only control myself," I said. "I'm breaking up with Mia. I don't care what her explanation is."

"Jack," she said slowly. "You don't owe me anything. I'm a big girl."

"I'm not doing it for you. And you can decide what you want for yourself. No pressure."

Nora took both my hands in hers and squeezed them, studying my eyes intently. "What is it you want?"

"You. And if everything is on the table, a time machine so we can go back and do it right. But I'll settle for you. We'll figure the rest out."

"It's lovely to imagine," she sighed, looking down. "Maybe I've got things to take care of too."

"You don't owe me anything either, you know."

She nodded, then glanced at her watch. "Listen, I'm exhausted. But I'm off tomorrow. Can we talk then?"

"Okay."

"We'll have breakfast. We'll make a plan, all right?"

"All right."

We kissed quickly, then Nora stood up and opened the door. I started towards Villabaia, then heard her hurrying after me. I turned into her as she wrapped me in a bear hug. She leaned back after a moment, taking my face in her hands and kissing me again, sweetly this time.

"You're a good lad, Jack. I'm sorry for being hard on you."

"It's okay," I said. "Everything is insane. It's time we embraced it."

I ducked back through the hedge and headed for the steps, where Fusilli and Katie were waiting for me.

"Everything all right?" Katie asked.

"I'm breaking the fuck up with Mia tomorrow," I said. "And Nora and I are going to figure this out."

Fusilli offered a gentle golf clap. "I like a man who takes charge of his future," he said.

"Are you ready for the trouble you're in for?" Katie asked.

"You asked me that before."

"No, I asked if you *knew* the trouble you were in for. This is a whole new game."

"I've had my thumb up my ass for too long."

"Perhaps a man *can* wake up in New Jersey with a righteous idea," Fusilli said.

"Do you have any to share?"

"I'm going back with Katie tomorrow night. We'll face her parents together. Start our life properly."

A smile emerged from the corners of Katie's mouth. I leaned down and hugged her, then offered the same to my cousin.

"Donnie," I said. "This might be the best idea you've ever had."

His eyes brightened at the sound of his Irish moniker. "Once more, I am proven the happy genius of the family."

24

I woke early the following morning, confused about where I was, an incessant ticking in my ear. It took me a moment to realize I was listening to my wristwatch. I rolled over, peeled it off, and was ready to hurl it at the wall before I stopped myself. Instead, I went to the dresser and yanked the topmost handle, pitching the watch inside. The titanium wristlet clattered against the hardwood. I was about to close the drawer when I saw my old Luminox was working again, a scrap of paper underneath it.

All it needed was a battery! Love, Grandpa.

I wondered if he'd known how close he was to the end as he fixed my watch. It was such a mundane use of such a limited amount of lifespan, and he'd spent it doing something for me.

I stretched the black rubber band around the untanned space on my arm. It was splitting in places but held together as I gently tightened the clasp and twisted the bezel to line the numbers up with the luminescent hands. The first time I put it on, Grandpa told me, "The Navy Frogmen wear these. They are regular bad asses." It was time to live up to that legacy.

There was no doubt I was setting myself up for trouble with

Nora. There was a geographic and cultural divide that might not be easily bridged. She was still a faithful, or at least observant Catholic, and I was bordering on atheist after my experiences. She called her mother daily, while I could go months without contacting mine. If things worked out, we would need to figure out a feat of intercontinental logistics, same as Fusilli. I tried to step outside myself for a moment, but the view only got worse. This was patently crazy. I'd known Nora for a few months in 1989 and a few weeks now. I was gaming out a positive outcome to an illicit affair with a foreign national, who, by the way, was hiding out from her fiancé in New Jersey of all godforsaken places?

I got cleaned up, then went over to the cottage. My anxiety gave way to excitement as I crossed the yard. I felt alive with Nora, in a way I hadn't felt with Mia in a long time. I felt . . . potential. That was worth something; it was another data point for my calculations. Another factor for the risk-assessment. There were red flags to be sure. Her drinking. The way her temper flared. We could work through those, couldn't we?

Something felt off. Nora's clothesline, which I usually had to duck under, was missing. Climbing the steps to the porch, the door was ajar. I knocked, which caused it to swing open. Jagged beams of sunlight pierced the room between the venetian blinds, illuminating motes of dust adrift in the still air. Nora's bicycle was parked near the couch, the living room beyond empty. The door to the bedroom was open.

"Nora?" I called.

Greeted by silence, I peered into the bedroom, where the sheets had been stripped from the bed. The closet was open and bare. I had a sudden, intrusive thought that Nora had done something terrible with the missing clothesline. I crossed the living room in two strides and yanked the bathroom door open, finding only bed linens in the hamper and the rope coiled neatly atop the pile. I reversed course, feeling spacey and detached. The other bedroom contained only Katie's luggage.

In the kitchen, I found a piece of white stationery on the table, vivid in a beam of morning sun beside the hurricane lamp. My name was inscribed on the envelope. The combination of light, glass, and translucent green fuel cast an off-kilter rainbow spectrum against the wall. A tremor in my hand, I reached for the letter. It was not a suicide note, or even some kind of Dear John nonsense, but an invitation to her wedding. When I turned it over, there was a single line in Nora's hand.

There is no such thing as time travel, love.

I turned slowly, surveying the kitchen with the emptiness of a partygoer suddenly feeling his age. Backing out of the room and into the shadows of the hall, I stopped at the bedroom for a moment. What might it have felt like to wake up beside her there? I paused again in the living room, imagining what she must have looked like as she folded her summer dresses over the old cane chair, then packed her bags before closing up the house. Such a sad thing to do. So devoid of hope for something better. Or maybe it wasn't like that at all. Maybe all my missteps had convinced her I just wasn't a good bet.

I went outside, then circled around the cottage, past the trash cans where the corner of her beach blanket was sticking out from under a lid. The only evidence of what we'd been to each other would shortly be on its way to an incinerator near Philadelphia. I wondered if she'd cried for me, for the death of our possibility. I ducked back through the hedge, following Fusilli and Katie's voices to the front porch.

"Thought you were having breakfast with Nora," Fusilli said.

I shook my head.

"What's wrong?" Katie asked.

I handed over the card. "Nora's gone. She left this."

Katie squeezed her eyes shut and shook her head. "Jack," she said. "Oh, Jack. I'm so sorry."

"I don't understand what happened."

"She keeps trying to find someone to save her from herself. I really hoped you might be the one."

"Jesus Christ."

"You weren't the first, love. You won't be the last."

25

I spent the morning helping Katie get her stuff packed. Fusilli went to collect the El Camino, but it was already gone. The cops claimed Aldo had come in earlier with a nun who was supposedly going to drive. They said it like the punchline of a bad joke. There was still no sign of the duo as Fusilli and I sat on the porch railing, drinking the last of the Heinekens, the sun warm on our faces.

"Come with us," Fusilli said. "You don't start work for a couple weeks. Maybe you can talk some sense into her. Christ, she's probably going to be on the same plane."

"I've got more pride than that," I said.

"Pride has no place in love."

"This isn't love anymore, Fusilli," I said, taking a long pull on my bottle. "I don't think it ever was. It was . . . a pipe dream."

"It showed you what was possible. That you can still have a different kind of life."

"It doesn't matter." I shrugged. "I gotta figure out what I'm going to say to Mia. Maybe it's a sign."

"Jack," he said, grabbing my shoulder. "Don't give up the ship."

"Did we even have a family here? Was any of it real?"

"I think a family is a story we tell each other until we believe it."

"Even the parts that are bullshit?"

"Especially the parts that are bullshit," he said. "You can't let facts get in the way of a legend."

"You going to be okay getting to the airport?"

He pointed to the street, where a black Cadillac Escalade was wheeling through a break in the traffic island.

"Classy," I said.

"I thought about just abandoning the Phantom at the airport, but I had a better idea." He reached into his duffel and produced a manila envelope that had seen better days. I peeled it open to find the keys to the Chevelle, along with the title signed over to me.

"Fusilli," I laughed, "I don't want this fuckin' thing."

He threw his arms around me. "Set it on fire. Drive it into the bay. Be dramatic. Send me pictures."

"I'll come when the baby is born," I said, returning the embrace.

"You volunteering for the mission?"

"He'll need a godfather."

"He?" Fusilli laughed, heading for the Cadillac. "God is going to give me a daughter. To spite me."

MIA's little flowered sundress swayed with her hips and the bay breeze as she walked to the railing on the deck. With each of my hollow footfalls on the boardwalk, I felt a growing darkness, as though shades were being drawn against the daylight. I was already judging the insincerity of the smile she was throwing at me as she waved.

We met in front of her house, where she hopped up into my

arms, kissing my lips and then my cheek over and over. "I'm so glad you're here," she said, hanging on my neck. "I wish I could have been there for you more the last few days."

"Mia," I said, my lungs filling with the familiar vanilla weight of her perfume. "I really need to talk to you. Let's take a walk or something."

"I know it hasn't been easy," she said, letting go and taking my hands. "I know it's been hell with Grandpa."

The darkness inside me grew thicker, spilling into my legs like old motor oil. Why was Mia still playing me? Would Daniel wonder the same as he greeted Nora under a graveyard Irish sky?

"What's that?" she asked.

My stomach dropped as I realized Nora's invitation was still in the breast pocket of my shirt.

"Oh. It's from Nora. She's on her way back to Ireland."

"Love letter?" Mia winked.

"Wedding invite," I said, passing it to her.

"Wow, Ireland!" Mia said, looking it over. "That would be tough with your internship and everything."

"I think she was just being polite," I said. "There's no way we could swing it."

"It was still thoughtful. We'll send something nice." She paused, running her fingers across the raised lettering. "Maybe we'll do something like this someday."

I willed her to turn it over and see the note from Nora. Instead, she pushed it back into the envelope and returned it. I slipped it into my shirt pocket, the linen thread catching the edges of the card stock. I wiggled it to make it fit.

Amelia called from inside the house. "Mia, should I throw the pasta in? When is Jack getting here?"

"He's right here, Ma!" Mia said, then lowered her voice. "My mother has been cooking all day. Let's just stay for a little bit. She really wants to do something for you."

Amelia burst through the front door, then hurried down the steps to us, her feet heavy on the treads. She wrapped me in a hug that would have smothered me, had I been a few inches shorter. Her tears were warm against my neck. "Jack, I'm so sorry about Francesco. He was such a beautiful person."

Her embrace felt like the first genuine comfort anyone had offered me over Grandpa's death. I'd been too wrapped up in the drama to really feel my grief. My own tears came in earnest as I melted in Amelia's arms. Everything had to get worse before it could get better, and I couldn't tell her. This would likely be the last time we'd see one another.

"Come in a minute," she said. "Have a little something to eat. I made bolognese. I know it's your favorite."

I WAS SEATED at my third funeral in two days, this one for the life I might have had with the people who had welcomed me as a son. My limbs buzzed, as if suffering the bends after a rapid ascent, my blood bubbling like soda water. How was I supposed to sit through this?

Amelia flitted around the table, filling our bowls with pasta, then loading the rotary grater with sharp goat cheese from her mother's hometown. Mia was seated beside me, studying me in the corner of her eye. She could feel something was wrong and was probably wondering what I'd wanted to tell her. I wondered the same.

Al tucked his napkin into the neck of his golf shirt to protect the clean white cotton. "How's your grandmother holding up, Jack?"

"About like you'd expect," I said, stirring the penne in my dish and hoping no one would notice my lack of appetite. "Worrying about everyone else and not taking any time for herself."

"The old-timers are like that," he nodded, pouring some extra sauce into his bowl. "I don't think I saw Mamma cry at my father's funeral. She just kept passing out Kleenex to the rest of us."

"It's good that everyone was together," Mia said. "Francesco was a legend."

"It's good that you finally got up there," he said, pointing his spoon at her. "You can't let your job get in the way of your responsibilities at home. Family first."

"It's all right," I said, unsure of why I was providing her cover. "It's not like we're married. People understand."

"*Mangia, Giacomo!*" Amelia urged as she sat down. I forced myself to take a bite. The sauce was tangy, perfect. The pasta, al dente. I desperately wanted it to fill the emptiness I felt inside. It wasn't just the mess with Mia. What I really needed was a bowl of my grandfather's hand-made gnocchi and a man-to-man talk. Who was he, really? Who was I? Is there a real person inside us at all, or are we whomever we decide to present ourselves as? As far as Al and Amelia were concerned, Mia and I were faithful and loved each other.

"I mean," Al laughed. "That's the thing, right? I just keep wondering when you guys are going to get engaged."

I almost choked on my pasta. Mia's porcelain smile froze on her face.

"Al," Amelia said. "You're embarrassing them."

"You guys don't want to be sneaking in and out of windows forever, do you?"

"Daddy," Mia said. "We wouldn't . . ."

"What," he said, cracking an amused smile. "You think we're stupid? That we didn't know you were sneaking out? That I wouldn't figure out you were meeting here in the winter? I was happy you were safe with Jack instead of at the bar with your girlfriends or something."

Meeting here in the winter? Candy's words reverberated in

my head: *I saw your girl with some other guy.* Mia was now staring straight ahead, past her father's shoulder and out over the ocean. The fingers that weren't holding her fork were trembling. She was wondering if I would be brave enough to step through the door he had just opened.

"Al," Amelia said. "What are you doing?"

"Relax," he said. "Like we didn't make out in the old days?"

Amelia turned barn-door red. "Al!"

"All's I'm saying is I don't want them to worry about sneaking around anymore. They're adults now. Professionals. Let's all level with each other."

"We can level," I said, finding my voice and putting down my fork. "I've never been here in the winter."

"Jack," Mia said. "Let's talk about this later."

"I appreciate you guys want to get your story straight," he said. "But I get the utility bills. And I don't think the mouse forgot his boxer shorts in the bathroom."

Amelia protested more vociferously in Italian, but her voice faded away like the doppler of a passing train. It hadn't even been a one-time thing. They'd been coming often enough that Al noticed on the goddamn Con Ed bill. They were so comfortable doing it that there was no paranoid cleanup in the aftermath. He'd left his fucking underwear behind. I'd been right. All the times I'd wondered if I was overreacting, if I was going crazy, I'd been right about Mia and Ian. I'd been right, and Nora was gone. Maybe she wouldn't be if I'd committed sooner, if I'd just shown a little fortitude. If I'd actually lived by the moral code I'd been raised with, even if life was more complicated than I'd ever imagined.

Mia was staring at me with wide eyes, her pupils dilating. The life drained from her cheeks, like a patient bleeding out in the trauma bay. There was no amount of implausible explanation that was going to fix this. There were no alternative theories of the crime.

"Jack?" Al said.

The sound of my name jerked me into the moment. "Yeah?"

"Are you okay? Jesus, I didn't mean to upset you. I thought all of us being honest might be better. I wanted it to be less stressful."

"Mr. Cerrone," I said, clearing my throat. "I appreciate your honesty. I appreciate your kindness even more. Both of you. The problem . . ."

I paused, expecting to be awash in anxiety or anger. Perhaps I was, but it was so overwhelming that the wires were melting before the current got through, as they do when lightning strikes a telephone pole. I looked down at the Luminox tight around my wrist, the crystal marred but the movement ticking. I flexed my forearm muscles, the dry-rotted strap at its limit but holding together.

Mia put her fork down, then folded her hands in front of her mouth and nose. Her eyes were telling me to stop, and perhaps that was the last kindness I should have shown her, but I was so tired. I was so tired of the deathmatch between my head and heart, so tired of telling myself to ignore my own misgivings. I was tired of carrying the weight of the past. I was tired of my own pretzel logic. I looked at the lips I had kissed, the ears I had whispered promises to, the body I had cradled but evidently hadn't satisfied. None of them were for me. Not anymore.

"The problem," I continued, "is that Mia was here with another guy."

Amelia gasped.

"What's wrong with you?" Mia said. "This obsession of yours with . . ."

"Why, Mia?" I asked. "Why put on the show? You know I'm telling the truth about never having been here in the winter. You know it for a fact."

"Oh," Al said. "Oh shit."

"Do you want to own it?" I asked. "Or do you want to tell your dad *he's* imagining things, too?"

Mia dropped her hands to her lap, her mouth making the shapes of words but nothing coming out.

"Tell me you don't love him, Mia," I said. "Tell me you'll never see him again. Tell me anything. I'm listening."

"Who?" Amelia said. "Who could you possibly be in love with?"

"Ian," I said. Saying the name out loud, in front of everyone, felt like letting my breath go after holding it for too long. His real, given name. Not the Witchdoctor or the Wizard of Yale. Not any of the jokes I'd used to temper my own humiliation. The sense of relief was overwhelming. This was the truth. Finally, after everything, we could have the truth, and we would see what the consequences were.

"*That* guy?" Al said.

"Can we please go outside and talk?" Mia said, springing upright and knocking her chair over, the hardwood back hitting the tile floor with the report of a gunshot. "Please, Jack? Can we please not do this in front of my parents?"

I nodded and stood. Mia ran for the sliding doors without looking back. Her footfalls were light across the deck and down the stairs. I stared at my plate for a moment. I couldn't stand to look at her parents. What would we say to each other? Amelia reached for my hand and held on, her eyes welling. The lightness in my gut felt like steering into the skid on a patch of black ice. I gave her a gentle nod, offered Al the same, then followed Mia out into the evening.

MIA WAS WAITING on the bench in the gazebo, sitting where Nora had been only days before, half-hidden from the rising glow of the lonesome streetlamp. I took my time walking towards her, hands in my pockets. A couple pushing a stroller passed to my left. I smiled at the baby as she passed in her pink pajamas, most of her right fist stuffed into her mouth. I had a sudden memory of the first healthy baby I delivered. I lifted him up for his parents before cutting the cord, unable to focus on them for my own tears. It was one of the most beautiful things I had ever seen. I wondered if I would ever get to be on the other side of that moment. I'd always imagined it would be Mia with me. I'd briefly fantasized about Nora in the same way. All of that was over now.

I stepped into the gazebo as the soft rubber wheels bumped away over the uneven boards, leaving us alone with the sounds of the breeze in the dune grass and the quiet peeling of knee-high surf. Hunched forward, Mia's chest swam in her gray sweatshirt, like an orange drying out beneath its skin. Her makeup was ruined from crying. We looked at each other for a long minute, then she rose and climbed the steps to the dune bridge.

"The first time I saw you," she said, stretching an arm out. "You were sitting on that lifeguard stand, reading something that looked smart."

"It was Hemingway that summer."

"Every year, it was something. You and your cousin."

"You'd understand why, if you ever read anything substantial."

It was a cheap shot. Mia was every bit as smart as I was. She lifted an eyebrow but didn't rise to the bait. Her voice sounded detached, as if she were waking from anesthesia.

"You didn't ask for my library card under the boat."

"It wasn't that night."

"A few nights later," she said. "You were pointing out constellations. I was thinking about the shoes I liked at the mall. So, I kissed you to shut you up."

It was a sweet story, in a way. The kind of thing you might

tell your kids when they ask how you fell in love. I was the cute dork. She was the popular girl making a man out of me. As we stood quietly, I could feel her looking for another way in, another hook, another way to defuse the darkness consuming me. I couldn't allow that. Righteous anger was my best defense, despite the fact that I'd done as she had. What if this was the way of things? What if monogamy was the exception rather than the rule? What if I were giving up a good future over common young adult mistakes, over ideals no one actually lived up to, not even the best man I ever knew? What if I needed to focus more on the story and less on the facts?

"You didn't have to do that," she finally said. "You didn't have to humiliate me in front of my parents."

I closed my eyes for a moment, unwilling to surrender to the anger boiling over within me. I needed to see things clearly, to see myself clearly, to see her clearly. To stop seeing what I wanted to see, or how I thought things were supposed to be. "You lied to me for years, and it turned me into someone I don't even recognize."

"I'm sorry," she said. "I didn't want to hurt you."

"You did anyway. At least now there are witnesses. At least now I'm not alone with it anymore."

"You were in a terrible place," she said. "Francesco was dying. You were barely speaking to your mother. You'd just accepted a position that was beneath you so that we could be closer together."

"Beneath me? Or beneath you, Ms. Georgetown Law?"

"That's not fair. I'm just saying you could have gone to a bigger-name place."

"Like Yale? Like him?"

"Maybe farther from your family? Maybe someplace where you wouldn't be so tied into their craziness?"

"Maybe authentic crazy is better than phony normal."

"What was I supposed to do, Jack? Tell you I was having

doubts? That I was falling for someone else in the middle of everything? I felt bad for you."

"I never needed your pity. I needed the truth."

"Yeah, okay," she said. "You want to hear me say it? Ian and I fooled around a few times. Feel better now? I was trying to figure stuff out."

I wanted her admission to feel like vindication. I wanted to tell myself that Mia had drawn first blood, and that made my infidelity with Nora righteous. None of that felt very convincing. Mia had done exactly what I'd suggested to Nora we do for the rest of the summer. Maybe I would have done the same, even if I hadn't suspected Mia. That felt like shit, and it might even have been true, but I couldn't get mired in guilt.

"What did he give you that I didn't?"

"It's not like that. It was never a serious thing. Long distance was hard. You were an eight-hour train ride away, on a good day. He was across campus. My friend since preschool. I loved *you*. Love you. I told him that last night. I want to make this work. I want the opportunity to have a normal relationship."

The sound of my words in her mouth made me flinch. How pathetic they must have sounded to Nora as she wondered when the next flight to Dublin was leaving. Maybe she'd already bought the ticket. I prepared to launch a broadside at Mia, then stopped myself. She'd loosened her hair, which was assuming its old golden wave. She swallowed hard, her larynx prominent between the strap muscles of her neck, her cheeks angular and hollow like a castaway. She reached for my hand, her small, cold fingers unable to circle mine. I pulled away from her.

"Please say something," she said.

"If you're always fronting, how do you know what's real?"

"Give me a break, Jack. Like you're always completely honest? Like you've never made a mistake?"

"I've made plenty of mistakes."

"Like what?"

"Sorry, I'm not going there with you."

"I don't believe you. That's not who you are."

"How do you know what I am? Maybe I just showed you what you wanted to see."

"Who then? The Irish girl? Someone from school?"

"Maybe all of them? Maybe none. Maybe, you'll just have to wonder."

If I had been a better person, I would have told her what I'd done with Nora. I would have told her that I'd explored my own doubts and that the results were a disaster, too. I would have said we could call it even and go our separate ways. I would have said that we were so young when we met, that we weren't fully formed people, that we were blindly executing a plan we'd been raised to value. That we should offer ourselves and each other a little grace. I just couldn't bring myself to do it. I'd been too angry for too long.

Mia's parents were standing in the bay windows. Her mother lifted a hand in sad farewell before disappearing into the kitchen. Her father might have offered a small nod, then followed his wife. My telescope was left alone in their place, its aperture pointed towards the tiniest fishing boats on the horizon as they faded from sight. I thought of standing on the bucket in the park as a child, Grandpa Francesco and I navigating the night sky, spacemen seeking the streetlights of Jupiter. Mia couldn't be given custody of those memories.

"If you don't mind," I said. "Leave my telescope out back. I'll pick it up in the morning."

"Jack," she said. "Please."

I looked over my shoulder to where she stood before the gazebo, her hand outstretched. The sky was starry above her, the twinkling lights blending with those of the carnival rides on the distant pier. Her eyes were barely visible in the darkness. I hated that I still felt her gravity, the pull of something that wasn't really love anymore. What would happen if I relented now? I would hate myself even more than I already did, be more willfully blind than I'd been before. It was time to stop doing that. This drowning man couldn't be saved. I would do better next time.

The night air was cool against my skin, as if summer was hanging in the closet, rather than just beginning. I imagined myself younger and stronger than I felt and continued down the block. Mia didn't follow. My dive watch hung heavy on my arm, like an old friend on the way home from the bar. The luminescent hands were split in a kind of Pyrrhic victory salute.

"We're more alike than you think, Jack," Mia called.

Mia might well have been right, and maybe that was okay. Maybe that could help me start forgiving myself. We'd both been raised to value tradition more than the trajectory of our hearts, or even the truth of our lives. I realized she probably couldn't help who she was any more than I could, and maybe that was all right too. And, after that, I tried not to think much about her at all.

The Friday of Labor Day Weekend found me working second shift in the fast-track side of the ER. The mantra was "treat 'em and street 'em." The board was full of Jersey holiday mayhem: drunks fighting, firework burns, and the occasional drug seeker with intractable back pain. Mysteriously, that last group always reported allergies to everything save the strongest narcotics. For my part, I was looking forward to a quiet weekend at the beach. My mother and sisters had abandoned Villabaia with the first day of school approaching. With Aldo disappeared to parts unknown, I'd have the place to myself. I'd spent most of the summer avoiding my family and trying to get my head together, the former made easy by my eighty-hour work week, the latter less so. Being single after so many years with Mia felt disconcerting, like forgetting where I'd left my wallet. Establishing my own identity was a strange process.

My supervising doctor that night was Dr. Schroeder, who was about ten years older than me. She had youthful freckles, a tinge of chlorine-green in her hair, and a swimmer's shoulders. She also had a husband and three kids, but a man could dream.

Schroeder was a good teacher, and I had the feeling that we would have made fast friends if not for our age difference.

"Jack," she said, passing me the chart. "Go see the girls in curtain twelve. You'll like them."

The top of the page read "Chief Complaint: Buttock Pain."

"Come on," I sighed.

"You're the intern," she said. "Runts, cunts, and assholes."

"Thanks."

"I don't make the rules," she laughed, going back to her note and peering over her glasses. "But I do enjoy enforcing them."

I rolled my eyes and shuffled towards the third alcove on the far wall. Behind the blue-patterned curtain was a pair of tall women, one standing uncomfortably next to the gurney. The other was seated and chewing gum like a cow, flicking absent-mindedly through a magazine she'd probably liberated from the waiting room. The seated one wore hoop earrings large enough to jump a motorcycle through. They had matching brunette hair with blonde highlights. It was cut jagged around their faces and fell to their shoulders. Their bangs curved across their foreheads like breaking surf.

"Schroeder was right," the standing woman said. "He *is* cute."

"I'm Dr. Frére," I said, my cheeks flushing. "Which one of you is Sarah?"

"That's her," the seated woman said, pointing with a well-manicured finger. "I'm Maribel."

"You two family?"

"Nah," Maribel said. "But we might as well be."

"We managed the respiratory unit." Sarah said.

"I thought you looked familiar."

"We got moved down to Neptune when they centralized everything," she added. "Didn't want to wait in that ER on a Friday night, though."

"Like hell," Maribel said. "You just didn't want them breaking your balls about falling on the fuckin' zucchini."

I'd already spent an inordinate amount of the summer fishing foreign objects from the assholes of people who really should have known better, given their sexual proclivities. We kept score on the whiteboard in the doctor's lounge. Vegetables were a frequent offender, but the most common find that summer was Barbie-doll heads. They pop off the body when a panicky recipient clenches and tries to yank it out.

"Give me a break, would you guys? I get off in twenty minutes."

"There's nothing up my ass," Sarah said. "I wiped out in my grandpa's garden. You should see this bruise."

Sarah gave a half-turn and hiked up her basketball shorts. A large purple smear was spreading beneath her skin, stretching from the crack of her behind to the back of her knee. She'd torn a hamstring at the very least. Maybe fractured the ischial tuberosity and possibly the coccyx, too.

"Yikes," I said. "We should shoot a film."

"Hey," Sarah asked, her eyes brightening. "Does Bregman still use the call room by radiology?"

"Yeah. He's on tonight, in fact."

"Fuck Andy Bregman," Maribel spat. "That guy's an asshole."

"He was good in the sack, though." Sarah sighed.

"Come again?" I asked, writing the order in the chart.

"Maribel worked with him back in the day," Sarah explained. "She didn't like him. He ripped a fart by her desk one time..."

"Fuckin' animal," Maribel interjected.

"... and she says 'Jesus, Bregman. That smells like your mom.'"

"What did he do?"

"He punched me in the arm!" Maribel said. "And he was

like, 'Oh, you gonna write me up?' And I go, what for? You hit like a fuckin' girl!"

"You gotta give as good as you get," Sarah said, "Or no one will respect you."

"Go get your X-ray," I said. "You're making me crazy."

"You got it backwards, Doc. We make you feel *sane*."

"You want for me to come with?" Maribel asked.

"Nah," Sarah said, accentuating her limp as she pushed through the curtain. "You stay here and see if you can get Doc's number. I'm gonna stop by Andy's room and see how he feels about a little charity for the disabled."

"He's gonna give you the fuckin' clap!" Maribel called after her, going back to her magazine. "You wait and see!"

The overhead speaker crackled to life. "Dr. Frére, please come to the main desk."

"Duty calls," I said.

Maribel looked up from her magazine and winked. "You know where to find me."

I pulled the curtain shut and stood there a moment. Sarah was exactly right. The reason I gravitated towards this kind of medicine, the reason I was so good at it, was because the chaos was my comfort zone. I told stories about it, I complained about it, I did my best to seem put upon by it, but it was where I belonged. I'd been trained for it from child-hood, groomed to remain nonplussed when confronted with the most ridiculous circumstances. It was my superpower, in a way. I didn't need to shrink from the insanity in my life. I needed to own it.

I found my way to the main ER, my senses assaulted by bright fluorescent bulbs and monitors twittering out of time with each other. Kendra was waiting for me at the desk. She'd gotten funky new cat-eye glasses, which combined with her heavy prescription and multi-color braids made her look like a denizen of a *Star Wars* cantina.

"Who?" she demanded, the phone cradled between her cheek and shoulder. "Like the damn pasta?"

My heart froze. Kendra pressed the hold button and passed me the receiver. "Some doctor. Terrible connection."

I pressed the phone to my ear as she released the hold. "Hello?"

There was a slight delay on the satellite link, followed by a familiar voice that tickled the fight-or-flight response in my reptilian stump.

"Cousin of my loins!"

Fusilli. Because of course it was.

"Jesus, what time is it there?" I asked. "Is everything okay with the baby?"

"Katie is pregnant as fuck," he said. "She's showing, and we finally had to come clean with her folks. This has had certain .. . consequences. Check the door to the ramp."

I leaned across the counter and peeked around the bend. The Castelli brothers had their truck double-parked in the ambulance bay. Paolo was standing in his southern-print poncho and Stetson, looking as though he'd just gotten off a horse on the western plains. Nunzio was wearing a ribbed white tank top and a gold cross on a chain, topped with a chauffeur hat. They were better tanned since I'd last seen them and wore matching stupid grins. Nunzio held up a hand-lettered sign with my last name on it, but missing the accent grave above the e. Paolo signaled they'd be waiting in the truck.

I slid back off the counter.

"Fusilli, I gotta be back at work in a few days."

"It wouldn't have come to this if you'd pick up your phone once in a while," he said. "We'll have you back in plenty of time. Our men will brief you on the mission."

He hung up before I could protest.

After signing out my patients, I stepped into the sticky Jersey night and stared down the tinted windows of the Castellis' truck. It was time to put my new self-image to the test. The greasy stink of steam-grilled onions hit like a subway car as I popped the door. Paolo didn't even wait for me to shut it completely before shifting into gear and chirping the tires as he pulled out of the ambulance bay. Nunzio turned around half-way, reaching between the seats to shake my hand.

"Check your jump bag," he said. "Make sure you got every-thing you need."

There was a knapsack behind the driver's seat. It was stuffed with a few pairs of underwear and socks, jeans, a couple of shirts, a toiletry bag, and my passport. A trio of suits, one of them mine, hung from the *oh shit!* handle on the opposite end of the back seat.

"How did you guys get into my place?" I asked.

"You got a few things to learn about home security, Doc," Nunzio said. "Our flight boards in an hour."

"You'll need your strength," Paolo said, passing a bag of White Castle sliders over the seat. "Everyone is counting on you."

"You still married, Paolo?" I said, stuffing a burger into my mouth.

"Brandi believes in murder, not divorce," he said.

"Too bad," I said. "I got a couple girls who would be perfect for you two."

ACKNOWLEDGMENTS

Thanks to everyone who read or listened to my stories over the years and laughed, cried, or cringed. Thanks to Kathy, Claudine, Jillouise, Cheryl, Meredith, Upham, Erin, and Kelly, my first and best gut-checks. Thanks to Doug and Alan, who know where the bodies are buried. Special thanks to the Quilluminati: Laura, Nicole, Sarah, and Amy, whose thoughts and encouragement mean everything. Thanks to Tasha, my literary soul sister and fellow shore denizen, who still knows the way to White Castle. Thanks to Pauly, my brother in dementia and auto repair. Thanks to the teachers who helped tame the mayhem I put on the page: Cari Luna, Jon Gingrich, and the late Professor Naton Leslie, who read the very first draft of this story long ago and told me it was destined to be a novel. Bonus thanks to Jon for his editorial kung fu. Finally, thanks to Jeffery Everett for cover art that provides all the feels.

ABOUT THE AUTHOR

I'm a physician-scientist by training, but I'm a storyteller by birth. I was raised in New York, in a small town haunted by the ghosts of early twentieth-century writers. I spent my summers at the Jersey Shore, in a smaller town haunted by the ghosts of some lobsters I failed to resuscitate after exposure to fresh water. In my defense, I wasn't a doctor yet.

After college, I worked and studied around the world. My characters reflect both the sorts of people I grew up with and the weirdos I've met in my travels. All are fictional, but they feel real to me. After three decades, maybe they are.

When I'm not tending to injured athletes or teaching at the medical school, you'll find me at the beach with my family and a totally unreasonable collection of fishing gear.

 bsky.app/profile/drphilipskiba.bsky.social

 x.com/drphilipskiba

 instagram.com/philipskibaauthor